Forgiving Spirit
A Journey of Reconciliation

A Novel

Richard D. Reavis

Copyright ©2020 – Richard D. Reavis

Acknowledgments

After doing a final reading I thought back at the hours spent writing this story. I can't help but dwell on those who have had an integral part in the process. First of all, we give all the credit to God through whom all things are possible. He is our true source of inspiration. I thank my wife, Bonnie, who has stood beside me over the last six decades. Her unwavering support as a sounding board has been my encouragement. To my granddaughter, Aurora, who continues to edit my books, what a great job you do. To the rest of my children and grandchildren who encouraged their dad and grandpa to continue to reach outside his comfort zone, I am forever grateful. Now, as I sit here holding a prepress copy of Forgiving Spirit, I am humbled and blessed by the hours so many others have selflessly given to make it possible. Thank you.

The Author

Prologue

The leather shoes stood out against the rich green leaves along the swollen river bank, sitting on a log with untied laces they told a story of anguish. With all surety, the young boy had waded into the water and was washed downstream. The perfect cover-up of a crime committed would stand for years to come as it would continue to eat away at the conscience of the guilty. As is typical with all sin, the time comes when it will be revealed.

Will this horrendous act tear the family apart? Come walk with us through the life of this early twentieth-century family as they learn how to have a forgiving spirit.

A Forgiving Spirit
Chapter One

It was a restless night. Sleep just couldn't come. Jake had so much on his mind he couldn't stop thinking. He wondered, "What should we do?" The letter had arrived today with the invitation to come out west. His cousin Jason had moved there five years ago. Jake was very happy with their farm and their church. The thought of leaving the place of his growing up years was hard. Yet with the unrest in the area following the Civil War, he felt he must do something. Finally, he fell into a restless sleep.

Living in Virginia was all Jake ever knew. His great grandparents, Carl and Bertha Bowman had emigrated here from Scotland in the early eighteen hundreds. They were hard-working people who loved to work the soil and bought eighty acres which were mostly wooded. They cut timber from the land and built a barn. They lived in one end of this barn for a few years, while they cleared off the land for growing crops. It was in that barn their son Delbert, Jake's grandfather, had been born. Cutting the timber had been hard work, but clearing out the stumps and roots was even harder. Through much persistence, little by little they cleared some fields to plant crops.

After ten years they had accumulated enough timber to build a house. They had felt it was a greater priority to clear more land and take care of what they had cleared instead of building the house. It was another ten years before the house was complete.

When Delbert was twenty-five he made a trip by horseback to Pennsylvania. When he came back two years later, he brought with him his bride. Delbert and his wife, Rebecca lived at one end of the barn while they cut logs and built a cabin. In this log cabin, they raised four boys and two girls. Jake's father, Henry, was the second of these boys.

Coming from Pennsylvania Rebecca was not comfortable living among folks who owned people as slaves. There had not been any slaves where she had grown up.

There was a conflict in the area about the ownership of slaves. Some, supposedly devout Christians, felt it justifiable. Others felt it was wrong. The church where the Bowman's belonged took a strong stand against it. However, there were some that did own slaves. They tried to justify it by saying, "To treat them kindly and not overwork them should not be an offense to God."

The Slaves were looked upon as another animal by some people. The Bowman's didn't see it that way. They felt they were part of God's creation and had a soul as all men had. This caused neighbors to be unfriendly to their church brethren.

When the Civil War broke out, the members of the church had their convictions tried. The soldiers came into their barns and took anything they wanted, including horses. Some of the brethren lost their lives. Jake's grandfather Delbert, was one of those. He had been helping slaves escape to the north when he was killed. Some fled to other areas where there was less conflict.

Henry was still at home when his father was killed. He and his brothers worked hard to support the family. There were times he would pitch hay out of the haymow to feed the Confederate army's horses. He did this only to pacify them, so they wouldn't hurt his mother. Henry married one of the church girls, Cassie June Jamison. Henry and Cassie had twin sons, Ezra and Jake. They were different as day and night. Ezra was a short blocky baby with dark hair. Jake was slender and fair.

The Bowman families were devout Christians. They attended church regularly unless there was sickness. Living by the Holy Word of God was their way of life. They were happy now the slaves were freed. However, there were folks that weren't happy with the outcome of the war. If Henry hired any of the freed slaves to work for him, those folks didn't like it. Consequently, they made it dangerous to do so. Living in that area during those times was difficult.

As Henry's boys grew up and found friendship with other boys, Ezra became friends with the neighbors. He sided in with them on their thinking of slave ownership. Henry and Cassie tried to reason with him but to no avail. He started attending a church where even the preacher thought President Lincoln was wrong. Some folks, if they could make it look like an accident, would slay these freed slaves. At times the Law enforcement would even help make it look like an accident.

It had been twenty years since the slaves were freed, but some of the bitterness was still there. Ezra fell in love and married one of the girls from this pro-slavery church. This church didn't hold to the truths of nonconformity, nonresistance, and forgiveness. The love of Christ was missing in their fellowship. Everyone just did as they pleased.

Both Jake and Ezra wanted to farm. Jake knew his brother wanted the farm and would do anything to get it. Ezra had the mindset, that if you don't get what you want, get a lawyer to fight for you. This caused Henry and Cassie much grief. Jake knew his parents were concerned about Ezra. He prayed the Lord would direct him in the way he should go. Some days as they were working together it seemed like they were getting along well. He thought, "Maybe I should slacken up on my conviction and flow with the world." One day Ezra bragged to him about treating a man badly. The way Ezra laughed and thought it was funny made Jake sick to his stomach. He knew then that he wanted to maintain his belief.

Jake read where Jesus said, "When the bridegroom is taken away, the people will fast." Also the time the disciples couldn't cast out a demon, Jesus said, "This kind comes out only by prayer and fasting." He felt he should pray and fast to see what the Lord's will for his life was to be. He spent three days in prayer with fasting. His mother was concerned about him but said nothing.

One week later he received a letter from his cousin. The letter told of good fertile land in Iowa. It could be rented on a crop sharing basis. The landowners were looking for plain Christian people to farm their land. He wrote that there was an old order church district starting up in that area. Jake asked himself, "Is this the door of opportunity the Lord is opening to me?"

The Decision
Chapter Two

It was a pleasant day. Ezra was in the field with the team plowing. Jake and his dad were cleaning out the tramp shed. Henry noticed Jake was unusually quiet. Once he noticed him wipe tears from his eyes. He knew his son well enough not to ask questions. If he had a concern to talk about, he would confide in time. The work went well and they had the tramp shed cleaned by chore time.

After they had finished eating and before they got up from the supper table, Jake handed his dad the letter he had received from his cousin.

"Dad, could you read this aloud. I want mom to hear it. I would like your opinion."

Henry read the letter slowly. He read it again. He sort of choked up and tears appeared in his eyes. Cassie didn't say anything for a while. When she was able to speak, she said, "Is that what you were praying and fasting about last week?" By now Jake was also shedding tears. His response was only a nod.

After thinking about it for some time, Henry said, "I was hoping you boys could have the farm and make it a family farm for years to come. Little do we know what the Lord has in the future for us. When our forefathers came to this country, they came for the opportunity both spiritually and economically. When my grandfather settled here, he felt it was a wonderful blessing. It was, although they had to work very hard to make it what it is today. No doubt their parents were sad to see them leave the old country to go into the unknown. Likely there were a lot of tears shed back then. It has been in the hearts of our family to praise God in words and actions. That is what has brought several families to this country."

Jake fiddled with his fork for a few moments before responding. "I am glad I can still worship God as I feel is right while living here. It is the stress of not being able to have that neighborly bond with those that live close by that bothers me. When I see what happened to Ezra, how a person can be led so far away from their faith, that got me to thinking maybe I should consider doing something else.”

After much discussion and prayer, Henry and Cassie gave their blessings on the new venture. Jake sent a letter to his cousin telling him of his plans to come after the harvest.

Late in the fall, Jake found himself sitting next to the window as the train slowly made its way over the Appalachian mountains on its way to Indianapolis. With every mile the steam-driven train rolled down the tracks, it took him that much further away from the conflict he had been experiencing. It was a long ride to Pleasantville, Iowa. The train seemed to stop at every little town along the way. The train pulled into the Indianapolis train station in the middle of the night. Jake was thankful for the conductor who directed him to the train for Pleasantville. He was tired and knew he needed to get some sleep on the next segment of his journey. It was late afternoon on the second day when he arrived. He retrieved his two suitcases and was standing there looking around when he saw a horse and carriage coming toward him. It was Jason. After their greeting, they loaded his luggage into the carriage and were on their way to Jason’s.

Jake noticed the fairly flat landscape. It wasn’t rolling, like back home. They passed a few nice homesteads. They noticed a mother and children cleaning off their garden for the winter. As they passed, the lady and all the children waved in a very friendly fashion. Jason waved back. As they passed the barn a man was watering horses, he waved heartily. Every placed they passed where folks were outside they greeted them with a friendly wave. “Do these folks all know you?” Jake asked his cousin. “No, I don’t personally know any of them,” Jason replied. “The way you all greeted each other, I figured you were friends," Jake said. Jason smiled, "Here in rural Iowa we are friendly to all our neighbors." As they turned onto a narrow road Jake pondered these observations, "Love and no bitterness." The horse showed excitement as they turned up a lane and drove down a tree-lined drive about five hundred feet to a large white clapboard house and large red barn. Pulling up on the reins Jason said, "We're home."

Jason tied the horse to the post by the yard gate. With the suitcases in hand, they walked up the board walkway to the house. Just as they stepped onto the porch, the door opened and out stepped Jason's wife, holding their eighteen-month-old daughter. Jason introduced Jake and his wife Dorothy and daughter Beth. At Dorothy's direction, they took Jake's luggage upstairs to a spare bedroom. Jake looked around at the well decorated and furnished bedroom. The quilt covered bed looked inviting after such a long trip. Jake sighed as he placed the suitcases in the room, "What a peaceful place."

Jake went back outside and found Jason putting the carriage in the shed and the horse in the stall. After two days on the train, it felt good to be helping in the barn. He was happy to help milk the twelve cows Jason had. Although they stood and talked sometimes, with the two of them doing the chores they got done in record time. When they returned to the house supper wasn't ready yet. Jason helped by setting the table and putting water in the glasses. Dorothy told them to go sit and visit. She would call when supper was ready.

The cousins had a lot of catching up to visit about. A lot had taken place since they were together in Virginia five years ago. It wasn't long before Dorothy called from the kitchen that supper was ready. Once they were seated around the kitchen table Jason said, "Jake, we have so many things to be thankful for, would you ask the blessing for the food and thank the Lord for these blessings?"

The vegetable beef soup was a really satisfying meal after the cold butter sandwiches Jake had eaten on the train. As they ate, Jason said, "Jake, I have a lot of things I would like to discuss with you but would like to wait until we have more time. For now, I would like to know how your folks are getting along health-wise." Jake updated him on their health conditions. He also shared how they were holding the faith in spite of the bitterness of worldly folks around them.

When they were finished eating, Dorothy excused herself and took Beth to get her ready for bed. Jason cleared the table and stacked the dishes. "Come into the living room," he told Jake, "Have a chair." Soon Dorothy and Beth came out. Beth had her nightclothes on. Jason looked at Jake, "We have a little evening devotion before we retire. You may join us."

Jason read a couple of pages from a little children's Christian book, and then he read a Psalm. They bowed in prayer. Jason said, "Tell our visitor, night night." Dorothy gave Beth a hug and kiss saying, "Good night, sleep tight." Jason picked her up and looking at Jake said, "Excuse me for a minute." He took his daughter into her bedroom, gave her a hug, kissed her goodnight, and tucked her in bed.

Jake was half asleep when Jason returned to the living room. "I have a little chore to do and will join you shortly," Jason told him. "In the meantime make yourself comfortable." In the kitchen, Dorothy was pouring water in the dishpan. She washed and Jason dried. It didn't take long until the kitchen was in good shape. Observing the couple work together, Jake asked, "Do you always help with the dishes?" "As much as I can," Jason replied. "There are times when the fieldwork is pressing she doesn't expect me to. When we got married we agreed to help each other as much as we could. Working together deepens our love for each other."

Dorothy excused herself, "I'll let you men have your time together. I am ready to retire." Jake thanked his host for the good supper and their hospitality. He was anxious to hear what Jason had in mind. He reminded himself just to be patient.

Jason soon began by talking about the church. "We believe Christians should evangelize, however, our thinking is different than the way other folks see it. We feel our way of life is the way the Bible teaches, to be a light about us. Where we live, we feel is directed by our God."

"God took his people down into Egypt by the hand of a boy named Joseph. That account is a very interesting story. Four hundred thirty years later God took them out of Egypt by a man named Moses. It was by a mighty hand He did that. That is also a very interesting story. There are many stories in the Old Testament about the hand of God moving His people."

"Through persecution, God brought Christians to this country. In this good land we live in, God moved His people. At times it was by persecution and at other times by opportunity."

"Because His people failed to obey Him, there were times He let them suffer at the hand of ungodly men. When that happens, there may be those who are following the commandments such as Daniel, Hananiah, Mishael, and Azariah who suffered, although they had not disobeyed. In the end, those folks came out victorious."

"Do you feel the Lord opened a door of opportunity for His true followers here in Iowa?" Jake asked.

"It may be His will, but we must be followers of Him."

"How do we know we are following God?"

Jason sat there with his head down for a bit as if trying to think of the correct answer to that question. "When we were baptized, we made a confession of our faith. We believe Jesus is the Son of God, and He brought from heaven a saving Gospel. We were willing to renounce Satan with all his ways, and the sinful pleasures of the world. We made a covenant with God in Christ Jesus to live faithful until death. After making these promises we were immersed in the name of the Father, and the Son, and the Holy Ghost. We were received into the church with a handshake and the holy kiss."

"I believe all this, and want to be faithful to my vows, but there are times doubts arise in my mind. Why does that happen?" Jake asked.

"You're able to rise above those doubts aren't you?" Jason replied.

"Yes."

Jason continued, "It is the gift of the Holy Spirit in you which gives you that ability to be faithful. As born again Christians, we believe the Bible to be the inspired Word of God. Therefore we accept the New Testament as the only creed of the church. We desire to obey the teachings written in it. If we do that we can feel assured we are a part of the elect of God."

"We have discussed the way we feel to live, now would you like to hear more about why I invited you to move here?"

Being tired from the past two days on the train Jake looked up at the clock. "I have really enjoyed our discussion concerning God's plan for His people. I do believe we are a part of his elect. Yes, I would like to hear what you have in mind."

"Five years ago when I came here, there were none of our faith living here. There were some living in Illinois, but farms were not available. We would have liked to stay there as the crops produced abundantly in the good black ground. Most of the farms are being handed down to the next generation."

"I saw an ad in the farm paper wanting a farm hand out here in Iowa. I inquired and got the job. We had only been married for six weeks. Dorothy didn't grow up on a farm, but it sounded like something she would enjoy. She grew up in Indiana in a large church and had a lot of friends there. After we were married we enjoyed the fellowship of several couples."

"Goodbye was a little hard, but we were young and had a pioneering spirit. We came by horse and buggy, bringing what we had with us. What little we couldn't get in the buggy we sold or gave it away."

"It was about lunchtime on a Tuesday when we drove up this lane, not knowing who or what we would find."

Jake spoke up, "That took faith didn't it?"

"Seeing the people wave to us in the community, as if they knew who we were, was an encouragement. John and Faye were eating dinner when I knocked on the door. They both came to the door. He stuck out his hand and said, 'You are Jason, right?' We had only conversed by letter. We shook hands and he said, 'Bring your wife and come in.' I went out and tied the horse to that post we tied Jack to today. Dorothy and I went in and introduced ourselves. Faye said, 'Come on to the kitchen and help us eat this food.'"

"John's are not of our church, but they are very nice folks. This may be hard to believe, but we spent that night here and have been living here ever since. I helped chore that evening and it just continued. A couple of weeks later, John had a heart attack and could hardly function. Their children are all living in other states, and not interested in farming. We came here at the right time."

"Are you telling me you just moved in and became a hired hand, just like that?"

"That is the way it was. I didn't even ask what the pay would be. They so much appreciated us helping them. We were treated like we were their children."

"How did things get to where it is today?" was Jake's next question.

"Two months after we were here, John came to the kitchen table with his checkbook. He told me, 'You have been doing most of the chores and other work ever since I had my heart attack. In our area, we pay young people like you by giving them a third of the milk check, a third of the calves born and a third of all crops raised with your labor. I got the milk check today for the first month you were here. I'll give you a check for your third.' I was shocked at the amount of the check. That plan continued and not having many expenses we've been able to build up a nice nest egg."

"How long did John's stay here?" Jake asked

"Their health was declining to the point we had to help them in and out of bed. Their daughter came and insisted they go to a Rest Home. We were expecting our first child. We felt a baby around would not work with older folks. Faye said, 'I like babies, but being older it is different than when we were younger.' We entered into a contract with John's which let us stay here on the thirds for a few years. They even gave us most of their furniture. At that time the price was set what we would pay for the farm when we bought it. Six months ago we bought it."

Looking at the clock Jake said, "Wow, it's after midnight."

Jason said, "Five o'clock comes awful early. Tomorrow I'll tell you about an opportunity there is for you such as we had. Good night."

The Change
Chapter Three

The alarm clock had been ringing for a while before Jake heard it. Even as tired as he was he had had trouble going to sleep. He constantly was thinking about the changes that may be coming his way. What would Lois think about living out here? He and Lois had been writing for two years. She didn't want to live where there were folks in favor of slavery. He did think about the possibility of trying to get a farm in northern Ohio where she lived. He found there wasn't much opportunity in that area.

Hurrying to the barn he found Jason already there, feeding the cows.

"Good morning. Did you sleep well?" greeted Jason.

"Good morning. Short night!" responded Jake trying to sound wide awake and cheerful.

They grabbed the milk buckets and milk stools and soon the sound of milk hitting the sides of the buckets made a soothing noise. This soothing sound had a tendency to make them sleepy, but Jason used this time to explain to Jake what he had in mind.

"After we get the chores done we can go see a man I have been talking to about you. He has a three hundred acre farm five miles west of here. One hundred and eighty acres of it is tillable. The rest is wooded. He and his wife live in the big house by the barns and the hired hand lives in a smaller house also there on the farm. His hired hand is moving out in a month. He wants someone of the plain folks to move in and work for him. After one year, if that works well, he will rent the farm to him on the thirds."

As the milk kept splashing in the bucket, Jake's mind was swirling. "Was God really opening an opportunity like this to him?" He emptied the bucket and sat down at another cow.

What would Lois think of such an offer? He was so excited about the prospect of working a farm that the milk was hitting the bucket faster than before. "Calm down," he told himself.

Jason returned from emptying his bucket and continued. "These are fine folks with a good reputation. They are in their sixties and want to retire in town. So after a year if all goes well, they will give you a contract to rent the farm on the thirds. In that contract, you will have the option to buy the farm at a set price when you are ready."

Jake thought, "Surely I must be dreaming."

After the chores, as they entered the house the aroma of bacon frying met them.

"Good morning men," Dorothy said.

"Good morning," was the response.

Little Beth as she came tottering around the corner, greeted Jason with a "Morn Da Da."

"Good morning sweetheart," Jason said as he scooped her up in his arms and gave her a hug. After putting her in the high chair, he helped Dorothy put the food on the table.

"Have a chair" Jason motioned to Jake. After they were all sitting Jason picked up the Bible and read a chapter. Then he thanked the Lord for the blessing of life given to them and the food.

The leaves were falling gently. There was a pleasant southern breeze as Jack trotted down the road pulling the carriage. Jake noticed there was still corn in the fields. "Do you have your corn in?" he asked.

Jason, fearing Jake would feel bad about him taking off on such nice days to help him, answered. "I still have some corn to husk, but I don't mind taking time to help you find a farm."

It was relaxing to hear the clip-clop of the horse as they rode along. Jason used this opportunity to explain more things about their community. He said, "In the five years we've lived here, there have been ten families of our church move in. There was a middle-aged minister and his wife. A deacon and his wife arrived a year later. Since that time eight younger families with their children have settled here. They didn't all come at once. It's always exciting to hear of another family coming. We were so happy to see the first family which came. We don't mind helping folks when they move here. The more that move in the more there are of us to help them.

Jake asked, "You being the first, who helped you?"

"Out here neighbors help neighbors. We didn't need a lot of help though, as John and Faye made it easy for us. We will help each other from time to time, even if your farm is five miles from ours, but you will find you need to help your neighbors and they will help you."

This sounded strange to Jake. At home in Virginia, the neighbors were at odds with each other unless they were brethren of the same faith.

The five miles passed quickly as they conversed. "Here's the place," Jason said as they turned in a short lane. Jake took in the view with amazement as they drove to the hitching rack. It was a picture of a well-kept farm. Jason tied Jack to the hitching rack.

"Let's go meet Bob and Carol," said Jason as he started for the house.

The door opened and a tall stately gentleman stepped out, "Good morning gentlemen."

"Good morning!" Jason and Jake responded in unison.

"Come on up on the porch and have a chair. Such a beautiful fall day we can visit out here."

He opened the door a little and called, "Carol, come out. Jason is here."

They had just sat down when Carol, a somewhat pudgy short lady with a smile on her face, came out the door. She had a mixture of brown and silver hair. Her blue eyes had a sparkle in them. Bob was easy to get acquainted with. He was a very friendly man. Jason made the introductions.

"Is this the young man you told me about?" Bob asked.

"It sure is. Jake just arrived on yesterday's train."

After much discussion concerning what Bob's were offering, and what Jake could do. It was decided Jake would live in the little house and work for Bob for one year as a hired hand. After a year, Bob's were to rent the farm to Jake on a one third. Jake was to do the work. Bob would furnish the farm, pay the taxes. He was to provide horses, livestock, and take care of the repairs of the buildings. At that time Jake would get a third of the income and one-third of all newborn animals. At the end of five years, Bob's would move into town and Jake would get the big house. At that time, Jake could buy the farm if he wanted at a set price.

Jake was excited about the plan laid out and wanted to jump at the chance to own his own farm. Still, he knew it was a big undertaking and such a decision required prayer. "Would it be alright if I took a little walk before making this decision?" Jake asked his potential landlord.

"Sure!" Bob answered, "Take all the time you need."

Jake walked around the barn and back a fence lined lane. Looking out over the fields, he spent time in prayer, asking God to give him wisdom in the decision that had to be made. As he slowly made his way back to the porch he took in all the senses of the farm. He looked over the corncrib and chicken house. He breathed in the smell of the hay and the livestock. He listened to the birds being interrupted by the bray of a donkey. By the time he was walking across the yard, he knew what the decision had to be.

"I'll accept the offer," Jake said as he stepped up on the porch.

Bob, being a thorough business type of a man, said he would get a contract drawn up. It was decided Jake would come back the next Tuesday to look it over and sign it.

Jake was deep in thought as they journeyed toward home.

After a time Jason said, "A penny for your thoughts."Jake just looked at him and smiled.

Jake had trouble getting to sleep. It was hard to believe the opportunity he had been given. He prayed the Lord would guide him in this time of decisions. After turning and tossing for a while he got up and wrote a letter to Lois.

He spent the next week helping Jason husk corn. On Tuesday Jason took him back over to Bob's to look over the contract. After carefully reading the document he asked Jason to look it over and offer his advice. After Jason finished he said, "It looks like Bob and Carol are giving you a great opportunity."

With a smile on his face, Bob said, "That is what we want to do. When we were young, we were given an opportunity. Now we are able to do the same for you. It has been a lot of hard work. It is work we love, but the time comes to slow down. We want to spend time with our children and grandchildren."

After signing the contract, Carol told Jake he could stay with them for a few days prior to moving into the small house.

The New Home
Chapter Four

Jake's hands were shaking with nervous excitement as he opened the envelope. "What would she say?"

"When you lived in Virginia you ask me to marry you." Lois wrote. *"I was not comfortable with a home among folks who wanted slaves. I have prayed about your request for my hand in wedlock. I feel the Lord is leading you in the right way. My answer is 'yes'. I would love to marry you and move into that little house as Mrs. Jake Bowman. Come as soon as you can. Lois."*

Jake stood there for a while, gazing across the landscape. He bowed his head and thanked the Lord for leading him to this point. He got a ticket and the next Tuesday he was on his way to Ohio. As he sat there on the train watching the landscape pass by, his thoughts traveled over the past years. He thought of his mother when he was a small boy. He remembered her holding him and his twin brother on her lap and reading storybooks to them. His thoughts traveled to when they played in the mud puddles after a spring rain. He chuckled to himself as he thought of the time when his brother was pulling him in their little wagon and upset him in a mud puddle. The more serious times were when their dad would read to the family from the Bible. Sometimes they would sing some songs. Reflecting over the bygone years, he knew he was blessed to have such loving Godly parents.

His thoughts were suddenly brought back to the present as the conductor announced the next stop would be "Lima, Ohio." His heart skipped a beat as he anticipated Lois being there at the station to meet him. He had trouble calming his nerves wondering if she would actually accept him. He was eighteen when he first asked her for her hand in wedlock. She said, "no" on account of the slave controversy there in Virginia. He wondered if that was only a way out. Would she actually become his wife? He felt unworthy to get such a lovely girl.

It didn't take long after she met him at the station to see she was sincere. They spent the next two weeks on planning their wedding. He learned to know her parents and siblings. He so much enjoyed the evening devotions at their house. He slept at one of her uncle's home.

The church was filled to capacity. As the first hymn began, it seemed the people were filled with the Spirit. Lois grew up among them and helped a lot of families when their babies were born. Children in the congregation called her 'Aunt Lois'. They were happy for her, even though they knew she would be missed.

The minister opened his remarks by talking about "The journey through life". He reminded them, "The Lord said, 'Seek ye first the kingdom of God and His righteousness and all these things shall be added unto you.' Life is not a bed of roses. There are happy times and times when sorrow comes. When we first look at the newborn baby, we are filled with awe to think a child is born to us. It may seem like a miracle. We know it is a blessing from the Lord.

The future of that newborn child rests on our shoulders. We will not only have the privilege to enjoy him but the responsibility to train him up in the nurture and admonition of the Lord. In Ezekiel chapter eighteen verse four we read the Lord said, 'Behold, all souls are mine'. I feel sure when Isaac and Rebekah first saw those two little boys, they were thrilled. Likely, they tried to teach them the way of the Lord. Little did they know the sorrow which lay ahead.

We enjoy our children as they are growing up. We should enjoy all of our blessings the Lord affords us and be thankful for them. The time could come they may be taken away.

Time moves on. We have only a few years to instill into our children's minds the important things of life. There comes the time they will make their own choice. What will it be? Esau, one of Isaac's boys, when grown, rejected his birthright. He chose a wife from the daughters of Heth. Rebekah was not happy about his choice. What footsteps are we leaving? Will our children follow them? Where we live, among whom we live, our priorities does the love of God reign among the people where we go to church; all these things could make a difference as to what our children will choose.

We said there will be happy times and sad ones. It would be sad to have our farm we worked hard to obtain taken away. Or lose the house we just paid off. There are many things we consider sad times. A loss of a companion when they pass away brings great sorrow.

There is one thing even more sorrowful than these. To have our children, that little baby we held in our arms, those small children we played with, the young teenagers we gave advice to; Should they choose to walk with the world would break our heart.

Look down the road. Make the right choices. Trust in the guidance of the Holy Spirit. Read the Bible daily. Pray every day. Fill your heart with the good things of God. Follow the simple teachings of the Bible. Now is the day to make the right choice."

Jake and Lois looked at each other. Both were thinking, "What a responsibility we are entering into." They had talked about a lot of these things. They felt the Lord was guiding them in this marriage.

After the closing hymn and prayer, the minister asked them to stand. He performed the marriage ceremony and introduced them as Mr. and Mrs. Jake Bowman.

****

The train ride to Iowa was an opportunity to discuss the events that had taken place in the last few days. They talked about the sermon they heard. They agreed they wanted to take heed to the counsel given. Should the Lord bless them with children, they must start their married lives walking close with the Lord.

Jason met them at the train station. After loading their luggage in the carriage they were soon on their way to their new home.

As they pulled up to the hitching post, Bob and Carol came out on the porch. "Welcome!" they said in unison. "Bring your things and come in." For Lois, it was a little uncomfortable going into a home of someone she didn't know. It didn't take long to ease her apprehensions as Bob's were the type that made a stranger soon feel at home. Carol gave the young couple directions to their room and had them go ahead and take their things to their room. Jason excused himself, as it would be chore time by the time he got home.

Carol was entertaining Lois, while the men walked outside to look around. Bob brought Jake up to speed as to what had transpired while he was back east getting married. "The folks in the little house have decided to move to California and will soon be having an auction sale. They are selling most of their things. If you are interested, it may be an opportunity to get some things."

"Does he have a horse and buggy?" Jake asked.

"Yes, he does. He has a good young horse and a fairly good older buggy."

"What about the furniture?"

"They do have some furniture they will be selling, but I don't know much about it. I can arrange a time for you and your wife to see it."

The newly married couple spent the week learning their new adventure. Bob and Carol let them have all the time they wanted to themselves. Being enthused with their new home, a lot of the time, they just wanted to be where the action was. One afternoon Bob and Jake took the time to go through the barn and sheds. Bob wanted to show Jake everything he could about the farm. They even walked around the fence lines.

"Is this all yours?" Jake asked.

"Yes and no!" Bob answered. "Someday it may be yours, but remember, 'The earth is the Lord's and the fullness thereof.' I may own it in a legal sense, and someday you may, it is only lent to us by the Lord. We have the responsibility to be good stewards of what the Lord affords us." These words coming from Bob, made Jake feel he had been guided to this farm by the Lord.

On Friday Bob's and Jake's went to see the things Levi's had to sell. Levi and his wife, Joan, were somewhat saddened about their possessions being auctioned off the following day. They knew it was better to sell and get more in California than to move it all the way out there. They were glad to show Lois their furniture. Jake had already seen the horse and buggy.

Saturday was a nice sunny day. Jake was happy to see Jason at the sale. He trusted him to help with the value of the merchandise. Lois purchased several items in the house she thought they needed at a very fair price. Jake bought the horse and also the buggy. He gave a little more then he hoped. Jason pointed out they didn't have to be moved and were acquainted with the farm. That made them worth more.

Levi's thanked them for showing a kind attitude and not trying to get their things at a very low price. Lois told them if they were in this area sometime stop in. Both Levi's and Jake's were satisfied with the sale.

That night as they were falling off to sleep Carol told her husband, "The attitude Jake manifested in the purchase of Levi's things today tells us what his character is like. They will be good on the farm.”

Prosperous Years
Chapter Five

Living with Bob's was an interesting experience for the newlyweds. Bob's were Christian people and were easy to get along with. They just had a little different way of thinking than Jake and Lois were used to. The two weeks at their temporary home passed swiftly as they immersed themselves into the workings of the farm.

While they were eating breakfast, Levi and Joan came over to say goodbye to the ladies and to let the men know what time they would be ready to leave. At ten o'clock the men hitched up the spring wagon and headed over to pick up Levi's. Their trunks and other miscellaneous items filled up the bed of Bob's wagon. Jake rode with Bob and Levi drove Jake's newly acquired buggy with his family. Reaching the train station a good hour before the train was scheduled to arrive they visited and talked about the past. Levi shared some of their hopes for their future out in California. Bob and Jake bid them farewell, wishing them the Lord's blessings on their new adventure. It was late afternoon before the men arrived back at the farm. At the supper table, Bob told Jake to take the next day off and move into their house.

Early the next morning Jake and Lois took their belongings over to the little house. Lois wanted to do some cleaning before they moved in, so they set their things on the porch swing. Walking through the house, they were surprised to see more than they bought. In the kitchen, there were more dishes than she bought and in the living room more furniture. They were surprised how clean Levi and Joan left it. It was ready to just move in. Jake went out and got their luggage off the porch swing.

Carol stopped by to see if everything was alright. Lois told her, "They left more than we bought."

Smiling, Carol told her, "Bob told me to buy anything you didn't that I thought you folks may need. He had two reasons for doing that. One was that Levi had been a good hand, and he wanted to bless them. Also, Bob says, 'If the wife is happy, the husband will be happy. If he is happy he will be a better worker.'"

"Thank you so much," Lois cried as she gave Carol a big hug.

"You're very welcome. We have been blessed and we want to pass that blessing on."

While Lois was making the potato soup for supper, Jake was unpacking the boxes of their belongings. He wanted to get the Bible out that he packed away when they came from Ohio. They had only been using the little testament he carried to church.

With two bowls on the table and the pot of soup in the center, they sat across from each other. They realized this was their first time to be at their own table as husband and wife. They just looked at each other for a little. After a bit, Jake said, "This is a new beginning for us. What will be in the future only the Lord knows. Let's start out with reading from the Bible." He then picked up the Bible and read the first Psalm. They bowed their heads and he prayed, thanking the Lord for such blessings. At Bob's, they always prayed before eating, but part-time Carol prayed. At other times she asked Bob to pray. Never was Jake asked to pray. They always had their devotions in their bedroom before going to bed.

Now Jake felt he was the head of his home, and Lois felt she now had her own kitchen. The house was small but comfortable.

****

Working for Bob was enjoyable. Bob was kind and gentle with his livestock. He never took advantage of anyone in business dealings. The neighbors all spoke well of him.

Six weeks after they came, Bob's had a new grandchild born in Ohio. He asked Jake if he thought he could take care of things for a few weeks. Not being planting time or harvest, there would just be the chores, and a couple of times to go to the mill for feed. Jake thought he could.

Bob and Carol were gone for four weeks leaving Jake's to handle the farm. They enjoyed the hard work and the freedom to work as their conscience dictated. Lois was happy to help her husband with the chores as that gave them more time together. One evening they were walking down the lane when they stopped and watched the sunset. "With hard work and diligence, this is what it will be like in just a few years," Jake told Lois. It didn't seem long at all before their landlord returned.

Spring came and along with it the working of the soil and planting. Lois asked Carol if there was someplace she could plant a garden.

"Sure, you may plant it in our garden," Carol replied. "There is a fence around it to keep the rabbits and foxes out. I don't plant one anymore. I have a back problem and I can't lean over to tend it. Joan planted their garden there for the last two years."

"Thank you for offering your garden. I'll plant enough for you and Bob as well."

"That will be kind of you. We won't need much." Carol smiled.

That evening after the chores were done, Jake took one of the horses and the single shovel plow and plowed the garden. Two evenings later he took the disk and worked it into fine soil. This made Lois happy. Together they planted several rows of radishes, lettuce, peas, and early potatoes. Later they planted the other things; they didn't leave any space unplanted. Jake and

Lois enjoyed working together in the garden after supper. The air was cooler and the birds would join them in song. One evening they were singing "In the Garden" when Bob and Carol came out and helped them hoe and sing for a while.

"Sundays are a day of rest," was Bob's thinking. He instructed Jake to do as many chores on Saturday as he could, and leave Sunday for the Lord. Bob's went to a church in town. Jake's enjoyed meeting with the members at their church on Sundays. There weren't many of them, but to fellowship with those of like faith and hear from the word of God was uplifting. There were two other couples that were married that year. They enjoyed being together with them, but they didn't neglect the older folks.

****

It seemed it couldn't be a year yet. Jake so much enjoyed his work and Bob was so good to him. He paid him well. Not having many expenses they were able to put back most of it in the savings. One Monday morning, Bob approached Jake with the agreement about him turning the farm over to Jake. Bob said he noticed when they were gone, everything went on the same. He said, "It is time for us to enter in the agreement of you becoming the farmer. One-third of everything will be yours. I'll help when we are home, but we want to go see our children and grandchildren more. The responsibility will be yours. Anytime you need any advice I will help you. If we are gone, your cousin Jason can give you good advice."

When Jake came in for breakfast he told Lois, "We're not a hired hand anymore."

She gasped, "Did Bob fire you?"

"Yes and no! We're now the farmers instead of the hired hand. It looks big to me, but Bob said he would help when they are here."

33

Lois responded, "Soon we may have a son to help you."

One week and two days later, there was a son born to them. They named him Rudy James. Carol came and helped while Jake worked. Rudy was a good baby. The rocking chair they got from Levi's was just right to rock the baby. Jake loved to rock and sing the baby to sleep. One morning when Jake came in from milking, Lois was sitting on the couch, having just fed Rudy. Jake sat down beside her and put his arm around her shoulder. Looking down into their baby's eyes, he said, "This little bundle of joy surely is a blessing from God."

"He sure is." his wife sighed.

Bob and Carol took a liking to little Rudy. Seeing him caused them to want to go see their children and grandchildren even more. Especially, being they had a grandchild less than a year old as well. Jake's saw less of Bob's as time passed on.

When Rudy was just over a year old, Jake and Lois were blessed with a second son. They named him Simon Levi. Lois told Jake, "Help is on the way."

"Looks like a long way off," was his response.

Their church friends each had babies too. Things were different when they got to gather. The minister said, "Babies crying in the church means a future church."

Jake and Lois hired one of the teenage girls from the church to come and help for a couple of months. Bob's would come and go, but they were faithful in being home during planting and harvest season.

Rudy was just over two when another son was born. His name was Henry Jay. Jake wanted a son named after his grandfather. Lois kiddingly asked Jake if he was going to need to rent more land to keep their sons busy. With a smile on his face, he answered, "It'll be a while."

One day while they were husking corn, Bob spoke up. "Jake, the work will overwhelm you if you let it. Your first responsibility is your walk with the Lord. The second is your family. Work takes third place. You may wonder how this can be done. Management is a lot of the equation. For instance, look at husking this corn. We need a certain amount for cow feed, but not all of what we have planted. There are times when you can let the hogs in a field and let them harvest it for you. It will take them longer to get fat, but you can have more of them. By the use of hog fence, you can use part of the woods to let them run. The little pigs need to be close to the buildings on account of the wildlife in the woods."

Jake tried Bob's plan with the hogs and found it worked well. Keeping up the fences was the hardest part. As long as the hogs had plenty of corn they were content. Keeping water to them was a chore.

Lois told Jake, "We need to figure something out before we have our fourth child. This little house is getting smaller all the time. We need a place to put the bigger boys before this next one comes."

Jake remembered what Bob told him about family comes before work. With a little planning, he was able to build bunk beds for the older two boys. Lois gave Jake a hug and said, "I knew you could do it."

"I love to help my wonderful wife and family." Jake responded, "We are so blessed."

The day Rudy turned four Lois had twin boys. That was a shock to them. The Doctor said he wasn't surprised. They were healthy little fellows. Only a little over five pounds, but they were normal babies. Jake thanked the Lord for that. They named them Thad and Chad. The girl that had helped them earlier returned for a few weeks to help Lois. One of the church ladies loaned them a second bassinet. The problem was where to put two bassinets.

Bob and Carol came over to see the babies. After some visiting and making over the twins, Bob got down to business. He said, "It looks like this house is about full. Our contract calls for us to move and you to move into the big house at the end of five years. With this many babies, I think we may up that date. The time has come that we are ready to let you have the big house. We have bought a house close to our daughters in Indiana and plan to move in a couple of weeks. After the house is empty we will have it cleaned. All you will have to do is move in. You are free to keep on farming until you want to buy the farm."

Two weeks later the movers came and loaded Bob's furniture. It was a sad, yet happy day for Jake and Lois. They had grown close to their landlords over the years they worked together. Bob's said they would keep in touch and would come on occasion. Then it was farewell. The next day there was a crew cleaning the house and left it spotless for its new occupants.

Moving day came and several church members came to help. The sisters brought dinner and being a nice day they ate outdoors. Jake thanked the folks for coming to help.

"We have a wonderful fellowship," he shared. "Today we feel the Godly love in your hearts as you have labored to help us. May the Lord bless you."

****

Their Christian walk was the most important part of the family. The little church Jason told Jake about five years ago had grown to a hundred members. Their creed was the New Testament. Jake and Lois attended as much as possible. Sometimes the boys complained about sitting through the two-hour meetings. At home, in their evening devotions, Jake tried to instill in their small minds the value of praising God.

Lois taught them how to plant seeds in the garden. Every few days, she took them to see if anything came up. She told them, "The seed you planted died, but it had life in it. The soil and rain will cause it to sprout. Soon a new plant will come up."

One morning the boys were excited to see the little green plant coming through the ground. They went every couple days to see these new plants grow into large plants. Their mother reminded them about the small seed they planted. They witnessed the small green plant when it first came through the ground, then the bloom, and finally the fruit. When they were eating some of the fruit she reminded them about the small seed they planted.

One day came she took them to the garden and they picked enough fruit to fill a basket. Again she said, "Remember that little seed you planted. Now, look at this bushel of fruit it produced. You may help me can it." When they had it canned she had them help take it to the basement and put it on the shelves.

Rudy said, "Mom, look at all those full cans. Did they all come from little seeds?"

"The peaches and pears came from trees, but the beans, corn, tomatoes and red beets come from a little seed," she replied.

In awe, he exclaimed, "Wow, all of those full jars from those seeds."

One evening Jake explained to the boys about Jesus, how He was willing to give His life to pay for our sins. "He died like that little seed you planted did. Jesus arose from the grave to save many from death. Like those little seeds rose from the ground to make food for us that we did not die of starvation."

Simon asked, "What makes the seed die and make a new plant."

Jake answered, "When God made the world He made all the plants and trees so there would be food for the people. He put in the seed a germ. When that seed is put in the ground, it would sprout and reproduce itself. He expected the people to plant the seeds and take care of the plants and trees, but He gives the increase. God is good to us. We want to learn more about the blessings He gives. That is why we read the Bible and go to church. To learn more and thank Him for all He gave us."

Under the Mighty Hand of God
Chapter Six

Prosperity had an effect on the family. Every year the crops and the garden produced abundantly. Lois told the boys, "We want to put up plenty. Not only for our needs, but we want to be able to help others who have unfortunate circumstances."

The news came there was a brother in their church that was very sick. Paul was not able to do his chores or fieldwork. They had no children. His wife, Gail, did the milking by herself. Some of the brethren had planted their crops.

Jake asked Rudy if he would like to help them. He could stay at their place and help with other things too. He wasn't so sure at first, thinking about the change it would involve, but finally agreed to go.

After two weeks he became homesick. He came home and was in tears when he told his parents about things over there.

"Gail works so hard all day, just to keep the things done that have to be done," he said. "I went with her to the garden and it was so weedy you could not see much worth picking. Mom, can we share with them?"

A smile came over Lois's face. "Boys, now you see why we put up extra when the Lord blesses us. Yes, we will share it with them. Simon, would you like to take Rudy's place helping them for a while?"

Although they were quite young, Rudy and Simon took turns weekly helping with the chores. They would spend some time talking to Paul, telling him about new calves or what was happening at the barn. Occasionally he was able to go to the barn and the boys showed him things he was interested in. He would show them things that needed to be done, but he was too weak to do anything and had to go lay down. Some of the neighbors came to do things the boys needed help doing.

That summer they took bushels of garden produce to Paul's place and canned a good supply. Gail enjoyed the fellowship as they worked together. Those days were a comfort to her. It was the end of the summer and the boys were putting the last of the canned goods in Paul's basement. They found satisfaction in what they had helped accomplish.

"Now they have shelves full of canned goods and we do too," Rudy told his mom that night.

Henry said, "All of that came from the little seeds we put in the ground."

"Those seeds had the germ God put there," Simon added.

Lois smiled as she, in her heart, thanked the Lord for sons who were interested in the plan of God.

After the brethren had finished husking their corn that fall they planned to husk Paul's. There was a workday planned for Monday. Saturday evening Paul passed away. Gail was very grief-stricken. The church folks came which was a comfort to her. Her family all lived in other areas of the brotherhood. They came as soon as they could.

Rudy and Simon were very broken-hearted. They had become close to Paul and were looking forward to his recovery. In their young minds, they wondered why God let him die. That evening as they gathered around the family altar, Jake read the scriptures about death. It is an appointment we all must face. He talked to them about Mary and Martha when Lazarus died. "Jesus was here and brought him back to life," he told them. "Jesus is now in Heaven preparing a place for us. Some day he will come back to earth and all those who died will come out of the grave, and the ones alive will be changed and all the righteous will go to heaven, never to suffer, cry, or die again. We have a good God."

Rudy and Simon continued helping with the chores. Others came and with the boy's knowledge were able to keep the chores done. The corn husking was temporarily postponed.

After the funeral, the deacons took charge of looking after Gail's affairs. Rudy and Simon were glad to be home again but felt sorry for Gail. They both had school work to catch up on, although they did some while working at Paul's.

Every day they thanked the Lord for the blessings afforded them. In the back of their minds, there was still the sorrow of the death of Paul.

One evening Simon asked his dad, "Did Paul and Gail sin? Is that the reason he suffered so much and died?"

Jake told him, "The Bible tells us all have sinned. Mortal man is under the curse of death from the fall of Adam in the Garden. Jesus came to pay for that sin. Just because someone dies young, doesn't mean they sin more than those who live to be ninety years old." It was hard for young minds to understand.

****

It was a hot day in July. Lois and the three oldest boys were hoeing in the garden. Suddenly Lois grabbed her head and cried, "My head, my head." As she fell to the ground.

Rudy hollered, "Simon, go get dad! Henry, go get a cold rag."

He fanned his mother with his hat. She was very pale. Henry came with the cold rag. Rudy wiped it across her face. She moaned and opened her eyes a little. Smiling at him she said, "Be a good boy, I love you." Her eyes rolled back into her head and she coughed. Rudy was in shock as Jake came running into the garden. When he made it to his wife's side, he saw she was gone. He sat down on the ground, put a kiss on her cheek and began to sob.

More Blessings
Chapter Seven

It had been two years since that sorrowful day when Lois left them. The adjustment was hard. Everywhere they turned there was something to remind them of her. Time does heal, but the love that their mother had for them was still needed. To go to the garden always reminded them of her. Jake hired a girl to come and help at times, but she wasn't Mother.

Folks from church often came to help. This was very much appreciated, but it still didn't take the place of mom. Jake tried to read more to them from the Bible and explain how God's ways are better than our ways. How we must go ahead through faith, looking forward to the resurrection day. It was hard for him to contain his composure especially when he saw tears running down their cheeks.

One day he went into his bedroom and shut the door. The boys heard him in there sobbing. Henry said, "Go help daddy." Quietly they opened the door. Their dad was on his knees by the bed as if he were in prayer. Rudy on one side and Simon on the other put an arm around him and a kiss on his cheek.

Rudy said, "Daddy, it will be okay. God will help us."

The other boys came in and stood behind. Henry and the twins started singing, "Jesus loves us, this I know, for the Bible tells us so."

Jake turned around and sitting on the floor, leaning back on his bed he said, "Thank you, boys. Yes, Jesus does love us. I know we should sing more praise to our God. It seems after mom passed, we just hung our harps in the willow tree. It is hard to even sing at church, but we must. Life shall go on. Jesus is still our Savior and we are still His children.

Israel was in a foreign land under another ruler when they hung their harps in the willow tree. We are in a free land where we can worship God as we know is right. Jesus is still our leader."

Rudy said, "Let's sing, 'Jesus lover of my soul'."

Jason and Dorothy had come to help encourage Jake and the boys. When they stepped on the porch, they thought they heard singing. Jason tapped lightly on the door, then opened it. They for sure heard singing coming from a room in the back. They stepped in and followed the sound down the hall. There on the floor sitting in a circle was the family singing with all their heart, "Jesus Lover of My Soul".

They quietly went back to the kitchen and sat down. Tears were streaming down their cheeks. The family they came to encourage was encouraging them. Sitting on the floor, as low as they could get, lifting their voices to the heavens in praise to the Lord through their faith.

> *Other refuge have I none, hangs my helpless soul on thee,*
> *Leave ah leave me not alone, Still support and comfort me.*
> *All my trust on thee is stayed, All my help from thee I bring,*
> *Cover my defenseless head, with the shadow of thy wing.*

Jason's had brought dinner for them, so when they heard the last verse of the song being sung they went out to the buggy and brought it in. Stepping back up on the porch they saw someone coming into the kitchen. Thad and Chad came running out to greet them. Jake opened the door and invited them in.

Everyone was happy to see them and the dinner they carried in the house. The boys did well with their cooking and the church sisters brought in good things, but nothing was better than Dorothy's good farmer's meal.

After saying "thank you for the good meal," the boys were gathering up to do the dishes.

Dorothy said, "Boys, today I am going to give you a break and do the dishes."

The boys looked at Jake. He winked at them. With another "thank you" they all went out to do their work at the barn.

While Dorothy did the dishes, Jason said he wanted to talk to Jake. They went into the living room and sat down. Jason got right to the point.

"Jake, you know Lois will not be back. Your boys badly need a mother. You also need a helpmate. It has been two years since Lois left. I know she was the dearest on earth to you. If you feel led to marry again we will support you in that."

Jake sat in silence for what seemed like an eternity. A lot was going through his shattered mind. Ever since Lois had died his boys were his life. He hadn't had a lot of time to think about getting married again. God had blessed him so much with Lois. Oh, how he missed her. Nobody could come close to replacing her. He knew only God could bring that kind of healing. It would take trusting in Him to make their home happy again.

Looking back at his cousin Jake replied, "It will take the Lord's leading to make that happen. I am at loss for what to do, but I have faith in our God. If it's His will for a wife and mother to join our family, who am I to resist?"

****

One day a letter came in the mail. After dinner, Jake said, "Boys, I got something to tell you."

"Are we getting company?" asked Chad, thinking there was news in the letter.

"Not exactly," responded their father.

"What is it?" Thad questioned.

"Just wait and let dad tell us," Rudy interjected, being anxious to hear what was in the letter.

Jake cleared his throat. "Boys, we are getting a mother for our home."

Rudy and Simon were deep in thought, saying nothing.

Henry smiled a little and asked, "Is she nice?"

"Is mommy coming back to life?" the twins questioned.

That question was a hard one for Jake. He sat there for a little, trying to think about how to respond to all their questions. No, Mother is not coming back, but God is sending us another mother. She will be a good mother and is a good Christian. She will be good for all of us. We must be good to her. She understands the sorrow we have been through.

Simon spoke up, "Is her name Gail?"

The boys were very excited. The thought of having a mother again gave them hope. It made them think of what it was like before their mother was taken away. Jake tried to explain to them how everyone has their own personalities. "Gail will have a different personality than your mother. We will have to adjust to that difference. If we have patience, God will help us make the adjustment. When we do, we will once again be a happy family."

Rudy and Simon remembered helping Gail a few years ago. They knew she was nice but different than their mother. She had no children. They tried to help the younger ones to understand, "Remember she has no children. Now we will be her children."

"Be a good boy," Rudy reminded his brothers what their mother told him as she passed away.

****

The wedding was a solemn occasion. The bride and groom both knew what it was like to experience sorrow and

45

loneliness. It was faith that carried them through. Now they were entering another chapter of their lives. What lay ahead? By faith and obedience to the word of God, they would take the next step.

The family adjusted well. The three older boys were old enough to help in the fieldwork. Gail accepted the twins as if they were hers. She took them to the garden and they enjoyed planting the little seeds. She took time to explain to them about the germ in the seed, just like Lois had to the older boys.

For the boys to work with their dad in the field or the barn was enjoyable. To come in at mealtime and there was a good home-cooked meal on the table was really appreciated. The evening devotions were special. It took a while to call Gail mom, but in time it became natural. They were once again a Godly functional family. The twins became very fond of their new mother. There was love at home.

A year after Jake and Gail were married they were blessed with a baby boy. Gail was overwhelmed, as she and Paul never had that blessing. They named him Joseph. This brought more adjusting in the family.

Gail, never expecting to bear children, had given a lot of attention to Thad and Chad. Now that there was a baby to care for the twins had to share their mother. Jake talked to them about loving their little brother. He explained to them a baby takes a lot of attention. Mother still loves you. You can be a help to her if you be good boys. They started becoming more daddy boys.

When Joseph was two there was another adjustment in the family when twins were born. They named them Benjamin Dale and Cassie Gail. Jake was really happy to have a daughter after having all the boys.

Jake and Gail both felt so well blessed. Having walked through the valley of sorrow, they were now indeed a happy family. They tried diligently to walk with the Lord endeavoring to bring the little ones up to serve Him.

The Trial of Faith
Chapter Eight

Joseph was a well mannered seven-year-old boy. He did as his parents instructed. Now he not only helped feed the calves, but he milked three cows every evening. His mother never asked him to get up early to go milk in the morning. He enjoyed playing with his younger brother and sister, but he also liked to go out to the field with the older ones. He learned from them how to do things. Thad and Chad taught him to play baseball and a lot of other games. He felt they were a big happy family.

In time the older children felt their mother was favoring the little ones. Little by little bitterness, soon turning into hatred, was creeping in among them. This came partly because the older boys were of an age to carry more of the workload. They felt Joseph was being babied. When they called him a sissy, Jake reprimanded them. He told them when they were younger they didn't do near as much as they were expected to do now.

Gail did show love for all of Jake's boys. She dried tears, rocked the little ones when they needed loving. Was a listening ear when one of them needed understanding. But try as hard as she could, there was not the same closeness as with the children she brought into this world.

Younger children usually are considered by the older ones as spoiled. No matter how old a boy gets, he still loves his mother. As they were approaching adult age, just seeing Mother give special treatment to the younger children caused deep hurt. It was natural for Gail to show love for the three young ones she bore. Jealousy and hatred grew in the hearts of Jake's older boys.

****

Word came that Jake's father was very sick. Jake talked to Rudy and Simon about doing the work at home while they went to Virginia to see his father. They felt they could keep getting the work done for a while.

When Jake, Gail, and the young twins boarded the train for Virginia, Joseph hugged his mother and wept. She told him to be a big boy and help his brothers with the work. He assured her he would do his best and stood watching longingly as the train disappeared down the track. When Jake's arrived in Virginia, they found his father was very low. Even in his weakened state, he was able to recognize his son and was thankful they had come to see him. It was evident to the family his time was near.

****

Things went well at home, though there were times they missed their dad a lot.

One day Henry asked, "Why can't Joseph milk more cows?"

Simon said, "Sure he can."

At first, Joseph thought it was fun milking more cows. Then his arms started hurting. Thad felt sorry for him and relieved him for a while. He had a good attitude in spite of the ridicule his brothers did to him.

One morning while they were milking the cows, Joseph told his brothers, "I had a dream about you last night. I was a wealthy landowner and you were working for me. You had to do what I told you to do."

They laughed and made fun of him. Henry squirted milk in his face, and laughing said, "Did you tell me to do that?"

Thad came running and ran into Joseph just as he started to get up from milking the cow. He lost his balance and fell on the floor between two cows spilling the bucket of milk. They all laughed called him a "clumsy dreamer." They blamed him for wasting dad's milk.

Joseph began to cry. The boys started chanting, "Cry baby, cry baby, go find mommy." They wouldn't stop laughing at their little brother. Joseph sat down to another cow and started milking. "Why are my brothers treating me so cruel?" he asked himself. The cows were more kind than they were.

He couldn't believe his brothers could be so mean. They weren't that way while dad was here. When they treated him badly, he would say, "I'm sorry." They would just walk away with a smirk on their faces

Joseph told his brothers, "We always said a prayer in the morning and evening when father and mother were here. Now that they are gone we never pray."

They began to chant, "Preacher boy, preacher boy."

Joseph would seek a quiet place and pray alone.

****

One day the boys spotted some people in the back field coming towards the house. It looked like they were coming from the woods by the river. As they got closer it became evident that they were gypsies. The boys had heard of these people but had never really seen them up close. The brothers were afraid of these strange looking and acting people.

They wanted food. Rudy told them to go away. This angered them. One of them grabbed Joseph and said, "If you don't give us some food we will take this boy."

Simon said, "For ten dollars we will give you two hams and the boy."

The older gruff acting leader said, "Three hams and the boy."

Rudy offered four hams, but not the boy.

Simon said, "If we get rid of Joseph we will not have to bother with him."

All this time Joseph was in shock at what he was hearing. "It has to be a joke," he told himself as he was desperately trying to understand. The leader of the gypsies offered to take the boy for ten dollars and no hams. He knew where he could sell the boy for a large profit.

Joseph pleaded with them to not sell him but to no avail. They tied his hands to two of the gypsies and led him away.

It didn't take long before the boys knew they had done the wrong thing. By the middle of the afternoon, Rudy was in a fit of unrest. He took off for the woods to find his little brother. Searching all along the river he came across the clearing where the gypsies had camped. Nothing was there. Just a few smoking embers from a campfire remained. He sat down on a log and cried. Returning to the house he shared with his brothers what he had found.

Simon only laughed at Rudy. "Now we will see what becomes of his dreams," he said. They divided the ten dollars between them.

"What will we tell the folks happened to Joseph?" Rudy and the twins asked, "We can't tell them the truth."

Simon explained the plan. "What we can do is tell them he went back to the river and never came back. That is what we witnessed. They just don't need to know the rest."

Jake's were gone for three weeks. His father passed away soon after they got there. After the funeral, Jake and his brother finalized the estate. Jake brought his mother with them to stay. On the way home, Gail said, "The boys will be happy to see their grandma." Grandma was anxious to see them, especially Joseph. She had never seen him.

Before they left Virginia, Jake had sent a card telling the boys when to expect their arrival. The card came the day before they got home. The boys fabricated a story to tell their parents.

The train was on time. Rudy was there to meet them with the horse and carriage. On the way home, Jake asked about things at home. He noticed his son was quieter than normal. All Rudy would say was that things on the farm were doing fine. He mumbled about a stillborn calf but that the cow was doing fine. Jake could tell that Rudy was hiding something but figured they would find out in time. The last couple of miles were painful to Rudy as he knew soon his parents would hear the devastating news.

Rudy tied the horse to the hitching post and helped carry in the luggage. The boys came running from the barn to greet them. They were surprised to see grandma. Grandma asked, "Where is Joseph?"

The boys looked at each other and tears were starting down their cheeks. Chad blurted out, "He's gone!"

"Where did he go?" his mother asked.

"Who's he with?" Jake added.

Simon answered; he told Thad yesterday that he was going wading in the river. Thad told him not to go as it was dangerous and he needed someone with him. It was chore time before we realized Joseph was missing.

"Didn't you go look for him?" Now Jake was visibly upset.

"Yes, we did."   Simon continued.   "Thad and I immediately headed for the woods while Chad and Rudy stayed at the barn and did chores. We searched until it was dark. We were scared, not only for our missing brother but of the dark. We were afraid we might run across the gypsies we seen down by the bridge."

"What about Joseph? Don't you think he might be scared too?" Jake was getting angry and emotionally troubled.

"Father, please don't be angry with us," Rudy pleaded, "We tried to find him. This morning as soon as we got the chores done we all went to find him. We didn't think he would go all the way back to the river. We searched every inch of the woods as far as the river. Along the riverbank over on the west end, Chad found a handkerchief. We don't know if it's his."

Chad pulled out a soiled piece of cloth.

Gail, with a frightened look in her face, said it all. "That is his handkerchief. It was my father's many years ago. Did you find anything else?"

Simon continued on with the now ever-growing lie, "When we were walking along the roaring water we found a pair of shoes with socks in them. We were pretty sure they were not his so we left them there. That was just before Rudy had to leave for the train station."

By now Gail was in tears and Jake's face was red with rage. He could not believe what he was hearing. "We must continue to search. Thad, you stay with grandma and the twins. The rest of us will go find Joseph."

Going through the woods at places they saw footsteps, but nothing they could recognize. The boys couldn't remember just where they had seen the shoes. They walked up and down the river looking. At last, it was Gail that found the small leather boots. They were sitting on a log with the laces hanging over the side. Stuffed inside was a pair of dirty socks that she knew all too well. She started sobbing.

Jake put his arms around a stricken mother. Looking at the wild river with little hope he told her, "If Joseph waded into that torrent water, he is gone. No doubt the wild rushing river has consumed him."

They stood there weeping for a long time. They bowed in prayer asking the Lord to help them through another deep valley.

Jake walked down the river for a long time hoping to see some trace of Joseph. With such roaring turbulent waters, he knew there likely was no hope, however, sometimes God does miracles. Darkness was coming over them as they went to the house.

Grandma had fixed some potato soup for supper, but no one would eat much. Jake tried to read from the Bible for comfort, but it just didn't seem to help. Grandma suggested they go talk to their minister. Jake had Simon hook up the buggy and ride with him through the dark to their minister's home. He was overwhelmed with sorrow when he heard the report. He sounded it to all the church members and stopped by the sheriff's home to tell him of the missing lad.

The next day there were several men volunteering to walk the river in hope of finding Joseph. Many of the church sisters came to comfort Gail and the children. The Sheriff sounded it abroad. The authorities searched down the river a long way.

After a week they told Jake, "With that high water they likely will never find him. Sometimes when the water recedes a body may be left on a sand bar."

The family tried to adjust to the loss. To keep one's faith is hard to do. It helps to have sympathizing church family and neighbors. Jake tried to remember Job's loss. He lost all his children at once. He said, "The Lord gives, and the Lord takes away. Blessed be the name of the Lord."

For the next two months, they had hopes of someone finding his body. They could hardly stand the thought of his body washed to the sea.

The prison of guilt the boys found themselves in haunted them every waking hour. The doors could not be broken down. The walls could not be scaled. The joy they thought they would find in having Joseph out of their lives was also a lie. There was no joy, only sorrow.

A Lonely Journey
Chapter Nine

Joseph tried to break loose from his captors. Each time he did, they slapped him across the back with a branch. He winced in pain with every slap. He was very disoriented and confused as to what was going on. He started to cry. They yelled at him and rubbed dirt in his face. The tears caused mud, which ran down into his mouth.

He didn't know how far they had come, but he was getting very tired. His bare feet hurt. Why had his brothers kept his shoes? His stomach was hurting from hunger. It was getting dark. He wanted to go to sleep. Finally, they came to a camp. There were women cooking some sort of stew over an open fire. They untied his wrists but told him if he tried to escape they would shoot him. They had walked far enough he didn't know where he was. He sat down on the ground and pulled his knees up to his chest. Laying his head on his knees he cried. He was a sad little boy.

One of the ladies brought him a bowl of stew. Through the tears he thanked her. Then, as he had been taught since he was a baby, he bowed his head and thanked the Lord for something to eat. The gypsies just dove in without prayer. When they went to sleep, they tied his hands and feet together. He slept between two of the older men.

The gypsies could speak both English and Spanish. They spoke Spanish most of the time. Every day they walked a long time. One time when they came to a town, they untied him. They said they were going shopping. He was instructed to not get anything, "If you try to run away we will kill you. Just do as we tell you." Eight of them went into the general store.

One of the gypsy girls just a few years older than Joseph told him to follow her. She was a slender girl and nice-looking with long arms and long slim fingers. "Let's look at the candy," she told him. It was close to the door. The clerk asked if she could help them. The girl pointed to Joseph and said, "He cannot talk." The girl asked for a candy that was on the bottom shelf. When the clerk got it the girl handed her a nickel. When the clerk opened the cash drawer to put the nickel in the girl said, "Oh! I want one too. That one was for my brother." When the clerk leaned down to get another one, quicker than lightning the girl snatched a twenty from the cash drawer and stuck it in Joseph's pocket. She paid for the second candy and as the clerk was putting the nickel in the cash drawer, someone dropped something behind her. Immediately the clerk turned around and just that quick the girl got another twenty plus two nickels. Because there were more twenties in the drawer the clerk didn't know two of them were gone. The girl was very kind and thanked the clerk. Joseph didn't know when the second twenty got in his pocket, but it was there. She told Joseph to put the candy in his pocket.

They walked back through the store. There was a customer looking over a grass seeder. One of the gypsy men asked the man if he could show them how it worked. While he was going into minute details about the performance of the seeder, a gypsy boy snuck up behind him and slipped his billfold out of his pocket. The man never felt it. Quickly he removed some money but left some in there. Without anyone seeing him he moved away from the man, laying the billfold on the floor.

While this was going on a gypsy woman had the clerk occupied asking if they had some certain dish. Joseph was witnessing some very confusing things. He knew it could not be right. His parents had taught him that stealing was wrong. The boy quickly slipped the money into Joseph's pocket putting it under the candy.

One of the gypsy men kept the seeder customer occupied until all the other gypsies were out of the store and spread out in different directions. They had a plan of where to meet. The girl told Joseph to stay with her. Their meeting place was outside of town after it got dark. As they were walking away from the store Joseph saw a paper in a vender with headlines that said, "Seven-year-old boy drowns in the river." "How sad," he thought. "That's my age."

When they met, the man that was the head of the group emptied Joseph's pockets. The candy went to the boy and the girl. They counted the money. It was two hundred dollars. The next day they were back on the road. Joseph was tired of walking, but gradually he got used to it. After what had seemed like a long time they stopped tying him up at night. He missed his dad and mother very much. At night when the men he slept between were asleep, he would pray and cry silently. He had been taught to love Jesus and to trust God. It was hard right now to do this. "Where is God?" he asked himself one night. "Why doesn't he take me back to my home?" Soon after that, as he was sound asleep, he dreamed he saw an angel standing beside him. The angel said, "Joseph, I will be with you. The Lord has a work for you to do. Obey your parent's teaching."

When he awoke the next morning, he thought of that dream and the one about his brothers working for him. He knew they were just a dream. He remembered the stories his dad used to read from the Bible of dreams that had meaning. He prayed the Lord would help him.

When they came to a town they would disperse, but all met in the same store. Their strategy was always the same. He knew he was being used. If something went wrong it was he who had the money. He was afraid of them and also afraid of what would happen if he was caught. He prayed the Lord would deliver him from these wicked people.

After several days they came to a small town. Most of the people were Mexicans. The group of gypsies dispersed. They had homes there. He was taken to the home of Durango, the older man from the group. There he met Durango's wife

Orlanda. She had been sick and unable to travel with the caravan. She looked Joseph over and said, "Jaycee!" From that time on, that's what they called Joseph.

The gypsies brought a lot of things home they had accumulated while traveling beside a lot of money. It was all acquired by stealing. There was a lot of canned food.

Durango took Joseph to the backside of their hut to a shed. In the shed there stood a Jersey cow. He asked Joseph to milk her, not thinking he knew how. Joseph asked for a bucket and stool. He took them, sat down, and started milking with speed. To sit beside a cow and milk made him feel more at home then he had for many days. Durango had a smile on his face. In the house, Orlanda showed him how to make soup. That soup didn't taste like his mother's, but it was something to eat.

Joseph lived with the couple for six months. It was the same soup every day. He milked the cow every day. He didn't waver from what his parents had taught him and prayed every day for his dad to come and get him.

Overcoming Sorrow in Iowa
Chapter Ten

Waking up in the morning and hearing Gail sobbing softly was hard. Jake would gently take her hand in his and softly give it a squeeze. Words just wouldn't come. Gail just couldn't believe her son would wade into such turbulent water, but the evidence pointed in that direction. They prayed for strength to heal their sorrow. She wondered how Job's wife was able to cope with the sudden loss of all their children. At times, Jake would put his arms around her and she would sob on his shoulder. She would say, "I just don't have enough faith." Jake told her, "It isn't about faith. You do have faith. You went through a very deep valley with Paul. You were left with no one. Having gone through the valley with Lois, I know a lot of tears were shed. God gave us tears to help in the healing. It's not a lack of faith to shed tears. Jesus did. At any time you want to cry on my shoulders, we can weep together. There may be times you want to weep alone. Go into the bedroom and shut the door and pour out your heart to the Lord. There are times I do that in the hayloft."

Life does go on. Time heals, but the memories are still there. At church, or other places when she saw boys Joseph's age, it always brought back the sadness. On his birthday it was extremely hard.

Church services seemed to draw them closer to Heaven where Jesus went. Hearing the words of Jesus, "Let not your heart be troubled." Thinking about Jesus' mother, looking up at the cross where her Son was suffering so much. Likely through her mind flashed the words of Simeon when he blessed them and told Mary, "A sword shall pierce through your soul." Also, "The thoughts of many hearts may be revealed."

Gail told Jake, "To relate with the mother of Jesus does help. However, we humans can't fully understand the love of God in giving His Son to pay for the sin of the world.

Jake responded, "Jesus' willingness to lay down His life, that He could take it up again, gives us hope of the resurrection. If we are faithful we will meet Joseph again."

A year after Joseph disappeared they were blessed with another son. They talked about naming him Joseph, but felt it would make it harder to forget their sorrow. They named him Aaron Lee. He was a healthy bundle of joy. Caring for him was a help to lessen their sorrow.

****

Time moves on. The five older boys were in young folks. They enjoyed being with other boys their age. There would always be parents attending. There was volleyball and baseball and other games. They were good players and good sports. They fit in well with the young people. At times they would sing. They would help sing some of the songs, but songs like, "Precious Memories" would cause them to get a choking feeling in their throat and they couldn't sing. Their friends felt it was the memory of their brother that bothered them.

Jake rented more land to keep the boys on the farm. The older three could do a man's work. They liked to work. One day, the five of them were husking corn. Jake went to the store to get supplement feed. Ben went with him. Rudy called them together.

He said, "We need to talk." He opened his mouth but got a lump in his throat. Tears were streaming his checks. "I, ah, I," then he broke down and sobbed.

Simon said, "I think I know what he wants to say. He wants, ah, he wants to." He just couldn't say it. He choked up and he also sobbed.

Through tears Henry said, "If we could just be with our mother in the garden planting seeds, she would tell us what we should do."

They all just sat down on the ground and sobbed.

Sunday the young minister had given them such good counsel from the Word of God about the need to be born again to enter the kingdom of Heaven. He very emphatically explained the horrible place of the lost. He said, "Do you want to go there? Today is the day of salvation, which can only be found in Jesus. Confess your sins and be baptized. Only then can you be free."

They were sitting on the ground, thinking about the sermon. One at a time they said, "I want to be baptized."

Rudy said, "We'll have to tell Dad what we have done to Joseph. I, ah, I don't think I can. I still hear his pleading not to sell him, and every time I shut my eyes I see the anguish in his eyes. We would not hear." He broke down and sobbed again.

Each one felt they would like to confess their sin to their father, but they thought it was more than they could do. Hearing their dad coming home, they jumped up and continued husking as fast as they could.

****

The boys didn't talk anymore about their brother. They tried to act as if everything was fine. Sometimes they almost had their conscience convinced that the story they fabricated was the way it really happened.

One day Chad was planting corn. He spilled some on the ground. How can you pick up all that corn? He spread it out a bit and covered it up with soil. He thought that was easier than picking those kernels up one at a time. If I covered it up, Dad will never know.

A few weeks later, Chad and his dad were cultivating corn in that field. Chad was coming back from his third round when he noticed his dad was stopped at the end of the field. He thought he was resting his horses. When he got there, he stopped. Dad said, "Come over here." There beside Dad's cultivator was a circle, about three feet in diameter of corn, very thickly populated standing as tall as the other corn. Dad remembered Chad planted the field. He said, "Son, do you know who planted these?"

Chad dropped his head, "I spilled some, and just covered it up with dirt."

Jake told him, "This loss isn't a great deal, but remember, it is hard to cover up a mistake. The truth will come out sometime. Had those kernels been very expensive, and you wanted to correct the mistake, you would have picked them up one at a time. You would have to humble yourself to do that. To cover up mistakes doesn't change the fact there was a mistake. There are times people make mistakes they don't know how to correct. The temptation is to try covering it up with the dirt of this world. They may get by for a while, but the truth eventually comes out. The best way is to confess it. Man is afraid to confess. When they don't, they live in a prison of guilt. Jesus taught us to confess our sins."

The church was growing. It was twenty years ago the first meeting was held in the building they were using. Every year there were baptisms. More folks were moving in because of opportunity. The time came they felt they needed more room to worship. The building they were renting wasn't large enough. The question came up. What should we do? One of the older brethren offered to donate five acres for a meeting house and a cemetery. The church appointed a committee of five brethren to look into it.

As the church population had grown, they had diversified. One brother became blacksmith, another shod horses. One family started a general store. Another bought the feed mill in the area. Jake bought a sawmill from back east.

They built a building to house the sawmill at the back of the lane in the woods. In the large woods on his farm, he knew there were several trees ready for harvest. He thought he could cut timber for the new meeting house. After that was complete he would let a couple of the boys saw for hire.

There was a lot of work to do, building the new meeting house. The week they planned to raise the building, Jake and all his sons were there every day. Some of the brethren wondered why Jake's five older boys, always came to meetings and now they worked with the brethren every day, yet they hadn't joined the church. Someone mentioned that it was Jake and Lois's children that hadn't come into the church. Jake and Gail's twins had. Is it something about the loss of their mother that bothers them? Someone said he remembered the crises of the drowning of their brother. He said, "Could it be they feel the responsibility of him drowning, and can't let go of it? Their folks were gone when it happened."

An older brother responded, "I remember that day well. At the time I thought something seemed fishy, but the boys were so remorseful. I couldn't accuse them of foul play. The twins were only ten. The oldest was thirteen and the other in between. It hadn't been many years since they were helping their mother in the garden. They loved to be with her. She was so kind and taught them valuable lessons about the way of the Lord. To lose her suddenly and later to suddenly lose their brother may be something they can't overcome. We need to pray for them."

Home on the Dairy Farm
Chapter Eleven

One day after Joseph had finished milking, Durango took Joseph a few miles to a farm. The farmer had advertised for a milkmaid, but Durango figured a hard worker like Joseph could do the job of a milkmaid. Durango told the farmer his "grandson" liked to milk. He said, "This boy can milk." as he patted Joseph on the head. The farmer agreed to pay ten dollars a month and give him room and board if he could milk three cows every morning and evening. Joseph nodded his head but didn't say anything. Durango had warned Joseph not to talk to the farmer. If he told him who he really was, he would disappear and never be seen again. That really scared Joseph. All he wanted to do was go home.

Durango stayed until milking time to be sure the farmer was satisfied with Joseph. The farmer had over thirty cows and needed several milkers. When the milking time came Joseph took a bucket, a stool and started milking. He could milk faster than any of the milkmaids. He milked three cows, while the others were milking two. Durango got the ten dollars, and said, "I'll come next month to see how he is doing."

Joseph had a room all to himself in the servant's quarters. He ate at the table where the other servants ate. Unlike at his captors, the meals were good and plentiful. There was always a prayer before the meals. Joseph was happy to have his own little bedroom, to be alone. It was there he prayed daily, not just for himself, but for his father and mother. Although he was afraid of them, he still prayed for his brothers who sold him.

Durango came every month to see how Joseph was doing and collect the ten dollars. The farmer never let him know that Joseph milked five cows instead of three. He knew if he told him, he would demand more money.

Joseph was a very good worker. On the farm is where he felt at home. It was what he was used to and he liked it. He not only milked, but he would clean out the stable and do other work around the place too. He liked to work. He never caused trouble with anyone.

Alva, the farmer and Eunice his wife thought there was something different about this young man. When they tried to talk to him, he would not say anything. They tried to pay him for the other work he did. When they did that he got fear in his eyes and shook his head no. They talked to him in both English and also Spanish. He just shook his head. One day the wife asked him to do something for them in their house. While he was there, she asked him if there was anything he would like to have. Tears started streaming down his cheeks. He pointed to a Bible on the stand. That night there was a Bible in his room. When he came in and saw it, he sat on the edge of his bed, opened it and holding it close to his chest started crying.

Alva told his wife, "Joseph has never once asked to go home to his grandfather. That boy is not Durango's grandson."

Joseph liked Alva and Eunice but was afraid of Durango. This and other things made the farmer and his wife suspicious. When they ask Joseph about it, he would look the other way and not talk.

It didn't take long before Alva and Eunice grew fond of Joseph and wanted to help him. After milking one morning they took him to their little school. They figured he just didn't know how to talk. The teacher, being fluent in both English and Spanish, soon found out he could talk.

Joseph liked his teacher and one day told her, "I have a secret I won't tell anyone."

"What might that be?" she asked.

"I can't tell you. I will get hurt, really bad. Please don't ask me to tell it."

The teacher did not ask him again but relayed their conversation to Alva and Eunice. That night they moved Joseph into their home. They told him that the next morning they would like him to go to church with them. He smiled but said nothing. He wanted to go to church. Not just any church. He wanted to go to his church, where all his friends were. He wanted to sit beside his father and sing again.

Joseph knew he had to tell someone his secret but he was afraid. Afraid if he told on his brothers they would harm him even more than they already had. He was afraid of Durango who had already hurt him many times. That night as he lying on his new bed, he thought of the dreams he had. He remembered the story his dad read to them about another Joseph who had been treated badly by his brothers. He had dreams too. "Will God work through me?" he wondered.

It became evident to Alva and Eunice that the boy they hired was a slave. One morning at breakfast Alva point-blank asked him if he was Durango's grandchild. They saw fear in his eyes. He shook his head no. From then on they wanted to help him escape, not only from Durango but from his fears as well.

Joseph had just turned eight when Alva and Eunice both showed up at school to take him home. Once all the other children had gone they called Joseph back into the schoolhouse. They told him he was a very good boy and they wanted to help him with his fears. They could protect him from the people of whom he was afraid.

Joseph sat there on the chair swinging his leg and fiddling with his fingers. He wouldn't look up for a long time. Finally, he looked up and said two simple words, "I'm scared."

"We understand." Eunice told him, "My brother is a long way from here in San Diego and he will protect you. He will give you a home and take you to school. Think about it overnight."

That night Joseph had another dream. An Angel stood at the foot of his bed and said, "Fear not to go with them." While he was milking the cows the next morning he thought about the dream. Was an angel actually talking to him?

Just as he was finishing milking Durango came wanting his ten dollars. He told Alva, "There will be only one more month for him to milk. We are going on a trip and want our grandson to go along."

Fear gripped Joseph. He knew to go with them he would be one of the gypsies stealing where ever they went. He felt the Lord was giving him a way to escape from that sinful life. After Durango left Joseph told Alva he would like to go to Eunice's brother's house to live.

Alva gave instructions to the farm foreman. He told him that he and his wife would be gone for a few days. He didn't tell him where they were going nor did he say a thing about Joseph. Only the school teacher knew and she promised to not talk.

After breakfast when the chores were done, Joseph went into the schoolroom. He gave his teacher a hug and said goodbye. They both shed some tears. She had been like a mother to him for the last six months. She said, "May the Lord bless you my child." Just as the other students were coming in the front door, Joseph slipped out the back. He got into Alva's buggy and lay on the floor in the back. He covered himself with the buggy blanket, as Alva instructed. Alva and Eunice soon came and put a couple of their lighter suitcases on top of him. They placed things around him. A worker brought their horse and hitched him up to the buggy. They bid him farewell and were soon going down the road.

When they felt it safe, they stopped and got Joseph out from under the luggage. They had him sit between them. It took four hours to get to the town where the train would arrive. Alva put the buggy in a shed by the livery stable. After giving the attendant of the livery stable instructions about the horse, Alva paid him and they walked to the train station.

It was about two hours before they could hear the train coming. Joseph got excited when he saw it coming around the bend. He had never ridden on a train. There were several people getting on the two passenger cars. Joseph noticed a boy getting on at the other car that he thought looked a lot like one of the gypsies.

They were all seated and the train began to move. What a thrill to feel the movement and the clack-a-ta-click as the train rolled along. Joseph looked out the window as the fields and houses sped by. With each passing moment, it was taking him farther away from his captors and at the same time farther away from home. Such a mixed feeling he had as he wondered what his parents were doing. Did they miss him? Was he now safe from harm? Then his heart sank. Down the aisle came the boy he saw getting on the other car. It definitely was one of the gypsy boys. He went on down the aisle and didn't act as if he knew him. It had been over a year since they had been together. At that time he had long unkempt hair. He was always dirty with mud caked on his face from the tears and dirt. Now he was clean and dressed in nice clothes. He even wore a new hat Alva had given him. Also, he was sitting between two well-dressed folks.

Joseph tapped Alva on the arm, "Watch your billfold," he whispered. "That boy is a gypsy. He has a way of getting money out of people's billfold without them knowing it."

The boy was going back up the aisle when Joseph watched him bump into a well-dressed man. Abruptly he pointed out the window, "Excuse me, sir, can you tell me what that is out there we are passing?" While the man looked out the window to see what he was looking at, the boy slipped his billfold out. After the man answered the boy thanked him and slid into the empty row behind his victim. After taking some money, he laid the billfold on the floor under the man's seat.

Joseph knew he didn't take all the money. That way the man wouldn't know he was robbed for awhile.

Joseph asked Alva if he saw that. Alva said he didn't see anything unusual. He saw the boy talk to the man, but didn't see the other.   The boy came back to the end of the train just as the conductor was taking tickets. He slipped into the restroom until the conductor was gone.

Suddenly Alva felt someone bump into him. There was that boy, "Sir I dropped my comb under that seat in front of you. Would you get it for me?" Alva started to lean over.

Joseph said, "Grab your billfold."

Alva's hand came on top of that boy's hand with his billfold in it. The boy hollered trying to jerk his hand away. Alva hung on tight as the conductor came to see what the commotion was.

"This young man just tried to steal my billfold," Alva told the conductor.

Scared, Joseph whispered into Alva's ear.

"Also you will find that he was money in his pocket that he took from that gentleman up there on the left. That's his billfold the boy put under the seat."

The boy scowled at Joseph and growled, "You'll pay for this, just wait and see."

The boy let go of the billfold and Alva let go of him.

The conductor asked the boy for his ticket. He had none. He asked Alva if he wanted to press charges.

"No," Alva answered, "but this boy needs to be taught something."

Joseph thought, "He has been taught something, but the wrong thing."

The conductor made the boy give the man his money back and apologize.

At the next stop, they watched as the conductor escorted the gypsy boy off the train. As the train began to roll again,

Joseph tensed up and his face went pale. There was their attempted thief walking away and who was alongside him? It was none other than Joseph's captor, Durango. Alva saw the man as well and grabbed Joseph's hand. An unsaid message was transmitted through the light squeeze he gave the scared lad.

It made Joseph shiver just to think about what things would be like if he hadn't been milking for Alva. He would have been just like the gypsy boy.

They were on the train for two days and two nights. They ate one meal a day in the dining car. Alva's bought him his meals. They treated him as if he were their son. The Bible was their companion on the train. They read for awhile each day. Joseph enjoyed the scenery. He slept well, although sometimes he had bad dreams of the days with the gypsies.

When they arrived in San Diego, Eunice's brother, Carl, and wife Rachel Bauman were there to greet them. There were hugs and kisses. Then Alva introduced Joseph to them. Carl and Rachel shook his hand and said, "Welcome to sunny California and to our home."

They loaded their things into Carl's automobile. Joseph was excited to ride in the horseless carriage. He had never ridden in one before. After a long hour and a half ride on a bumpy road, Carl announced, "Here we are. Welcome to our home."

Love in a California Home
Chapter Twelve

Carl was a talkative, likable man. Alva's stayed for a week to see how everything would go.

"What's your full name, Joseph?" Carl asked.

"Joseph Bowman," the eight-year-old mumbled sheepishly.

"Oulman?" Carl questioned, "Do you mean Bauman?"

Joseph said, "Something like that."

Carl replied, "Bauman is our last name. That is good. You have the same last name as us. What is your middle name?"

"Don't have any," Joseph replied.

Carl rubbed his chin, "Well, you look sort of like my grandpa and his name was Barnes. Being I have a cousin named Joseph Bauman, to keep from having confusion, how about it if we call you Joseph Barnes Bauman? For short we can call you J.B."

Joseph liked the idea. That would help to ward off Durango from finding him. Anyway, he liked the sound of J.B.

Rachel gave him a tour of the house and showed him his room. The house was a large one with two bathrooms. His room was upstairs. There were bookshelves full of books on one wall. It had been their son's room when he was growing up.

"He was a book worm," Rachel said. "He went to college and is now a doctor."

Carl said, "We'll not do too much this week. We want to spend it with Alva's. They drove out through the fields looking at the crops. He was amazed at the rows and rows of orange trees. There were several Mexicans working for him. He would always wave and they waved to him. He knew them all by name. Spanish was the main language spoken in the fields.

Joseph liked his new home from the first day. He and Carl became good friends. Carl had a lot of stories to tell. He had had some interesting experiences along life's way. Every evening, after supper, they sat around visiting. Before they retired for the night, they got their Bibles, read something and discussed it. They would bow in prayer. Then it was "Good night."

After a few days, it was time for Alva's to bid them farewell. Joseph gave them each a hug and thanked them.

He said, "Tell my teacher how nice it is here."

Carl took them to the train. It had been an enjoyable week.

****

After Alva's were gone, Carl and Rachel had a little serious talk with J.B. They shared with him about their life and its goals. They had been married for thirty-five years. The farm had been his father's. Carl had been an only child. He had grown up in this house. When they had gotten married, they had lived in an older farmhouse his father had owned. They had been married for three years before Carl Jr. was born. When Jr. was twelve, the old folks moved into a smaller house in the little village of Dulzura.

"That is when we moved here," Carl told him. "Oranges are our main crop. They do well here. Jr. never liked to work in the orange groves. His mother homeschooled him through the eighth grade and then he attended the church school for high school."

"He was an easy student to teach, he almost taught himself," Rachel interjected. "After finishing high school, he applied to college to get his pre-med schooling. He had decided to become a doctor. He has finished with his medical schooling and soon will be finishing his internship. He hasn't told us where he plans to practice. We hope it will be close here. Time will tell."

The onslaught of information was a little overwhelming for an eight-year-old, but he listened intently as his new guardians continued.

"We are Christians," Rachel continued. "We belong to an old order conservative church of which Carl is a minister."

"We feel to help others is part of our calling," Carl added. "When Alva asked if we would consider helping you, we prayed about it. We really don't know much about you. Alva's said you have a secret and don't want to tell anybody. That secret will be yours until you want to tell it.

As you have seen, we read the Bible, believe the Bible and endeavor to live the way it tells. Love is the theme of it. Obedience is a command. Eunice told us the only thing you asked for while living there, was a Bible. We want to make a home for you, just like we did for Jr."

Joseph thought about the love they had at home before his parents left to go see his ailing grandfather. Prayer ceased and love disappeared once they were gone. It made him miss his parents. He even missed his brothers. Seeing Carl and Rachel's love for the Lord and each other here made him miss all that he had had at home even more.

"Thank you," he said, and remembering the Sundays they went to church asked, "Do you go to church on Sundays?"

"We certainly do," Carl replied.

"May I go too?"

"We would expect you to, darling," Rachel smiled at the thought of taking a child to church on Sunday morning.

After the others were asleep Rachel dug out the old school books. Looking through them she realized it had been a long time since she had taught Jr. She had forgotten so much. It would take a lot of study time, on her own, to be able to teach this young man. Next, she looked over the report his teacher had sent along explaining where he was in his studies. Rachel was happy to see that Joseph was an enthusiastic student.

The first few times they went to church, he sat with Carl and called him dad. It didn't take long before some of the boys befriended him. When they became more acquainted, he started sitting with them. Kenneth and Daryl were two of the boys who were exceptionally kind to him. They became lifetime friends. He enjoyed the church service, especially the singing. The solemn sacred songs brought him closer to the Lord. There were times he shed tears, thinking of bygone days, sitting on his father's lap while these songs were being sung.

****

Five years had passed since Joseph came to live with Carl's. Time does heal, and the godly love shown helped him to forget the past. Rachel enjoyed teaching him. That brought back memories of the days she taught their son. J.B. was a good student and also a good boy. He was a big help around the house when he wasn't in school or helping Carl outside.

Carl's were faithful in their daily devotions. When Jr. was home he always became involved in the worship. It was evident the Bauman family not only talked Christian but also lived it. There were evenings they went to see older folks who were not able to attend church services anymore. One of these was the old Elder of their church. His mind was keen, but his body was not able to function. He and Carl had so many things to talk about. The experiences the older folks had during their life was interesting to Joseph. The advice they gave and the explaining of the scriptures enhanced his education.

Sometimes the folks they went to see were very senile. It appeared as if their mind was mostly gone. With these folks, Carl would talk to them as if they knew all he was talking about. He would briefly talk about what was happening among the members of their church. He read a comforting psalm and talked about it. At times they would sing a song. One time when they were visiting an old widow sister who didn't talk, Joseph saw tears running down her cheeks when they were singing.

On the way home, Joseph asked Carl, "People who don't talk or sing, do they know anything?"

Carl answered, "We never know. I think of it as a wall of glass. They are behind that wall. They know and can see us and hear us, but can't communicate. Did you notice the tears flowing down that dear old sister's cheeks as we were singing? We should always treat people kindly, regardless of their condition. We should act as if they know everything that is happening. We may be behind that glass wall someday."

One Sunday, after church services were over, Carl's were invited to take lunch with Joseph's friend Kenneth's parents. They also had his friend Daryl's family too. Not only did they have a delicious meal, but the boys enjoyed the afternoon. Kenneth showed them his rabbits that he raised and sold. They played horseshoe for awhile. Joseph found out he wasn't very good at that. Daryl did well, but Kenneth could throw a ringer most time.

Joseph told Kenneth, "If we were playing on teams, you certainly wouldn't want me on your team."

Kenneth kindly replied, "You would learn it. You can do things I can't."

Too soon the afternoon was gone and it was time to go home.

Dairy Boy
Chapter Thirteen

Carl, seeing Joseph was a farmer at heart, tried to make sure there were things he could do. When he found out he liked to milk cows, he bought four jersey cows. J.B. named them Mable, Maud, Roan, and Joyce after some cows they had back home.

There was an older barn in the back where they used to milk. It took a little fixing up, but he and Carl soon had it useable. Joseph not only did the milking but also made butter. They got more milk than they could use. Some of the farmhands bought the extra from them. Carl put that money in a special account. Seeing how well J.B. did with the cows, Carl bought two more.

When Carl's got up in the morning, J.B. would be finishing the chores and coming in with a bucket of milk. There was always a jolly "Good morning," with a smile on his face. While he was doing the evening chores, they could hear him singing or whistling.

The prayers he prayed, the thoughts of a loving God in his heart, the thankfulness he manifested to his loving adopted parents and the church they supported, all helped him rise above the sufferings he endured in the past. Carl's never once suspected what J.B. was going through. Underneath that godly attitude was a dark secret that had left a scar on the young man's heart. God is in control.

One Sunday Rachel had company after church for dinner. She loved cooking and hosting folks for a meal. Among those invited were Joseph's friends. She knew that would make him happy. In the afternoon the men folks took a walk around the place. When they went to the barn, they saw the six cows.

"Are these cows your dad's?" Daryl asked.

"Yes," Joseph answered his friend.

"Who milks them?" Kenneth asked.

"I do," Joseph responded, "Twice a day. Milk them every morning and every evening."

"Wow!" said Kenneth. "You may not be good at horseshoes, but you can do something I couldn't do."

"Everyone has a niche in life," Daryl added.

When they entered the house, Kenneth told his mom, "Joseph milks six cows every morning and evening, and he's only fourteen the same as I am. I couldn't do that."

Rachel, looking at Kenneth told him, "Joseph has known cows for a long time. You could do it if you had the opportunity. It takes a while to learn. Why don't you come and spend a few days with us sometime? Joseph will teach you."

"Sure I would," Joseph said. "Could they come and spend a week with us this summer after school is out? They could help make hay and I would teach them to milk."

The parents all felt the boys would all gain something from working together for a week and it was planned for the second week of summer.

The time came and Kenneth and Daryl spent a week with the Bauman family. Neither boy was used to getting up as early as Joseph did, but they were anxious to learn, so they rolled out at the first call. Walking to the barn that early did something for a person that is hard to describe.

First, they put a little ground feed in a box where each cow was to stand. Joseph said, "Come and stand with me outside the door. The cows are not used to you. If they see you in the cow stable they won't come in."

They opened the door and stepped out and to one side. Joseph called the cows and they came in one at a time. Kenneth and Daryl noticed each cow seemed to know just where to go.

"Do they always go to the same place?" asked Daryl.

"Yes they do," responded Joseph. Joseph told them to speak softly to the cows. Cows like kindness just like we do.

Joseph took his stool and the bucket. He explained everything to them, and then he started milking as they watched. He milked a little, then told Kenneth to sit and milk. Kenneth was nervous at first. Joseph spoke softly to the cow. She stood calmly as Kenneth finished milking her. Daryl was the next to try milking. Joseph used the same procedure and Daryl was able to get his cow milked. Joseph would talk to the cows and have the boys talk to them softly also. Some cows were a little uneasy, but talking softly helped calm them. Joseph stayed with each boy as he milked.

It took longer to get the chores done than normal, but each boy milked two cows. When they went in for breakfast, the ham and eggs smelled really good to them. After breakfast, Joseph said, "Lay down for a little nap. After a while, we will make hay. You will need some rest." Their arm muscles got a little sore after milking for a while, but by the end of the week, they were getting used to it.

Daryl and Kenneth felt the week went by fast. They told Joseph, "The work is hard, but we enjoyed it all. We feel blessed to get to spend a week with you."

****

Carl noticed J.B. was a natural with the livestock. He was kind and gentle with them.

J.B. told Carl, "If the cows are happy, they give more milk."

Carl said, "That is the way with Christians. Happy ones are better workers in the Lord's vineyard. Jesus said, 'If you know these things, happy are you if you do them.' He was speaking of the commandments in the Bible."

As the years passed there were more cows to milk. J.B. took good care of the calves born. Some were heifers. They became cows in time.

Carl told Rachel, "Give that boy time and we'll have a large dairy herd."

"That is the way Abraham got his wealth," she replied.

Time moves on and before long J.B. was a freshman in the church school. He had a lot of friends from the church folks. When some boys were getting away from their parents' teaching he tried to encourage them to walk with the Lord.

Lester, one of the boys was constantly getting into trouble. He had a haughty attitude. Any correction the teachers gave him didn't seem to help. Daryl suggested to the teacher to have Joseph take him home with him for a while. Joseph was a little uneasy about that. He said he would talk to his folks about it. After discussing it Carl and Rachel both agreed to give it a try. At first, Lester declined when Joseph approached him. After some encouragement from some of the other boys, he agreed to go if his dad was okay with it.

Lester had never been close to a cow before. Joseph explained the need to be gentle and kind to them. At first, he didn't want to try milking. After watching Joseph milk for a little, he thought he would try it. He got along well with the first one. He soon found it to be fun. When he sat down to milk the second one he forgot to speak to her. Just as he was starting to sit down to milk, the cow tried to swat a fly off her back. The end of her tail smacked Lester in the face. He let out a loud yell. The outburst excited the cow and she kicked him sending him sprawling on his back, the bucket went flying. About that time Carl stepped in the barn. Lester jumped up ready for revenge. When he saw Carl he just stood there. Joseph stepped in and apologized, "I'm sorry Lester. I forgot to have you to fasten her tail to the wire just above our head. When flies get bad that is the cow's way to protect themselves. The flies haven't been bad. I don't know where that one came from."

Lester was afraid of milking after that fiasco.

Joseph asked, "Did you speak to her before you started milking."

Lester shook his head.

Joseph explained, "It is very important to let her know you are there. Jersey cows are easily excited. Notice how she is shaking. This incident is bothering her as much as it is you. She is as afraid of you as you are of her."

"What can we do?" Lester asked.

"To calm her down we need to speak softly to her." Joseph got a little feed and walked in front of her softly calling her name. He put a little feed in her box. He rubbed her face lightly while still softly talking to her. He went around back and patted her, still repeating her name. He rubbed her back walking up beside her. She calmed down and started to eat the feed in the box.

Joseph said, "Now let's try another cow. I'll milk this one. Just in case another fly comes let me show you how to fasten the tail."

Once the tail was fastened Joseph continued, "Now speak soft to her and rub her back. She will think you are her friend and won't kick you."

Lester did as Joseph instructed. The cow was calm and he had no trouble at all. On the way to the house, Lester remarked how amazed he was at the way cows respond to kindness.

Joseph said, "Remember three things; kind, quiet and calm. They will like you and will be happy. Think about it, aren't we humans somewhat like that too?"

"Maybe so," remarked Lester.

Before they went into the house, Lester asked Joseph what he thought his dad was going to do to him because of what happened with the cow.

"What do you mean?" asked Joseph. "Will I get punished? No, my dad saw it all. It was as much of my mistake as it was yours. Don't be afraid of dad. He does punish when there is a need, but it is with love. We did not deliberately do anything wrong and dad knows that. What went wrong we corrected. There is a lot of love felt in our home.”

Lester seemed relieved with Joseph’s answer. “I notice you sing sometimes as you milk. Does that not excite the cows?”

Joseph answered, “The songs I sing are gospel songs. Those have a soothing feeling and the cows sense that. They actually let their milk down better sometimes when I am singing.”

“That is interesting,” said Lester. “Cows and people do have some things in common, don’t they?”

“They do have some things in common. They also each have their own personality.”

Lester noticed the kindness in the home was like it was in the cow barn. The devotions were very uplifting. The family always ate their meals together. They always prayed before they ate. Every morning it was a cheery “Good morning.” There were times of tears and times of laughter. Words like, “I’m sorry,” and, “I forgive you,” were definitely in their vocabulary. They were a happy home. Lester was there for two weeks. He learned to be calm around the cows. He got kicked a couple more times, but by the time the two weeks were over, he remembered to speak softly. That was a help in his personal behavior. He became close to the Bauman family.

Over the next two years, a couple more boys came to spend time in the dairy barn. One of them learned as Lester did. Even with all the patience and instructions, the other boy never learned anything. They let him stay for a month. He still manifested an arbitrary, self-willed spirit. Joseph told Carl, “If we keep him much longer he will ruin our herd.”

Carl said, “The Adam nature is still in him. We’ll pray for him and hope the Lord will touch his heart sometime before it is too late.”

Joseph answered the call and was baptized, becoming a member of the church. There were several other young people who had joined the church. They enjoyed getting together at times.

Several folks came from across the mountains to attend their Love Feast. Sunday afternoon, after the services were over, the young folks had a time of getting to know each other better. At this time, a boy could ask a girl to eat with him. They would get their food from the serving line and find a place at a table. The boy sat on one side and the girl he had asked would sit across from him. That gave them time to visit. There were the more aggressive boys, who were quick at asking the girl he wanted. Sometimes they were turned down, but not usually. Couples, who had been seeing each other, would go together.

J.B. noticed a girl from over the mountains who no one asked. She was a little heavy, but she carried a smile. She didn't act silly, like some of them did, trying to get attention. He slowly made his way close to where she was. It was hard to ask someone he hadn't seen before. Finally, he got the nerve and asked her to eat with him. She blushed and looked the other way. His heart was going fast. He stood there for what seemed like a long time. She slowly looked at him and nodded yes.

Neither one took much food. They were both very bashful. After breaking the ice, they had a nice visit. She told him her parents owned a dairy north of Bakersfield. She was an only child. She was a year younger than J.B. He told her his dad had a small dairy and he did the milking. By the time the evening was over, they agreed to write to each other as friends.

That evening, when he did the milking, his mind was in a whirl about the girl he had met. "She was modest and quiet," he told himself, "I am not worthy of such a nice girl." Then he corrected himself. "We are only writing as friends." Yet he couldn't get her out of his mind.

When he entered the house Rachel asked if something was wrong. He hadn't been singing while milking. He smiled at her and said, "May I tell you some other time?"

She smiled back, "Sure."

On Monday J.B. confided with Rachel about his friendship with Lovina.

Rachel told him, "Pray about it but do not push the situation. Let the Lord lead. He takes care of his people."

Letters went back and forth for two years. They both felt they were being drawn together.

Progressive Economy
Chapter Fourteen

The dairy herd increased. J.B. had doubled his milking cows to twelve. There were times he sold an older cow when a heifer he had raised came fresh. Besides the milk cows, J.B. was raising six feeder calves. Carl and Rachel were impressed with how J.B. took care of the cattle.

Rachel said, "I believe you're right. In time he could have a large dairy herd."

Carl hung his head and didn't say anything for a bit. Sometimes facing changes were hard to do. He had a son that wanted to work on the farm and now that was in jeopardy. Looking up he asked, "How are we to tell J.B. about the changes the economy is doing to us?"

After breakfast and the Bible reading, Carl asked J.B. to stay at the table for a little. They had something to talk about. J.B. noticed Carl was a little nervous. That made his pulse quicken. Carl never acted like this before.

Carl took hold of J.B.'s hand. "Son, you have been with us for a long time. You have proven yourself as you have grown from a well-behaved child into a godly man. We can trust you with anything we have. You have proven yourself to be an excellent cattleman. Above all, you have been a faithful Christian.

The times you reached out to wayward boys, bringing them home to teach them how to milk, and take care of the cows. Not only that, by example you showed them what respect to parents is and how rewarding it is. Some of the boy's parents told me how you changed their son. You have a heart filled with godly love. Son, there are better things ahead for you."

J.B. looked in Carl's eye and asked, "What is it?"

Carl said, "As you have seen, around us things are changing. More and more people are moving into the area. The economy is growing and the farm is now wanted by developers. They say it won't be long before this could all be part of the town. They are offering us an exorbitant price. It's a lot more than we ever thought it would be worth. Another factor in this is the taxes that are increasing as the value mushrooms. They are becoming unaffordable."

"Are you going to sell?" J.B. asked. "What about the house and barns?"

"Junior would like to buy our house and a couple of acres of ground. This house will make a nice home for him, his wife Carol, and their three children. He plans to have an office in town."

"What will you and mom do?" J.B. asked. "That is what we need to discuss."

Carl hung his head, "Son, your mother and I will be fine. We are getting older and need to slow down. A smaller home close to town will be fine for us. As I'm sure you realize for this to happen, the cows will have to be sold."

J.B. sat there a little with a serious look in his eyes. "This has been home to me for a long time. You and Mother could not have made it more pleasant. You have taught me a lot of things. So has the dairy. I know it is like I've heard you read from the Bible, *We have here no continuing city, but we seek one to come whose builder and maker is God.* It looks as if you have no choice. I hate to see the farm go, but you are between a rock and a hard place. I suppose the growing economy does that; however, the earth is the Lord's and the fullness thereof. All things work together for good to those who love the Lord."

Those words coming from the homeless boy they took into their home years ago caused Carl to feel very humble and thankful for the leading of the Lord.

J.B. continued, "I also need to tell you something. I proposed to Lovina and yesterday I got a letter accepting my proposal. Her dad has a dairy farm up north of Bakersfield. He wants me to work for him in the dairy and there is a house on the farm we can live in. Even though I will be moving away, you will still be my parents."

Although Carl's knew the friendship between J.B. and Lovina was serious, this knowledge sort of shocked him. "Yes we will always be your parents and you will still be our son. Time moves on."

They set a day for the sale of the cows and equipment. It was a nice day and the turnout was good. The cattle sold very well. J.B. was a little sad to see them go but knew life would go on.

Junior had come home for the sale. As they were watching the auctioneer calling the sale of one cow after another Carl told his son, Jr. "I bought four cows and this is what J.B. has done with them."

"That boy has a head on his shoulders," Junior replied.

"Yes he does, and the Lord is in his heart," Carl added.

Joseph was packing his things for his move north. He had accumulated some things over the years while on the farm. He felt he couldn't take much. Just the things he could get in a couple of suitcases. The Bible Alva had given him was the first thing he packed.

Carl called up the stairs for him to come down for a little while. Rachel and Junior were sitting with Carl at the kitchen table when J.B. walked in.

"Have a seat son," Carl told him as he slid an envelope across the table. "This is the money from the sale. I took out the expenses and the initial investment. This is the gains from milking."

J.B. ignoring the envelope, replied, "That is yours. I was glad you provided me a home and something I could do."

Junior smiled as the attitude of his adopted brother was one he desired to have himself. "The laborer is worthy of his hire."

Rachel smiled and said, "Your presence has been such a blessing to us. We certainly want you to have that. You worked hard for it."

J.B. finally relented and was surprised at the amount of money in the envelope. With tears running down his cheeks he said, "Thank you, may the Lord bless you." He gave them each a hug.

"We're not done yet," Carl added. "Mom and I bought a new car. We are giving you the old one. It is yours. Now you can take more of your things instead of just what you can pack in a couple of suitcases."

Rachel spoke up, "You can have the blankets on your bed. Also, there are some more things I want you to have."

"I'll help you load things up when you're ready," Junior added.

Joseph didn't know how to thank them enough, "Truly I have been blessed to live where there is love at home."

Rachel responded, "You added to that love."

Tears were streaming down his cheeks as he pulled out the drive. Carl and Rachel were standing on the porch waving to him. Changes are not always easy. Leaving the home and parents where he lived most of his life was hard. Looking on down the road, he was anxious about what the Lord had in store for him in the future.

It was the longest trip he had taken in a car. Going over the Grape Vine was stressful. He had to stop twice to let the motor cool. Coming down the north side was about as stressful. The brakes heated up and he stopped frequently to let them cool.

It was the third day when he got to the crossroad community of Five Points. A few miles north he came to Lovina's home. Sitting on the porch were Lovina's folks, Eston and Lucinda Spitler. After he had received a positive response from Lovina asking her hand in marriage, he had written to her folks asking their approval. He had never met her parents and was a little nervous about what they would think of him. He was glad they approved of the couple's plans. Joseph parked the car and went to greet them. Lovina came out and introduced them. They were a little shy at first. He could see where Lovina got it. What he didn't know, was that Carl and Eston were old-time friends. Eston's were happy Joseph chose to be their son-in-law. It was arranged for J.B. to stay at the neighbors until the wedding.

A New Day Dawns
Chapter Fifteen

Joseph started work the next day. He worked in the dairy barn helping with the milking. They milked fifty cows and used milking machines instead of milking by hand, which astonished Joseph. There were three Mexican men helping in the cow barn allowing the four of them to rotate schedules giving each one some time off.

Joseph and Lovina talked to her parents about the wedding. It was decided to have it after regular church services in six weeks. That would give them time to let family and friends know. In that time they could get their house furnished. The folks living there said they could move out in a couple of weeks.

In the dairy barn, Joseph was busy learning how things were done. He kept his eyes and ears open and his mouth shut. When he put the milkers on a cow, he spoke softly to them and would rub their back a little. The Mexicans spoke Spanish. Thinking Joseph only knew English they frequently talked about him. He didn't let on that he understood every word they said. He figured he could learn more that way. They did some dirty things to him sometimes, but he never retaliated. They referred to him as a dumb cluck. When they did those things, it brought back horrible memories of how his brothers had treated him in the cow barn a long time ago.

After the folks moved out of their house, he and Lovina took a tour to see what needed to be done. There was a lot of cleanup and some painting to do. Lucinda sounded it around, and several of the church sisters came and gave it a good cleaning. Three of them came back and helped paint.

While they were doing that, J.B. worked up the garden and planted several things. When he saw Joseph work the garden, Eston commented to Lucinda, "That young man has something about him I like."

One Saturday morning as the engaged couple was talking about going to a sale to buy furniture, Eston asked if they needed money.

"I don't think so, but thank you," J.B. replied.

When they returned from the sale with a truck full of furniture, they had enough to start up housekeeping. The furniture was used but in good shape. Lucinda asked Lovina if they had enough money to buy all that.

Lovina said, "Yes. We didn't spend it all."

Eston and Lucinda were satisfied Joseph was a thrifty man. "He will do well," they said.

****

The six weeks soon passed. Several of Lovina's friends came. Carl, Rachel, Junior, and his family were there. Joseph's friends Kenneth, Daryl, and Lester, from the church he used to attend, were at the church the morning of the wedding. Eston's were well-liked among their church family. The meeting house was almost full. They heard a very inspiring sermon.

After the meeting was over, the minister announced there was a couple getting married today. All are invited to attend this Holy ceremony.

He asked them to join right hands. He performed the marriage ceremony, then introduced Mr. and Mrs. Joseph Bauman.

After the ceremony was over the minister announced, "There will be a meal served on the lawn of the bride's parents. All are welcome to come and enjoy the first meal of this new family."

Most of the folks came and enjoyed the meal and fellowship. Carl's talked with them for a while, giving them some words of wisdom. Joseph felt this was a new day dawning on him. Little did he know of the blessings that lay in store.

****

J.B. took a couple of days off while they moved Lovina's things and got settled into their home. Back in the milk barn, he was gradually winning over his Mexican coworkers. They noticed that when they treated J.B. dirty, he never showed anger, nor did he retaliate. They commented on how the cows were getting calmer and giving more milk.

J.B. liked the milking plan. He always went to the barn early when he milked. After the chores were done, he had a few hours off. That gave him time with his new bride. He never had to work on Sunday evenings. At Carl's, he milked twice a day seven days a week. He enjoyed the milking, but there were times the Mexicans got on his nerves.

One day Lovina stepped into the barn just as one of the Mexicans squirted milk into J.B.s face and called him a dumb cluck. In Spanish, she said, "How dare you do that to my husband?" Looking at J.B. she asked, "Do they do that often? He responded in Spanish, "Not as much as they used to. I have been trying to win them over by love and patience." The look on their faces was priceless as he revealed that he understood what they had been saying about him. All three of them humbly apologized. They promised to never do anything like that again. They asked for forgiveness. He assured them that he had already forgiven them.

"Let's be friends," he told them as he stuck out his hand. They all shook hands. He thought he saw tears in their eyes.

Joseph and Lovina were enjoying married life. They frequently worked together in the garden hoeing weeds. They found fellowshipping with other young married couples from the church was always enjoyable. At times there were several families together for a meal. None of them had any children yet. Someone would get a Bible question going. They would talk about it. At times they talked about married life. Occasionally they would sing the good old songs of Zion. Joseph, while loving these old songs, would get a gloomy feeling as they were sung. It reminded him of his father and mother.

One morning when he came in from milking, he told Lovina, "There are green beans ready to pick." After breakfast and their morning devotions, they went to the garden and picked five baskets of green beans. As they were sitting under the shade tree snapping beans Lovina's folks pulled in. These unannounced stops were not unusual.

Lovina said, "Pull up a chair and sit a spell."

They were happy to join their children and with a couple of bowls in their lap started breaking beans. They stayed long enough to help get some canned. J.B. found it enjoyable to spend time working together. He was always glad to hear advice from Lovina's folks. It was a time to get better acquainted.

Eston looked at Joseph and said, "The day I saw you planting your garden, I wondered why you planted so much."

J.B.'s mind went back to the days he helped his mother plant garden, how he had asked her that same question. He remembered her answer, "If we don't need it, someone may." That is the answer he gave Eston.

Lovina sent some fresh beans home with her folks, as theirs weren't ready yet. On the way home Eston told Lucinda, "That boy thinks ahead."

Six months after the wedding, Eston asked J.B. to come into his office. Eston invited him to have a seat. "I have noticed how you behave yourself wisely. Even among those who don't treat you as they should. Lovina told me how you treated the Mexicans. How you forgave them and shook hands with them. After the kindness you showed, they started following your example of treating the cows kinder. Those men are doing a better job taking care of the cows. The production has gone up.

Joseph, Lovina is our only child, making you our only son. I want to turn the oversight of the farms over to you. All the things we have will be yours someday. I don't expect you to take responsibility all at once. You and I will work together. You will be my right-hand man. All the men will be under your supervision."

All J.B. could think about was those three men in the cow barn. "What would they say?"

Eston continued, "Come over here to the wall and I will show you the layout of the farms we have. The dairy barn is just a very small plot, compared to the other farms. We have six hundred acres of cotton. Over here on the east side is six hundred acres with a beef cattle operation. Next to that is the twelve hundred acres of Walnut trees."

J.B. just stood at the map in awe. He never had any idea that the Eston's were that wealthy. What a responsibility. He felt small and unworthy to even be part of this family. What had he done to deserve such a position?

Eston said, "There is more, but I don't want to overwhelm you. I will tell you about that later. Each of these operations has a man to manage them. They will answer to you."

J.B. felt he was dreaming. He needed to go home and confide with his wife.

The next week he rode around with his father-in-law. They went to all the farms. He was introduced to the man that was foreman of each farm. Eston told them Joseph was his son-in-law and co-owner of his estate. If any problems arise J.B. needs help with, he will come to me. Otherwise, he is in control.

When they went to the cow barn, the man that had squirted milk in his face was the foreman. When Eston told him J.B. was his boss, fear came in his eyes. Joseph put an arm around him and gave him a hug, "The past is past. You are doing a good job, just keep it up. Remember, what I told you about how Jesus forgave us? We want to have that forgiving spirit, only then will love reign. I still plan to help with the milking."

Joseph did continue to milk. Moretto, the Mexican that was foreman, felt uncomfortable working with his boss. He didn't understand the forgiving spirit. Joseph told him about the love of God, "Man was in an undone condition. God sent Jesus to us to free us from the grips of sin. He paid for our sins with his precious blood on the cross. We are only forgiven if we forgive.

Moretto, think about it. When you mistreated me, if I rebelled and treated you as you treated me, what a mess we would have. There would be hate and even fighting between us. The other workers would not like to come to work. The cattle would also sense it and production would go down. That kind of attitude grows to the other workers. If not stopped, the dairy would end up in shambles.

Moretto, you asked me to forgive you and I did. Now the hardest thing for you is to forgive yourself. I have prayed for the Lord to forgive you. The Bible tells us 'All have sinned and come short of the glory of God.' Also if we confess our sins, He will forgive us and cleanse us from all unrighteousness. I don't know how long I will be able to work in the dairy. I have several duties at other places. I plan to continue to milk with you until I see you have forgiven yourself. When that happens there will be peace here. When we greet each other in the morning with a cheery 'Good morning' and we have a warm feeling for the other, we are free."

Moretto responded, "Thank you. I hope someday I can be as patient and loving as you."

J.B. smiled at him, "You can."

The dairy became a place where the workers liked to be. Moretto became a very kind man. One day he asked J.B. if he could bring his twelve-year-old son with him sometimes, "I want him to see how pleasant it is working with men who feel love in their hearts."

After a few months, J.B. asked Moretto if his son would like to work part-time. "We could put him on the payroll." Moretto was happy with that.

Joseph spent a lot of time with his father-in-law. To learn the entire functions of the different farms took time.

Eston told him, "One of the most important things in running a business is to be kind and understanding to the employees. There is a man over each farm. Hear his concerns. Try to be a help, but don't lord over him. He may make some mistakes. That is to be expected. We are human. If you continue with the attitude you have, you will do well."
One year after they were married, they were blessed with a son. When he looked into his little eyes, he thought, "The blessings from the Lord keep getting better. This little bundle helps me forget the sorrow of my home in Iowa." They named him Daniel. Joseph always liked the story of Daniel in the Bible.

When Daniel was a month old, Carl's came to see him. Carl and Rachel felt he was as a grandchild to them. They brought a blanket Rachel made.

J.B. asked, "You are staying for Sunday aren't you?"

He liked the way Carl preached. He explained things, so he could understand it.

Carl replied, "We plan to."

Joseph was delighted. It was the Sunday they took in dinner and ate together. That would give them time to visit and talk about the love of God and how they had been blessed.

Church Service
Chapter Sixteen

Sunday dawned bright and balmy. Joseph and Lovina were happy to take their son to meeting for the first time. A lot of the sisters and girls wanted to see him. To make it more delightful, Grandpa Carl's were going to be there. Meeting time came. Jacob, their minister, opened the meeting with thoughts on thanking our Lord for the many blessings showered on us. After prayer, Carl got to his feet and opened his Bible to Hebrews, the third chapter. He read the seventh to the fourteenth verses.

"Today if you hear His voice, harden not your hearts. Do we want to hear His voice? We are journeying through the wilderness of iniquity. The Apostle said, *'Harden not your hearts, as in the provocation, in the day of temptation in the wilderness.'* They did not know the Lord's way. They murmured and complained. They didn't trust God. Their hearts were hardened to the point they couldn't hear if they wanted to.

Today is all we have. Tomorrow may never come. Each day we sow seeds of some sort. If tomorrow comes, the seed sown will sprout and grow. It will reproduce itself. Not only will it reproduce itself, but several times more of the same. A kernel of corn planted in the right condition will make one stalk. That stalk will make one or more ears. Those ears will each make around seven hundred kernels. When we think about the seeds we are sowing, would we want them to multiply like the kernel of corn?

When we prepare the soil for a garden, we want good, fertile soil. We put humus on the land and work it into the ground. This makes the dirt mellow and soft. Then the little seed can sprout and grow. We don't want hard clay soil with lots of rocks. That kind of soil is hard to do anything with.

The heart of man is like the soil. Some people have hearts soft and tender. When kind words are spoken by them, it sprouts and grows. That person feels love from the seed sown. The tender love continues to grow and brings more seed of its kind.

Good seed that is sown in hard, rocky soil likely will not grow.   Some people are like hard rocky soil. Weeds are the main seed that will take root. Cockle Burrs do well in that worthless soil. What do we want sown in our hearts? If we don't want weeds sown in our hearts, we need to remove the stones. We need to till the hard clay soil by reading our Bible daily and meditating on the Word. Apply humus by regularly going to the house of prayer, spending time with the Saints. Pray for strength to overcome.

Satan is the instigator of hard, stony hearts. He will not let go of one of his without a battle. The Bible is our road map to conquer this adversary. From the day Adam and Eve fell in the garden, man has struggled to obey God. For the redemption of man and to help him in troubling times, God sent His only Son into this world. He was born of a woman. A baby! Jesus, the Son of God, came into this world as a baby. He lived as other boys lived. He was subject to his parents.

Attending a wedding with His mother, He did His first miracle. In that day they used wine at their wedding feasts. Those feasts lasted much longer than ours today. They ran out of wine. Jesus' mother was told about the problem. She told them to tell Jesus about it and do what He says to do. Jesus told them to fill some vessels with water and then pour them out. They did, and when they poured the water out, it had become wine. Not only was it wine, but the best wine. That was the first miracle Jesus did. He did many more.

He not only performed miracles but taught us how to live happy lives with those around us. He taught kindness, compassion, forgiveness, faithfulness, long-suffering, to love the

Lord with all the heart, soul and mind, and to love your neighbor as yourself. When these attributes are in our hearts, there is no room for stones or hard soil. What Jesus said to those when they were out of wine to do, they did it. Today, we need to do whatever Jesus says to do.

Jesus gave a parable. The Kingdom of Heaven is as a man that gave talents to his servants. To one he gave five. To another, he gave two. To another, he gave one. The master took a far journey. In time he came home. He talked to the one he gave five talents. That servant said 'The five have gained five more'. The master said, 'Well done thou faithful servant. Enter into the joy of thy Lord.' The one he gave two said, 'Thy two have gained two more.' The master said, 'Well done thou faithful servant, enter into the joy of thy Lord.' The one who received only one buried that talent and did nothing with it. When the master came he was rejected.

What about our talents? How many do we have? Are we using them to the glory of our Lord? The one talent man may have felt he was no good anyway, just a hard rocky garden. "There is no use trying." He may have looked at the man given five talents, and become jealous. Then hatred set in. Next the feeling of unfairness, on and on that avenue of thought can take us. When these thoughts set in, the heart becomes hard as a rock. Only the love of God can break up that kind of soil.

Had that man taken his one talent, and thanked the master for including him in his gifts. Then prayed for wisdom to use it properly he likely would have heard the words, 'Well done, thou faithful servant, you have been faithful over little, be thou over much. Enter into the joys of the Lord.'

Are we one, two or five talent people? Most of us feel ourselves a one talent person or even less. It is good to feel humble. Moses was a humble man. Did he have any talents? Where did they come from? Many times he prayed for those with hard hearts. Had they obeyed, they could have gone with the ones who obeyed into the Promised Land.

Our text instructs us to not harden our hearts. We are to exhort one another daily while it is called today, lest anyone be hardened through the deceitfulness of sin. We want to exhort or encourage each other while there is still opportunity. We are partakers of Christ if we hold the beginning of our confidence steadfast until the end.

It is apparent the plain humble Christian has many different talents. The brethren that farm are usually good farmers. This goes down different avenues. The sisters are good cooks etc. Parents help each other to make a functional home. This happens by living according to the Word of God, the Bible.

Humble yourself under the mighty hand of God, and he will exalt you in due time. Yes, we have many talents given to us by our loving Savior Jesus Christ. Let's live in them, multiply them, and be an encouragement to others by the life we live. May we ever abound in the work of the Lord, for our labor is not in vain in the Lord. Today, this day, if you will hear the voice of the Lord, harden not your heart."

****

The sermon gave the congregation plenty to talk about in the afternoon while they enjoyed the pot luck dinner together.

Carl and Eston talked about the responsibility of handling the blessings the Lord sends our way. They agreed we are to be good stewards. Carl pointed out the Psalm, "If riches increase, set not your heart upon them."

Eston said, "We inherited from my parents a goodly inheritance. Not in money, but in farms. We try to use our resources to help others. We have been encouraged to invest in stocks, but we feel the Lord put the land here to produce food for the eater. To do this gives food and also jobs for the needy. We want to keep foremost in our mind, 'The earth is the Lords and the fullness thereof.' Also, 'The Lord gives and the Lord takes away. Blessed be the name of the Lord.' We trust the Lord to guide us."

Privately Carl asked Eston, "How is Joseph doing? We know he's has gone through some tough times before he came to us. He is always in our prayers."

"He is doing very well and has a wonderful attitude," Eston told him. "He just has a way to help people get along with each other."

"I really feel that boy will go places," Carl said.

A few days later Carl's said goodbye and headed for home. It was hard for Joseph to see them go, but he knew that that is the way life is.

Hard Decisions
Chapter Seventeen

Another year passed and the Lord blessed them with another son. Lovina wanted to name him Eddie. That was not what Joseph wanted, but he had named Daniel.

She said, "His middle name could be Joseph."

That was alright with him. They knew the children born to them were a gift from God. They thanked the Lord for giving them, healthy children.

Joseph was getting the hang of operating the estate. His father-in-law did not put more on him than he could handle. Little by little, he was able to take over more of the day to day operations.

Eston told him, "In all our doings, be sure to take the time to spend with your family."

One day Charles, one of the men who worked on the cattle ranch, came to J.B. and asked if he could talk. They went into his office, and Joseph closed the door.

"Please sit down," Joseph motioned to a chair. "What's on your mind?"

Charles dropped his head. He tried to talk but choked up. After a bit, he stammered about problems at home. "Our marriage hasn't been what it should be. I, ah, my wife and I started dating when we were young. I thought I was in love, but it really was only lust. We had an impure courtship. I found out after we were married, that when we were courting, she was seeing other boys from town." At this point, he broke down and sobbed.

When he got his composure, he continued, "We never read the Bible or prayed from the day we were married. When our first child was born, I thought we could repent and live a

Christian life. It didn't happen. Now we have three children, yet no prayer or Bible reading."

Charles wiping the tears off his cheeks looked at J.B. He could see nothing but tenderness in his boss's eyes, "We would visit the tavern late at night when we thought no one would see us." Again he broke down sobbing. "Our babies cry a lot. The older one does too as far as that goes.

A month ago Carrie left one night. I haven't seen her since. Yesterday I got a notice in the mail that she has sued for divorce. I also got a letter from her. She is living with another man and she doesn't want the children.

I have been trying to cover it up, hoping she will come back. I have missed a lot of days of work. I told my foreman I was sick. So far there has never been anything deducted from my paychecks. The days I did work, I left the children in the house alone. I would come home at noon to feed them and change their diapers. Then I would lock the door and go back to work. It has been hard. I can hear them cry as I walk away."

Again Charles broke down and sobbed, "What money we made was mostly consumed with alcohol. We didn't feed the babies well. When Carrie left she took what money we had left with her. I have to work to feed the little ones. I called in sick so I would still get a check. I have lowered myself to stealing to feed my babies. Satan has taken me all the way to the bottom. What can I do?"

Thoughts were swirling through Joseph's head. His emotional reaction to what he was hearing was overwhelming. He was about to break down and cry but knew he must be strong. The most urgent matter that needed to be attended to were the babies.

"Charles, you need help. Help will be available, but it will take time. The way I see it, the children have the most urgent needs. Where are they now?"

"They are at home hungry and probably crying."

"Considering the problems you have and the stress you are under, would you be willing for some of our church members to care for the children for a while? That will give you some time to think things through"

"Yes, of course," was all Charles could get out between the sobs.

Joseph told him to go home and get the children's clothing together. Someone would be there soon to pick them up.

Joseph was thinking, "With a one-year-old to care for, what will Lovina think of another three little ones? And one a three-month baby."

After Joseph explained Charles' condition to Lovina, she was shocked. "I knew they didn't attend church very often. Their babies came a year apart. They are fussy babies. I wonder if alcohol is part of that. And to think, they are all in diapers. What should we do?"

Joseph put his arm around his wife, looking down into her soft eyes he asked, "Could we relieve the situation temporarily?"

"You mean take those crying babies into our peaceful home?"

Joseph said, "Let's pray about it."

There weren't many clothes or diapers. The baby's milk was soured. As they put the children and their meager possessions in the car, Lovina wondered, "How will we ever handle this?"

As Joseph looked around the cluttered unkempt house, the stench was almost unbearable. "Charles, do you feel like you're in over your head here?"

A nod answered the question.

Joseph continued, "I want you to go back to work. I know you feel you owe me for the time you took off, but don't worry about that. We will take care of that in time. For now, stay away from the alcohol. We'll pray that God will heal your heart and give you the strength to do what is right."

As they left for home, Lovina said, "I think you better pray for me too."

J.B. patted her shoulder and said, "The Lord is our shepherd we shall not want."

Lovina's mother came right away. She had a suggestion, "There is a single sister hunting work. Why not hire her?"

Within a couple of days, the young single sister was enjoying her employment helping with the children. It didn't take long before word got out about what Joseph's were doing. Soon there were sisters bringing clothes and diapers. They had their doctor come out and examine the children. The baby and the one-year-old were obviously suffering from malnutrition. Through a proper diet and care, he felt they all would grow out of their challenges.

Joseph contacted the deacons. All three deacons agreed to meet him that afternoon.

It was a long and intense meeting as J.B. explained the whole situation. One by one he answered their questions. He wanted to turn the job of rehabilitation over to them. He would continue to employ Charles. He had talked with his foreman and found that Charles had shown improvement over the last few days. The stealing part he would forgive.

After talking a bit, one of the deacons asked, "Do you think Charles would consider letting his children out for adoption?"

"I don't know. What are you thinking? Joseph asked.

"We have been working with Wilber and Joyce Sims. They recently lost a baby to miscarriage. She had something wrong and they had to have surgery. Now they are telling her she will never be able to have a baby. They have been very discouraged."

Joseph knew the couple quite well and was excited about the prospect of the solution, "That may work. I'll leave it to you, brethren. May the Lord guide you."

A few days later Joseph was working in his office when the deacons stopped in. They had spent some time with Charles. At times he seemed pliable, and then he would go into a rage. At their second visit, he had calmed down quite a bit. To totally give up his whole family was hard for him, although he admitted alcohol is what actually took them away. He admitted he prayed or tried to pray for guidance from the Lord. He admitted the children needed a godly daddy and mother. That was something he could not provide. He had finally consented to meet with the Sims. The meeting had gone well and he had agreed that, if the children couldn't stay with Joseph's, Wilber and Joyce would be next best.

Arrangements were made and Joseph made sure he was home the day Wilber and Joyce came to meet the children. They had asked that the sisters that normally came to help take the day off. This would give Wilber's more alone time with the children. Joseph and Lovina welcomed the apprehensive couple into their home and the four of them sat in the living room. The conversation started out with small talk, but soon the seriousness of the day was brought up.

The children had come through a lot of changes in the two weeks they had been at Joseph's. Following the doctor's recommendations, the babies were a lot calmer. They had been fed properly and it was showing in their demeanor. Lovina explained that the two-year-old was not potty trained yet. She wanted to get that started but felt it best not to rush into too many changes all at once.

Seeing the look of anxiety in their faces, Joseph asked the maid to bring the children into the living room. He picked up the Bible and after reading the twenty-third Psalm, he commented,

"Sometimes things look big, and to us they are, but we are not alone. Let's kneel in a word of prayer."

After prayer, Wilber and Joyce's anxiety seem to have calmed. To look to God in times like these is always helpful. The time of interaction between the children and their future guardians showed that they were a very compatible family. From thinking they never would have any children to having two little girls and a little boy, Wilber and Joyce were overwhelmed.

Joseph added to the emotional avalanche taking place in their lives, by saying, "We have discussed it with Alice and she's open to the idea of helping you for a few weeks until such time as you no longer need her. You don't need to worry about the cost as her pay has been covered."

Wilber looked perplexed and Joyce looked relieved.

It was decided that Joseph's would follow them home, bringing Alice and her belongings. That would give them a chance to see the children in their new surroundings.

It was late in the day when the children were settled in their new home and Joseph's bid them all goodbye. Joseph pressed two hundred dollars into Wilber's hand, "There will be added expenses, and you may need to take a little time off from work. May the Lord bless, and strengthen you and your new family."

****

Charles was a very sad man. Having gone from a home with a yelling wife and crying babies, he now lived in a quiet empty house. He sat alone thinking of the road he had traveled down. When he was in the young folks, Cassie was the lively one of the party. She was beautiful and dolled up. She was always crowding the fence on the church standards. She would laugh and be loud, constantly flirting with the boys. She was the youngest of a large family. Her parents were not good examples of obedient church members. She, being the youngest, got most of the things she wanted.

He thought she was the life of the young folks. She appealed to him, although most of the church boys wouldn't have anything to do with her. After a couple of years, they got married. He soon found out she didn't know how to cook, nor did she want to. He had to do most of the cooking. When he mentioned having an evening devotion and prayer, she scoffed at it. There was no depth of love in their home. Unity was driven out by their constant yelling, neither hearing what the other was saying. They had hidden their frustrations in their consumption of alcohol. An evening spent in the taverns with so-called friends only worsened their relationship. He thought when they had their first child things would get better, and they did for a little while, but soon they reverted back to their old ways. He knew the life they were living was unsustainable. Something had to change. Little did he know the change was going to be this devastating. His depression was so deep he didn't know where to turn.

In that moment of despair, he dusted off the Bible his parents had given him and started reading. It wasn't long before he realized that he needed help.

When Charlie welcomed the deacon's into his home, they were kind to him but firm. They asked him if he was sorry for all of his past sins.

He dropped his head, "I am very sorry. I have sinned for years. How can I ever be forgiven and be happy again?"

Speaking solemnly, they told him, "It will be a long hard road. You have made the first step. You came for help. You can't do it alone. You need the Lord for help. The first thing you should do is make things right to those you wronged. You need to apologize to the church and your boss. If you need someone to go with you, one of us will."

It was decided Everett would go. The first one they went to was J.B. He had them come in and offered them a seat.

Everett got right to the point, "Charles has some things to say."

Shakily Charles, said, "I have sinned terribly before God and to you. I'm sorry. What can I do to make things right?"

Joseph said, "You have already confessed about the stealing time from work and that has been forgiven. To clear your conscience, give to charity a little out of each paycheck, which will make you feel better. Use the money that you would use to buy alcohol for charity. It will make you feel a lot better, knowing that your struggles are helping others. Stay away from the taverns. Anytime you're tempted to just stop in for "one drink," think about the pain that "one drink" has caused.

I have been considering your job. Your current work is mostly alone. If you are sincere in wanting to walk right with God, I will change your work. I have been talking with Moretto, the foreman of the dairy. He could use more help. The workers in the milk barn are happy, friendly people. Working in that environment could be a help to you.

Last of all, you need to make amends to the church. You have caused a lot of pain not only to your family but your church family as well. Do what's right."

Charles became a different man. The day came when he was able to share with J.B. about the process of the cleansing of the church and how he was restored. Going through that process lifted a load off his shoulders.

He said, "Now I feel I can pray."

"Pray often," J.B. told him, "read the Bible. Meditate on holy things."

Charles enjoyed working with the men at the dairy.

Moretto told him, "We have a kind, lovable family of workers here. We don't play dirty jokes on each other. When we are happy, the cows are happy. When the cows are happy, they give more milk. When they give more milk, the boss is happy. When the boss is happy, he gives us bonuses. When we get bonuses, we are happy. It is all in a circle that makes working here a joy. We greet each other with a 'good morning' to start the day right. Start a day right and it will likely end right. If you have any grumbles, don't bring them in here."

****

Wilber and Joyce had their struggles with the little ones. To get an alcohol baby over the effects of its mother drinking while carrying it takes a lot of patience. They worked closely with the doctor, sometimes wondering if they made a mistake in taking them.

Alice who already had a few weeks experience with the children was a big help. The church sisters were good at coming in to help. Slowly the children's health began to improve. The new parents' hearts were growing fond of the little ones. Alice also was starting to feel as if they were her siblings.

The day Wanda, the oldest, turned three, they had a little birthday party for her. Alice made a little cake and put three candles on it. Wilber and Joyce gave her a little doll. She was delighted and went to Joyce giving her a hug.

Looking up into her eyes with a smile she said, "I love you, Mommy."

Then she went to Wilber and jumped on his lap. Putting her arms around him she kissed him on the cheek, "Daddy you are so nice. Aunt Alice, you are nice too."

Her little brother Jesse was sitting in his high chair. Still trying to learn to talk he lisped out, "Lob ewe too."

Baby Ella was sitting on the floor, contented, playing with her toys.

After they sang "Happy Birthday" she jumped up and down clapping her hands with joy. Jesse in his highchair was

109

clapping his hands.   Joyce, when stooping to pick up Ella, noticed she was trying to clap.

After getting up from the table, Wilber put his arm around his wife and said, "Honey, we made the right choice."

She looked up at him, "With the help of the Lord and many others."

Enjoying the Lord's Blessings
Chapter Eighteen

It had been a few years since Eston had given Joseph the oversight of the ranch. Life on the ranch was becoming more enjoyable as J.B. and Eston worked well together. They both seemed to know how to keep their priorities straight. Joseph had time to play with his sons, and have family devotions. He took it to heart what his father-in-law told him about having family time. He instructed all the foremen to be sure every man had time to be with his family.

Lovina grew up with her mother having company on church Sundays when it wasn't potluck. Lovina was like her mother. The members felt comfortable coming to their place. Though they were quite wealthy, it didn't show in their homes. Eston felt the true Christian should live a humble meek and thankful life. He acknowledged the earth is the Lord's. "All we have and are comes from our loving Father in Heaven." His life portrayed that belief.

Lovina, like her mother, had company often, although not as often as her mother. The children liked their mother to have folks who had children their ages. She did that often but didn't leave out the older folks. The Sunday table is a blessing some folks don't have. It is not just good food, but to visit with others is also enjoyable.

****

The years continued to roll around. J.B. and Lovina were enjoying their life together with their two boys. When Eddie was two they were blessed with a little daughter, they named Shelly Lovina. Grandma came often to help and enjoy the grandchildren.

Eston had mostly withdrawn from the day to day managing of the farms. He was happy to have Joseph, whom he called his son, taking care of things. He and Lucinda would go often to visit older folks and those with sickness. The grandchildren could expect to see them pull in at least once a week.

Joseph visited the different farms frequently to see how things were going. There were times he helped the foreman to settle disputes between employees. Periodically he would spend a few days working with a foreman. If he felt the foreman showed signs of stress and there were problems with the men, he would give him a two-week vacation with pay.

He would hand the foreman some money and say, "Take your family on a trip."

During these two weeks, Joseph worked closely with the employees. He tried to get them to see the value of forgiving. He told them it may mean to go the second mile. Try to always have a smile. Cultivate a pleasant disposition. That attitude can be catching.

After the foreman came back, he worked with him for another week. If there was a man who was insisting on being hard to get along with, J.B. would instruct the foreman on how to work with him. If nothing changed in a month they would move the difficult employee to another farm. There were times that happened. J.B. talked with Moretto to see if he would try the difficult employee in the dairy. If he didn't change in there, he likely wouldn't change.

Joseph did well in working with the challenges of the estate. There were times he confided with his wife for encouragement. They daily worshipped and prayed together. To feel the guidance of the Spirit was such a comfort.

****

One day Joseph received word that the cheese plant where they sold their milk was going to be sold. The plant had been in operation for many years and the owner was getting old. There was a rumor a large cheese company in Bakersfield was thinking of buying it. Their plan was to close down the plant which would put several men out of work. This would create a challenge for Eston's dairy farm.

Joseph and Eston talked about the possibility of them buying the cheese plant. Their biggest concern was their lack of expertise in running such a plant. They met with the owner and made him a conditional offer. If he would be willing to stick around a few weeks as a consultant while a new manager was trained, they would like to acquire his company.

The owner was in tears at the thought of someone local purchasing his cheese plant. Someone with the integrity of the Eston's, who would keep the plant open, was a dream come true. He was glad to not have to lay off any men. Some had been with him for a long time.

He explained that he managed the operation himself and only had a couple of supervisors who had no desire to become a manager. All the employees were willing to stay working in their present positions. He agreed to stay for a few weeks to train a new manager. Joseph knew just the man he wanted to put in that position.

Charles had worked out well in the dairy. Moretto had just told Joseph last week that he felt Charles was ready for a more responsible position. He had shown such spiritual growth that he was a joy to be around. When Joseph mentioned the cheese plant Moretto agreed that would be a good fit.

"What do you mean?" Charles asked.

"You heard me right," J.B. responded from behind his desk. He had called Charles into his office to explain the opportunity.

"I really don't know if I can manage a business. You know my history."

"God knows your history as well. It's history, Charlie. God has done great work in your life. You need to thank Him and be willing to go down the road He leads you."

Hanging his head for a minute, Charles looked up with a smile. "You're right, boss. If you're willing to help me for a while, I will give it my best try."

It only took a couple of weeks before Charles had learned all the operations of the cheese plant. There was a great group of employees, who all knew their position and were willing to answer all Charles' questions. Joseph stopped in periodically and found everything running smoothly. It was obvious that Charles was a natural manager.

A few months later at their monthly meeting, Charles asked to speak with Joseph in private, "As you see from our report, the plant is running smoothly. I enjoy working with the men and all goes well at work. It is the evenings that bother me. I feel so alone. I know I made my own bed and I have to sleep in it. Also, maybe you noticed, I don't come to church as often as I should?"

Joseph nodded as Charles continued, "Seeing Wilber and Joyce with the children so happy should give me peace, knowing they are well taken care of. It doesn't. If anything, it reminds me of the sin I committed by not building upon the rock, Jesus Christ. Is there anything I can do to be happy?"

That stumped Joseph. He scratched his head and gazed out the window for a couple of minutes. Finally, he said, "I wish I had the perfect answer for you. I don't. Let me think about it for a little while."

Joseph wrote to Carl and explained the situation. It didn't take long before he had a reply. "There is an elderly widowed brother in our church that would love to have someone live with him." Carl wrote. "He is seventy-five and has trouble getting around. His children come every few days, but he is so lonely. He really needs someone to help him at times. It wouldn't be a full-time job, but there is part-time work in the orchards. I have talked with him and his children and they are interested in giving it a try. All Charles would need to bring would be his personal things."

"What about the cheese plant?" Charles asked once Joseph explained the offer.

"Don't worry about the plant. Our concern is for your spiritual growth. It would be best if you spent some time praying that God would give you direction."

****

Early Monday morning Joseph, Charles, and Daniel headed south for Carl's. Daniel's little brother wanted to go too, but Lovina told Eddie she needed him to help her take care of his little sister, making him feel important.

It was a long day's drive to Dulzura. Charles could have taken the train but Joseph wanted to see his adopted parents as he had not been home in a couple of years. Carl and Rachel were happy their grandchild was along.

"I knew I'd better not come without at least one of the children," J.B. told them.

Rachel fixed a good supper. Carl wanted to hear more from Charles. He knew some things but wanted to know they weren't making a burden for dear brother Sol. Charles manifested a meek and humble attitude. He shared with Carl the story of his life, holding nothing back. At times he shed some tears. He shared about the peace he had with how his children were being raised. "Seeing them in a Godly home," he said, "makes me wish I had provided such a Christian home. Had I put the Lord ahead of the worldly ways, things would be different. Now my wife is married to her third husband. They can't be happy and I am lonely. I hope, by taking care of Sol, it will help me forgive myself. Just to have the feeling the Lord has forgiven me and to be working in His vineyard."

Carl was convinced this plan may work out well. After breakfast and the Bible reading the next morning they went over to Brother Sol's. His children were there to meet Charles. After the introductions, Sol said, "Sit down and tell me about yourself."

"I'm a lonely man," Charles said, "My wife has left me. I like to be around people. If you will let me live here, I'm willing to help you in whatever way I can. By doing this you will help me by being someone I can talk to."

Sol rubbed his chin a moment and responded, "I too am a lonely man. My wife died a couple of years ago and although the children come often, the evenings are so lonely. I believe you and I will hit it off. Can you cook?"

"I can do that," Charles smiled. "All you need to do is tell me what you like and I can fix it."

"Can you read? My wife and I always read the Bible every morning and evening."

"I can read, but am a little slow at times."

Sol said, "Brother you're home. Bring your things in."

Carl noticed a smile on the faces of Sol's children.

Carl and J.B. bid them farewell and wishing them the Lord's blessings left for home. J.B. and Daniel spent the rest of the day visiting with Carl's. Carl Junior and his family came over for supper. Their children were happy to see Daniel but were disappointed the others weren't along.   They enjoyed another good home-cooked meal.

J.B. said, "Lovina is a super cook, but there is nothing better than mom's meals."

This brought a smile to Rachel's face. She came to him and gave him a kiss on his cheek.

Early the next morning J.B. and Daniel were on their way home. Rachel sent some sandwiches along for the journey. Pulling into the drive as the sun was setting, they were happy to be home. Lovina came onto the porch. The other children were playing in the yard. They came running.

Eddie said, "Daddy I helped mom take care of Shelly."

After the hugs and kisses, Lovina asked, "Are you hungry? Come on in. I fixed a pot of chili soup not knowing when you would be here."

That sounded very good to J.B. and Daniel. All they ate on the way home was the two sandwiches Rachel sent. After the prayer, as they enjoyed the soup, Lovina asked the children to eat first before talking. The children had so many questions and had many things to tell.

Early the next morning Eston came over to talk to J.B. and to make plans.

Looking to Jesus
Chapter Nineteen

"How will we do it?" Joseph felt as low as he had for some time. With the responsibility of managing the farms, now the church had placed him in the ministry. Lovina handed him the Bible opened to the twelfth chapter of Hebrews.

She said, "Read the second verse."

He read, *"Looking unto Jesus, the author and finisher of our faith, who for the joy that was set before Him endured the cross, despising the shame, and is sit down at the right hand of the throne of God."*

He sat there meditating on what he had read.

Lovina said, "Read the next verse."

He continued, *"For consider him that endured such contradiction of sinners against himself, lest ye be wearied and faint in your minds."*

Lovina told him, "For as long as I have known you, your actions showed me you always look to Jesus. Now the church has asked you to share it with the people from the pulpit."

His mind went back to a time long ago. As a boy sitting with his dad in church, he heard the preachers say, "Look to Jesus." At home around the family altar, the children's Bible stories were, "Look to Jesus." When his brothers were treating him mean while he was milking cows, he "Looked to Jesus." Trudging between the two gypsies for hours, he was "Looking to Jesus." When milking cows for Alva's he was "Looking to Jesus." The day the Bible showed up in his room, he "Looked to Jesus" in thankfulness for that Holy Bible.

Joseph remembered the kind school teacher who taught him and was willing to keep his secret. He turned his eyes heavenward and thanked the Lord for her kindness. He remembered the train ride when the gypsy boy tried to steal Alva's money. How the boy got escorted off the train. He remembered the day he met Carl and Rachel and the day they adopted him. He thought of how they taught him the love of God. In all these things he felt he "Looked to Jesus" in prayer and thankfulness.

These things flashed through his mind in an instant. Here he was, holding the Bible, the Holy Word of God. The book his wonderful wife handed him opened to a beautiful scripture.

Tears were running down his cheeks. Here he was with a godly wife and three wonderful children. Not only that, but his wife's parents supported him. He also had adoptive parents in the ministry supporting them. His mind went to his parents back in Iowa. How he wished he could find them. If they knew, they would be praying for him. We have all this and a godly peace-loving church.

He read again, *"For the joy that was set before Him."*

Lovina said, "If Jesus was willing to suffer as He did, what was the joy set before Him?"

Joseph answered, "Satan caused man to sin in the garden. Because of that sin, God placed the curse of death on man. There was a law given by Moses, but because of the weakness of man, sin and death continued.

Jesus was with the Father from the beginning. All things were made by Him. Without Him was not anything made. Seeing the undone condition of man, God sent His son into this world as a baby. This made Jesus both God and man. He was the only one in Heaven or Earth who could pay the price of that sin. He knew He would have to suffer and die to be separated from God, and to come forth anew to destroy the power of Satan. Jesus said, 'No man can take my life from me. I have the power to lay it down and to take it again.' In doing this, He was the first to be resurrected to the new body. When He died on the cross and shed His precious blood the veil of the temple was rent in two. Now all men may have the privilege of a spiritual relationship with God.

This blessing is ours, along with all true Christians. We are freed from the power of Satan that we may walk with the Lord blameless. This a true joy for us. Jesus, when He was looking down through the annals of time, seeing the thousands who will reject Satan and gladly keep His commandments, I believe this was the joy set before Him. He said, 'Greater love hath no man than this, that a man lay down his life for his friends. Ye are my friends, if ye do whatsoever I command you.'"

Lovina added to what her husband was saying, "Before Jesus went to His death, He told us if He went away He would send the Holy Spirit to dwell in us and lead us. Joseph, we have made confession of our faith and been baptized. Part of the prayer on our behalf was that we would have the indwelling of the Holy Ghost. Joseph, it is evident by the way you conduct yourself you have that Spirit within you.

Now the church has called you to preach, yield to the Holy Spirit. Sure, you will need to study, pray, and meditate. Let go of self and let the Spirit reign. May the Lord be praised and glorified and the church edified."

Joseph put his arm around his wife and looked down into her eyes, "Having a good wife is such a help."

Adjusting his life to have time to learn the Word of God took effort. He found to take a few minutes each morning to study was a help. He thought of the advice his father-in-law had told him, "Read simple Bible stories to your children at bedtime and then discuss with them what was read. If they have questions, explain it in a simple way. You'll be surprised how much you will learn. Remember it was the common people who heard Jesus gladly."

The next two years were trying. He was constantly being interrupted when deep in scriptural thought, by one of his foremen or a phone call. The challenges that came with overseeing the estate were never-ending. There were days he was late coming home. Lovina could tell he was getting stressed out.

"Have you been sleeping well?" Lovina asked Joseph one morning.

"Not too good," he replied. "If I'm not thinking of the Word of God, I'm thinking of a problem on one of the farms. I sure miss your father not coming into the office anymore."

"I remember the days when I was young," Lovina shared, "sometimes dad came home after a stressful day. He wasn't his old jolly self. Those times made our happy home not so happy. He didn't have to preach either.

Mother told me after we were married and dad made you his right-hand man, there were not as many of those days. You and dad shared the burden. Could you get a dependable man to share the burden of the farms?"

J.B. sat there thinking. Who could he get?

"What about Wilber Sims? I hear he has been having trouble getting enough work to support his family. He's found it takes a lot more to support five than two."

"I don't know if he has what it takes when it comes to managing all these farms. It's not like milking a handful of cows anymore."

"It may not be my darling, but you were just a novice yourself when you started. Wilber has a good heart and has shown his love for the Lord. As long as he's willing to learn you can teach him how to be a manager."

"I suppose so. I guess it wouldn't hurt to meet with him and see where it leads. I do have my reservations."

Lovina called Joyce the next day and asked if they could bring supper that evening. Joyce was delighted.

Arriving at the Sims home they were greeted with children playing in the yard. It sure looked like a happy home. Wilber's children looked like a picture of health.

Daniel wanted to help his dad carry in the supper. Joseph handed him the cookies and the bread. It always made him feel like a big boy to help his dad. Joseph followed along with the rest of the food as Eddie ran ahead. He was anxious to play with Jesse.

After they enjoyed a good supper together, J.B. and Wilber had settled into the overstuffed chairs in the living room.

The children were enjoying themselves playing together. Joyce and Lovina gathered up the dishes. Lovina started washing while Joyce poured coffee for the men.

J.B. asked Wilber about his work situation.

"It's been tough," Wilber said. "There's just not a lot of work to be had around here. I have to drive quite a distance just to keep busy."

"Well, I have a proposition for you if we can work out the details," Joseph told him.

"I'm all ears," Wilber responded.

As they sipped their coffee Wilber was very attentive while J.B. explained the work involved and the stress he was experiencing. "The bottom line is that I need a man to help me. Would you be willing to be that man?"

You could see the wheels turning in Wilber's head as a frown formed on his brow. "I don't know anything about that kind of work. All I know is construction."

"When I started I didn't either, but my father-in-law taught me. I will teach you too if you are willing to try it." When J.B. told him the starting pay, Wilber's face told the answer.

Having finished cleaning up the kitchen the ladies joined their husbands.

"What do you think, Honey?" Wilber asked his wife after explaining J.B.'s job offer.

Tears welled up in her eyes, "I believe this is an answer to our prayers."

Lovina looked at Wilber, "I think you will enjoy working with my husband."

Another two years passed. Wilber had been easy to train. He was not afraid to tackle the toughest problems. Very seldom was J.B. late coming home. There were days things got a little tight, but most days were stress-free. Wilber was a kind soft-spoken man, but when he gave an order, he followed through with it. The foremen soon learned he meant what he said.

The Love Feast
Chapter Twenty

Joseph slowly read the letter again. Carl's were inviting them to go with them to a love feast in Illinois. He had only been in the ministry for a short time and was not ready to venture out. Grandma Spitler offered to watch the children, but Joseph was reluctant to leave them for the three weeks they would be gone. After talking it over with his wife, he finally agreed that only fear was holding him back. To help ease his fears, it was decided they would go if they could take the children along.

They arrived at Carl Junior's Saturday afternoon. The cousins were excited to see each other. They all enjoyed the evening around the supper table, sharing things that were newsworthy with the families. As the old grandfather clock struck ten Joseph asked to be excused as he needed his rest for the following day.

Joseph and Lovina slept in the bedroom which was his when he lived there. They didn't get to Junior's often and it sure brought back memories. Soon Lovina was sound asleep, but Joseph tossed and turned as his apprehension of the upcoming trip would not let him rest. He knew his dad would be shouldering the greatest part of the load, but there would still be responsibilities for him. Not only that, tomorrow morning at the church service, they expected him to lead out. Lying there thinking about the burden he had been given, he heard a still small voice, "Where is your faith?"

Time passes and so does the night. Joseph looked around the full meeting house. He recognized a lot of the folks from his youth. He was humbled by his position but knew where his strength came from. Opening his Bible to the first chapter of Romans he read, *"For I am not ashamed of the gospel of Christ: for it is the power of God unto salvation to every one that believeth; to the Jew first, and also to the Greek. For therein is*

Joseph was well able to proclaim the Word of God. Faith was his subject. Faith had carried him through many a day, from the day he was sold until the present. He opened his heart to the people. He said, "Looking down the unknown road ahead, can be scary. Looking to the Angel of the Lord going before us is comforting."

****

Early Monday morning, after spending the night at Carl's, they were on the road to Illinois. Carl's wanted to go by Alva's on the way. Even though it had been many years and Joseph was now a grown adult, it still brought uneasy feelings. The thought of being close to those that had enforced his slavery created tightness in his chest. "It's silly," he told himself, "They are all old people now and wouldn't know me."

It was a long and exhausting trip. They got to Alva's on Wednesday. The children were happy to get out and run around. Joseph noticed Alva and Eunice both had aged since he saw them last. When he asked about his school teacher, he was sad to hear she passed away.

"Whatever happened to Durango?" Joseph asked. Not too sure he wanted to know the answer.

"He came by the day after we left," Alva answered. "Nobody here knew what had happened to you. He asked where I was and they didn't know that either. They said he got extremely angry and said I owed him a lot of money. He left in a rage.

Later I read in the paper he got caught with a kidnapped boy. They were on one of their stealing sprees when the boy dropped a note behind the counter. The police found the note explaining his enslavement and what they were doing. The

125

police set up a trap and apprehended them all. Now they are in jail."

With a little bit of sadness in his voice, J.B. looked at Alva, "Thank you for delivering me from those wicked people."

"We left just in time," Alva replied. "I believe the Lord was with you."

They enjoyed a delicious meal and a nice visit. Soon they were ready for a good night's sleep. Early Thursday morning they were on their way. They arrived at Solomon Wills' on Friday afternoon. Solomon, being a little older than Carl, was the presiding elder of their local church. When they pulled in, Solomon and his wife, Elsie, came out to welcome them in.

They were jolted awake on Saturday morning by a loud clap of thunder. As the thunderstorm raged around them Joseph thought about his childhood days. A lot had changed since he had been in this part of the country. He remembered the days with the gypsies as they walked through thunderstorms. Cold and wet he would trudge along, crying for the protection of his warm dry home. Another clap of thunder and the children came running into the bedroom and jumped into their bed. They were not used to the loud clap of thunder and the close lightning. Where they lived in California they didn't get these kinds of thunderstorms.

The rain was hammering the metal roof as Joseph walked into the kitchen where Solomon was sipping on a cup of coffee.

"Does the storm dampen your spirits?" he asked.

"Only if you let it in," Joseph smiled.

****

The meeting was opened with hymn 488

Thou Shepherd of Israel and mine,

The joy and desire of my heart,
For closer communion I pine;
* I long to reside where thou art.*
The pasture I languish to find,
* Where all who their Shepherd obey,*
Are fed on thy bosom reclined,
* And screened from the heat of the day.*

Ah! show me that happiest place,
* That place of thy people's abode;*
Where Saints in an ecstasy gaze,
* And hang on a crucified Lord:*
Thy love for a sinner declare,
* Thy passion and death on the tree;*
My spirit to Calvary bear,
* To suffer and triumph with thee.*

'Tis there with the lambs of thy flock,
* There only I covet to rest;*
To lie at the foot of the rock,
* Or rise to be hid in thy breast.*
'Tis there I would always abide,
* And never a moment depart,*
Concealed in the cleft of thy side,
* Eternally held in thine heart.*

The meeting house was almost filled to capacity. The congregation sang with enthusiasm. It was easy to see they were looking forward to this meeting.

Carl stood and started reading the fifty-third chapter of Isaiah. *"Who hath believed our report? And to whom is the arm of the LORD revealed? For he shall grow up before him as a tender plant, and as a root out of a dry ground: he hath no form nor comeliness; and when we shall see him, there is no beauty that we should desire him."*

As these words of prophecies rang out across the congregation, visions of his youth flashed through Joseph's consciousness. He pictured himself sitting beside his father in this very church. "But I have never been here before," he thought. "I must just be imagining things." He pushed the thoughts out of his mind as he concentrated on the passage.

When Isaiah prophesied about the coming Savior, he had to have been amazed at what God was revealing. The impact of the Lord coming in meekness and with humility would have been hard to understand.

He is despised and rejected of men; a man of sorrows, and acquainted with grief: and we hid as it were our faces from him; he was despised, and we esteemed him not. Surely he hath borne our griefs, and carried our sorrows: yet we did esteem him stricken, smitten of God, and afflicted. But he was wounded for our transgressions, he was bruised for our iniquities: the chastisement of our peace was upon him; and with his stripes we are healed.

Joseph again had what appeared to be a flashback to his youth force its way into his thoughts. This time the picture was just a little bit clearer and included his brothers. He hadn't even thought of them in a long time. This brought a little uneasiness to his thoughts. He had to concentrate.

All we like sheep have gone astray; we have turned every one to his own way; and the LORD hath laid on him the iniquity of us all. He was oppressed, and he was afflicted, yet he opened not his mouth: he is brought as a lamb to the slaughter, and as a sheep before her shearers is dumb, so he openeth not his mouth. He was taken from prison and from judgment: and who shall declare his generation? For he was cut off out of the land of the living: for the transgression of my people was he stricken.

Joseph shut his eyes as the words rang out with authority throughout the church house. He knew every word. He started visualizing that he was standing on the bottom rail of the fence beside a barn. He was just a little boy and his dad was standing next to him with his hand on his shoulder. They were watching the sheep grazing peacefully in the pasture.

And he made his grave with the wicked, and with the rich in his death; because he had done no violence, neither was any deceit in his mouth. Yet it pleased the LORD to bruise him; he hath put him to grief: when thou shalt make his soul an offering for sin, he shall see his seed, he shall prolong his days, and the pleasure of the LORD shall prosper in his hand.

The seriousness of the words of Isaiah brought Joseph back to the here and now.

He shall see of the travail of his soul, and shall be satisfied: by his knowledge shall my righteous servant justify many; for he shall bear their iniquities. Therefore will I divide him a portion with the great, and he shall divide the spoil with the strong; because he hath poured out his soul unto death: and he was numbered with the transgressors; and he bare the sin of many, and made intercession for the transgressors.

As Carl sat down, Joseph named hymn number 28.

Kindred in Christ for his dear sake,
  A hearty welcome here receive,
May we together now partake
  The joys which only he can give!

To you and us by grace 'tis giv'n,
  To know the Savior's precious name,
And shortly we may meet in heav'n,
  Our hope, our way, our end the same.

May he, by whose kind care we meet,

The sincerity and joyfulness of the singing seemed to fill the house with the Spirit.

Joseph opened the meeting by using words from the hymn he just lined. "We are kindred in Christ. We have come from different parts of the country. Yet we have a kindredship. The law was weak through the flesh. Jesus came to make a way that we, being lost, could be saved. It is by the grace of God. To come to the house of prayer is a sign we want to follow the Lord. Satan will endeavor to distract us from this love of God.

This house is filled with folks who have accepted the offering of salvation through faith. They have repented and have been baptized. We are looking to this evening hour when we will commune with our Lord. The day leads up to partaking of holy things."

J.B. noticed five men come in and sat down on the back bench. "Under the Law of Moses, God had the priest to go before him only once a year with the blood of animals. They could never take away sins. Jesus shed His precious blood to take away our sins. He said, 'Come unto me all you that labor and are heavy laden and I will give you rest. Take my yoke upon you and learn of me; for I am meek and lowly in heart; and ye shall find rest unto your souls. For my yoke is easy and my burden is light.'

Some say we have closed communion. It is not closed. It is open to all who will accept Christ and be baptized. Come while there is time. Just as the Lord closed the door of the ark, He will someday close the day of grace. Let us kneel in prayer."

At Carl's request, the twenty-fourth chapter of Saint Luke was read. Carl centered his thoughts on the twenty-sixth verse. *"Ought not Christ to have suffered these things, and to enter into his glory?"*

"They were walking with Jesus on the road to Emmaus and didn't know it was their risen Savior. They were sad because Jesus had been crucified. They supposed He was the one to redeem Israel. They believed He was the Son of God but didn't understand the scriptures concerning the plan of God. Because of disobedience, death had reigned from Adam to Moses. Then they were given the law. The law was weak through the flesh.

They couldn't understand the scriptures. As they walked along, Jesus explained all the prophecies concerning himself. In spite of the explanation of the scripture about the coming of Christ, they didn't know it was Jesus.

The evening was drawing nigh. They invited him to abide with them. They served a supper. He blessed the bread, and while he parted it to them He opened their eyes and they knew Him. He vanished out of their sight. This caused some excitement. They said, 'Did not our hearts burn within us while He opened the scripture to us?'

They were walking with the Lord. He was telling them the meaning of all the scripture. Every word of God is pure. They were hearing the pure word of God. It's no wonder their hearts burned within them.

He made out as though He would go farther, but they constrained Him to abide with them. Had they not, they may have never known He was Jesus, nor understood the Word of God.

We come together to invite the Lord to abide with us. Jesus told them, 'If I go away, I will send the Spirit to bring to remembrance the things I have told you.' Not only do we need it brought to our remembrances, but to teach us by inviting Him in. He opened their eyes to know Him. He likely explained the love of the Father. It's not His will that any should perish, but all should be saved and come to the knowledge of the truth.

We that have been baptized and made promises to be faithful have come together with full faith that He will be in our midst during this meeting. We have invited Him to abide with us. We read in the morning lesson, 'Who hath believed our report?' We that are born again and have invited Him to abide with us believe. We plan to partake of the emblems of His broken body and shed blood. He opens our eyes to understanding. We believe the report. To whom is the arm of the Lord revealed? On the Emmaus road the arm of the Lord was revealed, but not until they said, 'abide with us' and sat with Him at the table.

To come to church, but not invite Him into your heart would be like not understanding the Scripture concerning the love of God. We are enjoying each moment as we draw closer to the Lord. This evening as we sit around the communion table, we will feel the spirit of a loving God drawing us close to Him, to each other and to heaven.

If you're not in, invite Him in. The day is far spent. The night is at hand. Today if you hear His voice, harden not your heart. Jesus wants to abide with you. He wants to break the bread to you. Yet there is room."

The meeting was a very uplifting service. Carl led the communion. His closing remarks put the cap sheath on the close feeling that overshadowed them. He said, "This evening hour as we were walking in the steps our master taught, we could just feel the closeness of our Savior. Each ordinance was bringing us closer to the cross. The sacred solemn songs we sang as we were partaking of the cup made us feel so close to each other and the Lord. I noticed the little children reaching for the cup sometimes as mothers slowly rocked them back and forth. For over four hours we have been sitting here, yet we were enjoying the love of our Father in heaven. That feeling has been passed down to us from our parents who have kept the faith. We want to pass it on down to our posterity. The spirit of the Lord was certainly with us tonight. Someday He will come and take us to be with him. Are you ready?"

J.B. led out Sunday morning with the farewell address. He was still experiencing a close relationship with the Lord carried over from the night before. This closeness removed all ties with any worldly sorrows. He cast his eyes heavenward as he lined hymn 494.

There is a happy land,
  Far, far, away-
Where saints in glory stand
  Bright, bright as day;
Oh, how they sweetly sing-
  Worthy is the Savior King!
Loud let his praises ring
  For evermore.

Come to this happy land,
  Come, come away,
Why will ye doubting stand?
  Why still delay?
Oh we shall happy be!
  When from sin and sorrow free;

The first verse had just begun, when the door opened and in walked the five men Joseph had noticed the day before. It was evident they weren't members of the church. As the day before, they sat in the back. Joseph thought, "they likely are neighbors." Then he noticed they had hymn books and joined in the singing. "Who are these men?" He wondered but quickly dismissed it from his mind.

He opened his Bible to Saint John eleven reading verses twenty-five and six, *"Jesus said unto her, I am the resurrection, and the life; he that believeth in me, though he were dead, yet shall he live: And whosoever liveth and believeth in me shall never die. Believest thou this?"*

Looking around at the attentive eyes Joseph shared his thoughts, "Life and death! Ever since Adam fell in the garden, man has lived in the fear of death. The Word tells us it is appointed for man once to die and after this the judgment. It is normal for all the animal kingdom to want to preserve life. Man is different than animals. Animals don't have a soul. When God made man, He breathed into his nostrils the breath of life and he became a living soul.

In Ezekiel eighteen the fourth verse, God said, 'All souls are mine.' In the garden when God told Adam not to eat of a certain tree, He said, 'the day you eat thereof you shall surely die.' God and Adam had a close relationship in the garden. To sever that relationship would be to die spiritually. In other words, he would lose contact with God. Man is mortal. Was man immortal before he fell? There are some things hard to understand. One thing we do know is that mortal man will die.

What becomes of man after death? There were people who lived righteously with the Lord. There were more that didn't obey His commandments. Jesus told about two men. One was rich and didn't use his resources as he should. The other was a poor man. Likely he trusted in the Lord and obeyed his commandments. They both died a natural death. The poor man's soul was taken by the angels into Abraham's bosom. The rich man was buried and in hell he lifted up his eyes. He was in torment. He was in flames and couldn't get away from them. What was in torment? His body would soon burn up. His body was buried. The soul of man will never die. I believe that man who knows to do good but chooses not to, his soul will be separated from the protecting hand of God. Yet God would not allow his soul to die. Think of the terrible suffering.

I like to remember the three Hebrew children in the book of Daniel. They were faithful to the Lord. They would not worship the golden image. They would only worship the Lord. Their heart was firmly grounded in the Lord. They knew the Lord could deliver them if he chose. They also knew if their bodies were burned up, their souls would not be hurt. Men can not destroy our soul. They may kill our body, but that is all they can do. What about a man destroying his own soul? Can he? The answer is no. God has that in His control. Man does have the choice of accepting or refusing the offer of salvation. Jesus said, 'I am the resurrection and the life.' Do you believe it? Accept him.

Lazarus was dead. Jesus was not close by when he died. When He came, Martha said unto Jesus, 'If you had been here my brother had not died.' Jesus said, 'Your brother shall rise again.' She said, 'I know he shall rise again in the resurrection at the last day.' Likely Jesus had told her about the time coming when this dispensation of time will be no more and He would rule in a kingdom where there will be no more sin, or sorrow nor death. It will be a land where we will never grow old. Jesus did bring Lazarus back to life. That was back to mortal life. Jesus is the first fruit of the resurrection of the immortal life.

'Whosoever liveth and believeth in me shall never die.' Believest thou this? Do you believe the words of Jesus? We are passing through this life at a fast pace. We have time to choose where we want to spend eternity. Jesus came into this world in the flesh so that He could die to the flesh for us. We read in Hebrews chapter two verse nine, '*But we see Jesus, who was made a little lower than the angels for the suffering of death, crowned with glory and honor; that he by the grace of God should taste of death for every man.*'

Last night we sat around the table of the Lord, partaking of the emblems of Jesus' shed blood and broken body. We were remembering what Jesus said, 'Except you eat of my flesh and drink of my blood, there is no life in you.' In our mind's eye, we saw Him hanging on the cross. He cried out, 'My God, My God, why hast thou forsaken me?' He cried, 'It is finished' and gave up the ghost. The power of death had been conquered. The veil of the temple was rent in two from the top to the bottom. The Holy of Holies is now open to all who choose to accept salvation. Oh, the closeness we felt to our Savior.

Jesus didn't die just for me. He died for you. Have you considered coming into the fold of God? There is still room. The door is still open. Tomorrow may be too late. Don't think you're too much of a sinner. He came to seek and save the lost. The Spirit and the bride say, come. Let him that heareth say come. Let him that is athirst come, and whosoever will let him take of the water of life freely.

Jesus said, 'I am the resurrection and the life.' Do you believe this? Don't tarry, come."

Carl rose and lined the first verse to hymn number 476.

Jesus, my all, to heav'n is gone,
  He who I fix my hopes upon;
His track I see, and I'll pursue,
  The narrow way till Him I view.

"Do you love this life? Are you happy with your condition? What keeps you from enjoying the blessings of a home in heaven? The brother said, 'The Lord came to save the sinner.' In Genesis, we read where Jacob's sons got themselves in a prison of guilt they didn't know how to get out of. The day came they had to confess. Had they confessed it long before they did, they could have saved themselves years of sorrow.

A man living in sin is stealing from God. How? As the brother told us, we have a soul. Our soul belongs to God. Jesus taught us to let our light shine that others may see our good works and glorify our Father in heaven. When we feel the wooing of the Spirit and turn a cold shoulder, we are saying, 'We don't want to work for the Lord.' Just think about being a worker in the Lord's vineyard. That is a very rewarding, pleasant job. Not only is it a joy, but it is comforting to the soul. When we come to the last day of our life, and come to the Judgment seat of God; to hear the words, 'Come ye blessed of my Father. Inherit the blessings of the Lord.' What a joy. What is required to have eternal life? Faith! Saint John three sixteen, a very familiar verse says, *'For God so loved the world, that he gave his only begotten Son, that whosoever believeth in him should not perish, but have everlasting life.'*

Repentance and baptism! We read in Acts chapter two, verse thirty-eight, Peter on the day of Pentecost told the new believers, *'Repent and be baptized every one of you in the name of Jesus Christ for the remission of sins, and ye shall receive the gift of the Holy Ghost.'*

Walking with the Lord you can do what we sang in the last verse of the hymn; *Then will I tell to sinners round, What a dear Savior I have found; I'll point to thy redeeming Blood, and say 'Behold the way to God!'*

Farewell one and all until we meet again."

Joy In Sorrow
Chapter Twenty One

After the services, a simple meal of beef and soup was served in the basement. They all were filled both spiritually and physically. Carl decided to go for a little walk around the church while the local folks were cleaning up the dishes. That was when he came across the five gentlemen who had come in after church had started. He introduced himself to them and asked who they may be. They explained that they were the Bowman brothers from Iowa.

The older brother asked, "Who is the minister with the young boy?"

"That is my son J.B. He has only been in the ministry for a couple of years. The young lad is J.B.'s son Daniel." Carl answered.

One of the brothers looked sad as he confided with Carl. "He looks a lot like our brother who died when he was about that age."

"I'm sorry to hear that," Carl responded. "Do you still miss him?"

They didn't answer but Carl could see in their faces that there was a pain far deeper than the conversation revealed.

****

Carl's informed Joseph that they were invited to come to Iowa for a meeting Thursday evening. They would be leaving early the next morning in hopes of being at the home of their host before supper.

It was on the way to Iowa when Daniel told his dad about a conversation he'd had with a lady on Sunday afternoon. "There was a woman asked me how old I am."

"Well, that's not unusual," Joseph responded to his little boy.

"She said she had a little boy that was seven and looked just like I do. I asked her if I could play with him and she started crying."

"That is a little strange. Did she tell you why she was crying?" Joseph asked.

"She told me her little boy died when he was seven and that it was a long time ago. Am I going to die daddy? I'm scared."

Joseph reassured his son nothing like that was going to happen. "What did she look like?"

"She was really nice. She had tears in her eyes when she talked about her little boy."

After Daniel had fallen asleep, Carl shared with J.B. the conversation he had with the five men from the church.

****

It was about two o'clock Monday afternoon when they got to the home of Elder Jason Bowman. As they were driving up the lane, J.B. thought something looked a little familiar. He couldn't think what it was. *I have seen this place before.* They parked by the old hitching post. Jason came in from the barn and Carl introduced them to him. Jason's wife, Dorothy, came out on the porch, as they were walking toward the house. Carl and Rachel happily greeted her.

"This is our son, J.B. and his wife Lovina, and their children, Daniel, Eddie, and Shelly," Carl introduced his family to Dorothy.

Jason said, "Come in and find comfortable chairs."

Walking in the house, Joseph had some really strange feelings. *I've been in this house,* he thought, "But when?"

"You folks have been traveling awhile, let me get you a glass of water," Dorothy told her guests.

Jason helped her pass water to the adults. The children wanted to run and play.

Carl asked, "Have you got chores to be doing?"

"No, our son does all that. We turned the farming over to him last year. He and his children take care of everything now. I only go to the barn when I want to. Here they come now."

Jason's three grandchildren came along to do chores. Dorothy called them in to introduce them to J.B. and Lovina's children.

Daniel came and asked, "Dad, can I go watch them feed the calves?"

Joseph looked at Jason for approval, "Sure son. Just don't get in the way."

"Thank you, Dad, I will help." He bounced down the steps running to the barn.

After some talk about the church and the members in the local district, Carl asked Jason about the five men he had met over at the meeting in Illinois, "They said they were brothers from over here in Iowa. Do you know them?"

"Yes," Jason looked down as if he really didn't want to continue.

"I noticed they all had hymn books and sang. Do they attend church here?" Carl asked.

"Yes, they do. They hardly ever miss a meeting."

"If they show that kind of interest in the church, why haven't they become members?" Carl questioned.

"That is a puzzle to all of us," Jason answered.

Looking around to see there were no children close by Jason continued, "They all still live at home on a large farm about five miles from here. When they were young, their mother died suddenly. The boys had been helping her in the garden on a hot day and I think she had a heat stroke. The boys did all they could to save her but to no avail. Her final words to the boys were to be good, and that she loved them." The crackle in Jason's voice showed the emotions of the loss so many years ago, was still there.

Jason had to wipe his eyes before he could continue, "That was a very sad funeral. They struggled along for two years. We took dinner there one day and found them all sitting in a circle on the bedroom floor, singing with all their hearts."

Carl asked, "What were they singing?"

"Jesus lover of my soul," Jason answered. "They didn't hear us. We tiptoed back out to the kitchen and sat until we heard them singing the last verse."

"So, did their father raise the boys by himself?" Joseph, who had been listening quietly asked.

Turning to Joseph, Jason explained, "No, a couple of years later they got a new mother. Jake married Gail. She was a widow sister without children. It was hard for those five boys to accept her, but they tried. Jake and Gail were blessed with children. The younger two are twins. The home seemed like it was a happy place, although it was obvious that the older boys had not gotten over the loss of their mother. Things were going as well as could be expected until…"

Jason was visibly getting choked up. He pulled out a hanky and wiped some tears away before continuing, "It was really sad. Jake and Gail had gone to Virginia to see Jake's ailing father. They took the twins with them, leaving their son, Joseph, with his older brothers. Jake's father soon passed away. It took a little time to take care of his affairs. So it was a few weeks before they returned home.

The day they arrived home the boys were beside themselves. They couldn't find their little brother. After a long search, his shoes were found by the river. He was only seven years old and likely drowned, even though his body never was found. That has affected those five boys to this day."

Lovina suddenly jumped up and went to J.B., "Honey, what is wrong?"

Joseph was in a sweat and very pale. They helped him into a bedroom and onto the bed. Lovina continued placing cold cloths on his face. After about half an hour, he started getting color in his checks. He asked the others to let him and Lovina be alone for a while. They closed the door.

Weakly he asked her to sit next to him.

Holding her hand he said, "I am Joseph."

"I know dear. You are Joseph."

"No, I am the Joseph that Jason was talking about."

"You're the little boy that drowned in the river?"

"Yes, only I didn't drown. My brothers sold me to some gypsies for ten dollars."

Over the next half hour, he told her the whole story of his life, "I also was afraid of my brothers. I was afraid of Durango, who told me he would shoot me if I told anybody. The only person I told any of this to was my teacher at Uncle Alva's and she promised to not tell."

"Are you still afraid of your five brothers?" Lovina asked.

Joseph was silent for a few minutes as he worked through his feelings, "I think they likely, long ago regretted what they did. They are in a prison of guilt, not knowing how to get out. I wonder if they made up that story about me drowning. That would be the reason dad never found me. That may be what is keeping them out of the church."

"Do you think we ought to tell dad and mom and get out of here?" Lovina asked.

"I feel we need to talk to them and get their council," Joseph said, adding, "If there is proof of sorrow in their hearts, I hope we can someway help them to get out from under the grips of Satan."

Lovina went out and returned shortly with Carl and Rachel and found Joseph sitting up.

"What's the problem, son?" Carl asked.

Joseph told the vivid story of his youth to his adopted parents. He finished with his feelings that his brothers fabricated the story about his drowning, "That would explain why they never tried to find me."

"They must be in a prison of guilt," Carl said. "Do you think they would like to repent?"

"I don't know, but if they will I would forgive them. They would need to make a full confession."

Carl looked down at his son with mixed feelings. J.B. had been their son for many years. The thought that the parent son relationship could be taken away was heart-wrenching, but he knew that a long coming healing process was being orchestrated by God. "Son, you know that you are called to forgive your brothers regardless of what they do?"

Joseph looked up at Carl and Rachel and smiled, "Yes, but I'm not sure I want to. Whatever happens, you are my parents. You took me in when I was ten. You instilled the love of God in my heart and life. You are and will always be dad and mom."

Carl and Rachel gave him a hug and kiss, "You will always be our son. I think we should talk to Jason and Dorothy."

Jason and Dorothy sat there in shock as Joseph told the story of his life from the day he was taken captive with the gypsies until his time with his adopted parents. He tried not to show any ill feelings or hatred towards the five men who had been, and would always be, his brothers.

When Joseph had finished there was not a dry eye in the room.

The room was silent for what seemed like an eternity. Finally, Jason spoke up, "I think it would be best if we spent some time in prayer."

The six of them knelt in prayer as Jason prayed for wisdom and guidance on how Joseph and all those involved should move forward. He asked God to give them peace and a forgiving spirit to all those that had suffered as a result of such an atrocious act.

****

"Sure, we would love to," Rudy replied to Jason's invite. "I'll need to talk to my brothers, but I see no reason why we can't be there around seven. You say Carl Bauman from California is there?"

"He is and would like to meet you boys. They're on the way back home with their son J.B. and his family," Jason explained.

"Great, I would enjoy visiting with them. That was a great meeting with a lot of good preaching. See you tonight." Rudy ended the call.

Dorothy was busy putting supper on the table as Lovina called the children to come in. The meatloaf was steaming hot with an aroma that should make everyone hungry. The slab of butter was melting down into the pile of mashed potatoes. Side dishes of corn and honey glazed carrots completed the banquet fit for a king.

Uncharacteristic of J.B., he ate very little. It all looked good but he didn't feel like eating. The butterflies in his stomach told him that he was more afraid of his brothers than he was letting on. The vision of the mean look in their eyes the day they sold him was haunting.

Sitting next to J.B. his young son noticed and asked what he thought was an obvious question, "You're not eating much tonight Dad, do you have to preach?"

"Daddy isn't feeling too good Daniel," Lovina whispered to her son.

As per the plan, after supper, Jason ran the children over to their son's to spend the evening with his grandchildren. There were considerable questions about the extent of the conversation in which J.B. should participate. It was mutually decided he would keep the interaction with his brothers to a minimum.

"Just listen and don't say much," Carl told his son. "If they are still hard-hearted, I don't think it's wise to reveal your true identity. We will give you a sign when we feel it is time."

"If your emotions get to you, slip into the bedroom," Jason added.

Jason thought it best if the ladies were not involved in the meeting. "I feel the men will be more open if they're alone with other men."

"No problem," Dorothy said. "We can visit in the kitchen within earshot."

****

At five minutes before seven, a car drove up the lane. The men got out of the car and walked up the sidewalk. "This is the older three," Jason said as he got up to open the door. He welcomed the brothers and introduced Rudy, Simon, and Henry to Carl and J.B. They were still making small talk when another car made its way up the drive. A few minutes later the twins, Thad and Chad had met Jason's guest and they all were comfortably seated.

Carl started out the conversation, "I was asking Jason and Dorothy if they knew the five men we met over in Illinois and were surprised to find out your father is Jason's cousin. Tell me where does your family come from?"

Rudy, being the oldest told the story of their father's move to Iowa many years ago.

"Speaking of your father. Are your parents still living?"

"Yes," he answered. "They are getting older but doing well."

"Do you have any other siblings?" Carl was working his way into the heart of the conversation.

Rudy coughed a couple of times and asked for a glass of water.

Henry took over, "There are eight of us children."

The puzzled look on his brow caused Henry to continue, "There were the five of us born to our father's first wife. Mom died when we were young. Dad remarried and had four more children."

The puzzled look on Carl's face didn't ease as he was doing the math.

Rudy caught on to what Carl was thinking, "One of our younger siblings died," he said matter-of-factly.

"What happened?" Carl asked, knowing the trap was laid. Would they out rightly reveal the truth, or had the lie grown such roots that the truth was inconceivable?

The silence was deafening as the weight of the question caused hearts to sink.

Over twenty years of torment was pounding in the consciences of the brothers. It was showing in their faces. They looked at each other remembering the promise of secrecy they shared. It was Rudy that finally mumbled, "He drowned in the river. He was only seven years old." He took out his hanky and wiped away the tears that were running down his cheeks.

Carl looked around the room. All of the brothers were looking down. The outcast demeanor revealed five lost souls. The tension was building as the elders knew that the dam of guilt was about to break.

"I noticed at the meeting last weekend, you all sang as if the words meant something to you," Carl's firm, yet loving, words cut through the silence. "Jason tells me you men attend church with regularity. Yet, you have not come into the church.

I feel there is something in your life that is stopping you. Satan would love nothing more than to keep us out of fellowship with our Lord."

At this point, all the brothers were wiping tears away. J.B. was having trouble maintaining his composure, yet he had to stay in the room, he was sure they were witnessing God working in the hearts of his brothers.

Carl continued, "You are amongst friends here. We would welcome you to share with us what is tearing away at your hearts. We would be happy to help you resolve it. Don't let anything keep you away from the salvation of the Lord."

They sat there for what seemed like several minutes with only the sound of the old grandfather clock ticking away. The glistening of sweat running down their faces was revealing years of buried guilt.

Rudy was the first to speak, "I believe the Lord has sent you to help us. For a long time, we have wanted to untangle a very disturbing mess. We were young and never understood the consequences of what we were doing. If we had known, things would be much different today."

"Please explain," Carl prompted as Rudy's hesitation seemed to drag on.

"Our little brother did not drown when he was seven," Rudy's soft words crackled as he could hardly believe he was revealing what they had done. Looking up at their three interrogators he continued. "You see, we were very jealous of Joseph. We perceived that our parents favored him over us. We know now that that was not the case, but in our adolescent state we were blinded by hate."

"Were you instrumental in your brother's death?" The sharpness of Carl's question brought a very audible gasp from Joseph. His head was spinning as he looked down at the floor not sure he even wanted to hear how his brother answered the question.

"We did not kill our brother," Rudy looked up at Jason. "You remember the day when Joseph went missing? All the searching we pretended to do looking for him was a hoax. We were only doing that to hide that we had sold our brother to a band of gypsies so they would leave us alone. We have no idea what happened to him."

Carl decided it was time to bring the other brothers into the conversation, "What Rudy has said, not only indicts himself but also levels some very serious accusations against you men. Is this true?"

One by one the brothers lifted their tear-filled eyes and with sadness in their voices said, "It is true."

Joseph could no longer control his emotions. He excused himself and left the room. Slipping out the back door he walked around the barn and started back a lane towards the woods. He was shuffling his feet in the gravel as he heard someone come up behind him. Turning around he was greeted by Lovina. She didn't say a word as she slipped her hand into his. Together they walked, no words were spoken, and none were needed.

****

Jason's memories took him back many years to when these men were little boys playing in his yard. He recalled them pushing each other on the swing that hung in the old maple tree. He relished the days they played baseball in the backyard. "What happened? Where can things go so wrong in a young man's life?" Satan drove the wedge of envy into the hearts of these men while they were still in their youth. It has only been through prayers of their family and friends that God has sought their redemption.

"It may be obvious," Jason spoke up, "but I need to ask. Are you men sorry for what you did to your brother and the lies you have told covering it up over the years?"

One by one all five brothers said, "Yes, I am."

"If you had the power within you to make things right, would you?" Carl asked.

Rudy answered for them all, "Oh! There is no question we would do things differently if we could go back. Joseph did not deserve what we did. It not only hurt him. It has hurt our father deeply. He still grieves the loss of our brother."

"I remember how much your father missed Joseph," Jason commented. "He spent hours lamenting about not taking Joseph with them. Boys, you know, life's road only goes one way. There's no going back. We can't undo what we have done. When Jesus walked here on earth he taught us how to change the road we are on. When we see that we are walking down the wrong road, we are not at the end of the road but at a fork in the road. A decision must be made to go the right way. Watch for the signs. The first sign is confession. This evening we have heard you boys confess to what you have done. The second sign is repentance. We have listened as each of you has repented of the horrible things you have done. The next sign is to humbly ask for forgiveness. These three signs will direct us down the right road."

"If it were possible, would you want to be forgiven?" Carl asked as he looked intently each one in the eyes, studying their response.

Henry was the first to respond, "Yes, if there is any way possible, but we have gone so far down the wrong road. I just don't see how anyone could forgive us."

Through the tears streaming down their faces, each of the boys nodded in agreement with their brother.

"Have you sinned more than those that condemned Jesus to be crucified?" Jason asked. "Yet on the cross did not Jesus ask that those who had treated Him so wrongly be forgiven?"

The five brothers could feel Jason and Carl were reaching out to them in love.

Jason thanked the brothers for their outpouring of honesty and asked if they could come back the next evening. They nodded showing their agreement. He asked them to spend the night in prayer and fasting as tomorrow was going to be a brand new day.

****

Joseph and Lovina stood there leaning up against the fence as the sun dropped below the horizon and the sky lit up in reds and orange. Lovina could see Joseph was looking well beyond the sunset.

"Do you see it?" she asked.

"See what?" he replied through the tears that were forming in his eyes.

"Do you see forgiveness for your brothers?" Her soft voice brought with it a soothing sharpness.

Joseph only squeezed her hand gently as his thoughts raced through time. Finally, he wiped the tears out of his eyes and smiled. "Who am I to withhold forgiveness?"

****

A light rain was falling as the brothers hurried up the sidewalk. Their disposition was a little better than just twenty-four hours earlier. They had spent the night in prayer and fasting. They felt the weight of many years had been lifted from their shoulders, yet the agonizing reality of their sins had left a deep scar. They knew that it was only time before they must reveal to their parents what they had done so many years ago. Only their imaginations could conceive how this news would be received.

Jason met them on the porch. As they made their way into the living room they were greeted by Carl and J.B. No sooner than they were seated the ladies joined the group. The brothers looked perplexed as they expected it would only be the men.

"Our wives have been brought up to speed on the situation," Jason told them, breaking the building tension in the room. "As with the rest of us, they too have been praying for you. Reconciliation is a joyous time and should not be missed."

"Not so sure it's a joyous time, we still have unresolved issues," Rudy stated.

"Yes, but we expect some of those will be taken care of this evening," Jason replied. "Remember, with God all things are possible. Carl, I think you should tell them about your experience."

Carl smiled as he responded to his cue, "Boys, let me tell you a story of a young man I met years ago. Rachel and I went to the train station in San Diego where we met some of our family from Texas. They had a young lad with them who was looking for a home. He was a perfect fit for our family and we adopted him. He became our son and we became his parents. He was a blessing to our lives, yet we could tell something was missing. He had obviously had a rough past that we could not get out of him. He was suppressing the memory of his early years. Whoever had mistreated our son had done some lasting damage. However, he loved the Lord and in his early teens gave his life to Christ and was baptized. This young man found hope in his faith and grew even closer to his Lord as he matured.

One day he met a girl and, in time, he got married and moved away. We were blessed by his time with us and within a couple of years we had grandchildren. We don't see them often enough but how we love those little ones."

Not only the brothers but everyone in the room was intently listening to Carl tell the story. Everyone was studying the faces of the brothers to see if they understood who Carl was talking about. Their furrowed brows showed that it was still a mystery.

"One day," Carl continued, "this young man we had met at the train station was called to the ministry. Today he proclaims the Word wherever he goes. I guess what I want to relay to you is the power of God's love is far greater than we can ever understand. In God's timing, the underlying hurt within our son was brought to light. We continue to be amazed at how God orchestrates the events in our lives." Carl looked at J.B. and nodded.

****

With butterflies in his stomach, J.B. rose and walked in front of the ones that had sold him into slavery so long ago. He stood there in the middle of the room looking back and forth at his brothers. How he longed for the clock of time to spin back to the time before they had done that horrible deed. But it was not to be. That was not God's plan. Over the last twenty-four hours, he had become certain that his brothers had repented and had started down the right road. It was time they knew who he was, "I am Joseph."

The words echoed throughout the room like the sound of a hammer beating in an empty well. The brothers sat there with a look of total confusion gripping their thoughts.

Joseph repeated himself, "I am Joseph, your brother, the one whom you sold to the gypsies for ten dollars."

What they were hearing was finally sinking in and the brothers were speechless.

As the reality of the words they were processing continued to sink in, the brother's demeanor showed signs of emotional collapse. As expected the original shock turned to feelings of shame. Rudy was the first to respond. Like a whipped animal he arose from his chair and approached Joseph.

153

With tears streaming down his face he humbly stood before the one whom he had betrayed. Looking down he muttered, "I am so sorry. There is no excuse for what I did." Looking up he asked for one of the most difficult requests ever asked of Joseph, "Will you forgive me?"

Joseph choked back his emotions the best he could as he opened not only his arms but his heart as well. "Yes, my brother, I forgive you." As the two of them cried on each other's shoulders the other four brothers stood in line behind Rudy.

Around the room, many happy tears were being shed as the brothers now stood in a circle in the middle of the room. Finally, Joseph had them sit back down as he himself pulled up a chair in front of them.

"Satan has a lot of power," he said as he leaned forward. "About the time the spirit of the Lord would have drawn you into His fold, Satan took advantage of your weakness. You were sorrowing over not having your dearly loved mother when evil thoughts were planted in your hearts. The opportunity to act on this sin came when the gypsies showed up while the folks were gone. This action put you in a prison in which you could not escape."

The brothers were listening intently to their younger brother. They were still having trouble putting it all together. It was like they were living in a dream. The last they had seen Joseph, he was crying out as he was walking back to the woods tied between two strangers.

"How did you know where to find us?" Henry asked.

"God has a way of working out His plan. At the meeting over in Illinois, I noticed the five of you as you entered the church on Saturday morning. It was a little unusual, but I didn't think anything about it other than you must be neighbors. I did notice you singing and listening intently. Still, it did not even dawn on me that you could be my brothers.

On the trip over here our son Daniel was sharing that a lady at church told him he looked like her son who had drowned many years ago.”

“That would have been mother,” Chad interjected.

“I believe God saw your sorrows,” Joseph continued. “He understood the dilemma you were in. He heard you as you sang songs of praise. He noticed you as you came to church. He knew the inner thoughts of your hearts as you repented of that atrocious crime. We serve a just God and He has a plan for each and every one of us. God has taken care of me since that dreadful day over twenty-two years ago. He put it in the heart of my adopted father to come here and invite us to come along. Little did we know the plan of our loving heavenly Father.”

The conversation turned to the rest of the family as Joseph asked, “How are the folks doing? Are they well? And tell me more about Benjamin and Cassie.”

“They are doing well,” Rudy answered. “We are apprehensive, yet anxious for them to find out about you. We pray they will take it well. We love them dearly and the knowledge of the hurt we have done to them may be unbearable.” The grimace on the faces of his brothers was not missed by Joseph. It was obvious this was a hurdle they still faced.

“Ben is married and has two children,” “Rudy continued. “They live in the little house of the farm and still help with the farm work. Cassie is married and has a daughter. They live over close to the church in Illinois. We also have a younger brother, Aaron Lee, who was born after you were gone. He still lives at home with mom and dad.”

“Are any of them church members?” Joseph asked.

“They all are,” Rudy answered. “They were at the meeting last weekend.”

“Yes, they were all at the communion table Saturday night,” Simon added.

"What about the folks? Were they there all the time?"

"They took in the whole meeting. They went a couple of days early to help Cassie and spend time with their granddaughter."

Things had moved fast and yet there was more to be done before the night was over. Joseph felt it was time to turn the floor back over to the elders in the room as he nodded to Jason and moved his chair back. Asking to be briefly excused, he went to the restroom, giving himself time to gather his thoughts.

Returning to the room, Joseph overhead Carl asking the brothers what was keeping them from accepting the call of salvation and joining the church. From what the brothers were saying it became evident that they felt their past was their only hindrance.

Joseph told the brothers he would like to see his parents in the morning. This would give them time to make a full confession. "You don't want to omit anything or blame anyone. Make sure, as you have done here, take full responsibility. If at all possible I would like to also meet my other siblings and their families."

****

On the way home the brothers talked about how to approach the folks on their confession.

"Shouldn't we wait until morning?" Chad suggested.

"If we do, we won't sleep," Thad responded.

"If we tell them tonight, they won't sleep," Simon said.

Rudy was the one that made the final decision. "If they are still up, let's do it before Satan tries to change our mind."

"We are at the dividing of the road. Remember the sign that says confession is the right road?" Henry reminded as they pulled in the drive.

They sat in the car for a few moments trying to get up the nerve to go in. Finally, Rudy said, "Boys, now is the time. We've known we should confess for years. Come on, let's go."

When they walked in, their parents and Ben's were all sitting around the table. It was evident Ben's had been there for supper.

"How did you find Jason's?" Jake asked.

With a lot on their mind, they half-heartedly acknowledged the question with an assurance that Jason's were doing fine.

"Did they have any other company?" Gail asked.

"Yes they did," Rudy answered. "The ministers from California who were at the meeting in Illinois were there."

"Was the little boy that looks like Joseph there?"

"Yes, he came just before we left."

"He was such a spitting image of Joseph," their mother said with tears forming in her eye. "I would like to pick him up and give him a hug."

"Possibly you can. We are all invited to Jason's for dinner tomorrow."

"Are you saying that the young preacher will be there with his son?" She didn't give them time to answer. "I don't know if I could stand to hold that little boy. His daddy and grandpa are sure good preachers. It is easy to see they are father and son, by the way they preach. They are so filled with the Spirit. Will they both be there? I am excited to meet them."

Rudy cleared his throat. There was more than one question in his mother's statement. He felt now was the time to move this conversation to a new level.

"Yes, they all will be there. The ministers will be preaching tomorrow night at church. Mother, you will especially be excited to meet the younger minister, the father of the boy."

"How is that?" Gail had a puzzled look on her face.

As Rudy mustered up all the courage he could his brothers were silently praying for God to help them all through this life-changing time.

"That little boy's daddy is your son Joseph."

The silence was deafening. The scene within the room changed from family member to family member. The brothers stood there waiting for judgment to fall. Their younger brother sat there with a look of bewilderment on his face. Their father was processing the statement as he shook his head back and forth. It was their stepmother who finally responded to the strange statement.

"He can't be. Our son Joseph drowned. Why are you doing this to us?"

"I'm sorry mother, Joseph didn't drown. That young minister you listened to over in Illinois, is your son Joseph."

"How can that be?" Jake asked as he still was now slowly shaking his head.

All five of the older brothers with a defeated look hung their heads as Rudy again cleared his throat. "We have come to a fork in the road. Jason told us, 'When a person knows they are going down the wrong road, they must turn and go another way.' He said we must be sorry for our sins and repent. Confession is a sign leading to the right road."

The rest of the family was now looking more confused than before Rudy started speaking.

"Joseph?" Jake prodded.

"Father, the five of us have a very serious confession to make. I pray that somehow you will be able to forgive us." He wiped his eyes, and with sadness in his demeanor, he told the complete story. He told of their hatred for their brother. He shared how they longed for his demise. He told of the gypsies leading Joseph away. He choked his way through the moments afterward when they regretted their actions and went looking for their brother. He explained the sinful lies of the cover-up story.

His voice was failing him and he asked Simon to explain how Joseph had been revealed.

"God has a way of working out His plan," Simon stuttered. "While we were causing pain and living a lie, God was working in Joseph's life. While he had no idea where he had come from, God started bringing back his memory over in Illinois. God led him to Jason's home where a conversation about the five of us brought up the story of Joseph's drowning. That is when it was revealed to Joseph. Father, mother, I too am sorry for what we have done. I too pray that sometime you will be able to forgive us." Simon fell to his knees as his whole body was shaking with sobs.

The other three boys added to the confession until there was nothing else to say.

Jake pulled his chair close to his sobbing wife and put his arm around her. He sat there holding Gail close to him. His mind was in a whirl, but he kept his composure. He knew he needed to in order to calm his wife. "Did you boys confess to Joseph and ask him for forgiveness?"

"Yes, we did. It was difficult to face the horrendous thing we had done to him." Rudy answered. "He said he forgives us. We were shocked at the love we felt as he wept on our shoulders. His heart is filled with the love of God."

"Boys, there is no question about forgiveness. We are called to forgive, no matter what someone has done to us. I need to spend some time with your mother. So if you will excuse us we are going to our room."

Gail wiped the tears from her eyes and was able to smile a little. "I forgive you too."

Ben spoke up, "I'm totally confused, but nevertheless, I forgive you as well."

Jake stood up. "Let's try and get some sleep. Tomorrow is a very special day."

****

Jake could feel the apprehension as he reached across the car and took his wife's hand. It had been a silent ride on the way over to Jason's. It was approaching ten a.m. as they drove up the tree-lined drive.

Gail broke the silence. "Did I dream that Joseph is still alive?"

"If so, you were not the only one to dream that dream," her husband replied.

As they pulled up to the old hitching post, they recognized the young minister coming out of the house. "Could that really be our boy?" Gail questioned as she was still coming to grips with the possibility.

Joseph ran to his mother. Throwing his arms around her he gave her a kiss and hugged her close. "Mother, mother how I have missed you!"

They stood there weeping.

Jake came around the car and stood beside them wiping the tears from his eyes. After a few moments, Joseph turned to his father and threw his arms around him. "Dad, I have missed you so much." He kissed him and in an embrace, they wept.

They made their way to the house where Jason's and Carl's were waiting. They told Joseph they would stay on the porch and let him introduce his parents to his family without interruption.

Walking into the familiar house Jake and Gail met a young lady who graciously stood up and opened her arms to the mother of her husband.

"Mom, Dad, this is my wife Lovina. She is also the mother of your grandchildren."

Lovina motioned to the children, "Come children."

Three timid children slowly came to her.

Joseph introduced them, "Meet your grandchildren. Daniel is seven years old. Eddie is six. Here is little Shelly, she just turned four. Children, you have been blessed with another grandpa and grandma."

Grandpa and grandma stooped down and gave each of them a hug. The children acted perplexed. Joseph told them, "There are things we will explain to you later."

Once they had all taken seats Joseph asked if his older brothers had revealed to them what had happened. They nodded.

"So did they make a confession?"

"Yes they did," his dad answered.

"Did they ask for forgiveness?"

"Yes, and we forgave them."

"What about Benjamin?"

"Yes and he forgave them as well."

"Praise the Lord," Joseph sighed. "I need to tell you about Carl and Rachel. When I was ten years old they adopted me. They gave me a very good home, and taught me the way of the Lord, just like you would have. We will have more things to talk about later. I feel well blessed. I have three sets of parents. You two," Joseph stood up, walked over to his parents and gave each of them a big hug. "I also have Carl and Rachel, and Lovina's parents."

Joseph expressed his desire that they do not dwell in the past. "Let us be thankful for what the Lord has done. We want to look forward to the joys that are ahead."

Daniel had been intently listening to the conversation. He came to Gail, took hold of her hand, and looked up at her. "I love you, Grandma."

Gail could not hold back the tears as her thoughts went back to just last week when she first saw Daniel. He looked so much like his father when he was that age. To think, his father, her son had stood there that day, powerfully preaching the word of God. Listening to that sermon, and having no idea he was the son she thought was dead. "Am I dreaming?" she wondered.

As Jason's and Carl's joined the rejoicing family in the living room, Carl said, "God moves in a mysterious way."

Jake said, "His wonders to perform."

"He plants His footsteps on the sea," Jason added.

"And rides upon the storm," Joseph said finishing the well-known verse.

Jason said, "I think it would be beneficial for us to spend some time in prayer before the others arrive. Carl, would you lead us in prayer?"

They knelt while Carl prayed a touching prayer. He prayed for their guidance this day and on the morrows. He thanked the Lord for bringing this sorrow to a conclusion. Then in a very tenderness of voice, he prayed for those brothers in need of being lifted from their prison of sin. Together they all prayed the Lord's Prayer.

Ben and his family soon arrived and he was able to be reunited with his brother. Cassie and her family arrived from Illinois. Her mother had told her about Joseph being found but left out the details of the involvement of her older brothers. Jake had told her it was up to the boys to share that information. He wondered if they would show up.

Jake's doubt was answered as the boys drove up the driveway. When Jason met them at the door, it was apparent they had been weeping. Shaking hands with them he told them to have courage.

The living room was getting crowded so Dorothy had taken Cassie's family into an adjoining room where they could have privacy. Jason directed the brothers in that direction. Before he left them alone Jason told Cassie, "Your brothers have something to tell you." He and Dorothy went out and shut the door. Several minutes later Rudy came out and asked that Joseph and his family join them. They were there for a long time. When they all came out they had been weeping. In the meantime, Aaron arrived.

Once they had all settled in around the crowded living room Joseph announced, "Repentance and confession have been made. Forgiveness has taken place. We are together as one unbroken family. Let us not look back." Joseph then quoted the scripture, *"Forgetting those things which are behind, and reaching forth unto those things which are before, I press toward the mark for the prize of the high calling of God in Christ Jesus."*

Rudy humbly stated his thankfulness to those who forgave him. "For years I have wanted to be baptized and become a member of the church, but I have been in the prison of guilt and in the clutches of Satan. Is it possible to be forgiven by God and be baptized?"

One at a time they each expressed the same thing.

"Let us turn to the scriptures for the answer to your question," Jason told the brothers. "Romans 6:23 tells us, '*For the wages of sin is death; but the gift of God is eternal life through Jesus Christ our Lord.*' Do you boys believe this?"

They all answered verbally and with a nod.

"When would you like to be baptized?" Jason asked.

"As soon as possible," Rudy answered. "I would like Joseph to be present."

All the others nodded that they were in agreement with Rudy.

We have a meeting appointed for this evening," Jason said. "We will call the church to meet earlier and have the baptizing beforehand."

The family enjoyed a joyous meal together.

Overcoming Satan
Chapter Twenty Two

The news quickly went out there was to be a baptism at three that afternoon. There was a good turnout. To see someone turn unto the Lord is always a joy. There were a lot of questions in people's minds who it may be.

The meeting was opened with a hymn, a little preaching, and prayer. Jason arose and told the members there were five who desired to turn their backs to the world and walk with the people of God. After naming off the five brothers he told the congregation, "Before I ask if you are willing to receive them into the church by Christian baptism, they have a statement they want to make."

The congregation sat in stunned silence as one by one each of the brothers confessed the sin they committed to the smallest detail. They stated they confessed to each of their family and asked to be forgiven. "We are humbled by their forgiveness. Will you forgive us and may we become a part of this church by Christian baptism?"

Their parents and each of their siblings acknowledged that it was true. Jason asked if anyone had any questions to ask. There were none. He asked the brothers and their near family to withdraw while he asked the church if they were willing to forgive and receive them into the church by Christian baptism.

As the voice was being taken some of the men who had grown up with the brothers broke down and wept. For years they wondered why they didn't come. Now it was all out in the open and evident. The church unanimously approved of the brothers' request.

Jason called the family back in and told them the church was unanimously willing to forgive and receive them into the church by Christian baptism.

As each of them came up out of the water it was an impressive sight. It was like a bad sore in the community had just been healed. Jake and Gail were standing on the bank. Jake was on one side of his wife and Joseph was on the other side. They each had an arm around her. When Jake and Gail received them it was so impressive, yet all eyes were on Joseph as he fell on their necks and wept. No doubt there were no ill feelings.

The members of the church received them, the brethren with a kiss and a handshake and the sisters with a handshake. After all those turbulent years, Satan had lost the battle.

****

When seven o'clock came, five newborn Christians walked into the meeting house. They did not sit in the back as they had for many years. They sat about halfway up. They mingled with other brethren about their age in life. Their faces glowed with joy as they were singing, *Oh for a closer walk with God, a calm and heavenly frame, A light to shine upon the road, that leads me to the lamb.*

Gail sat there thinking, "That young minister is our son and the boy beside him is our grandson. Just last Sunday while I was listening to him preach, I had no idea he was our lost son. The words now flowing out of his mouth radiates the depth of his heart. Being so filled with the spirit, there certainly is no room for hate, envy, jealousness, bitterness or any of the other devices of Satan. Only the love of God comes forth." She wondered, "Was it his trials that made him strong in the Lord?"

Carl stood and continued with thoughts on "The Christian Battle". "God's love is so great. He can see us here this evening. He sees into each of our hearts. We each feel our heart's overflowing with thankfulness for the blessing of times like we enjoyed today. It was the Son of God that was willing to come into this world and shed His precious blood for the

165

redemption of fallen man. Every one of us who have set to our seal that God is true and been baptized are redeemed by the blood of Christ.

The Word tells us we must eat of His bread and drink of His blood if we want to have any life in us. In former times it was the shed blood of animals that rolled back sins. Their blood could not pay for sins, only roll it back. Jesus, the Son of God, when He shed His blood on the cross, didn't roll our sins back, He paid for them. His blood was holy. He was God in the flesh. When we are born again of the water and the blood, we become a new creature. We have been planted in the likeness of His death. We shall also be in the likeness of His resurrection.   One time only did He shed His blood. His blood was so holy, so precious, that in shedding it He conquered death, hell, and the grave. He arose and is now on the right hand of the Father.

Satan will try to discourage us to the point we could give up. There are times the Christian will suffer. The Word will help us from falling. We read in Romans 8:16-17 *The Spirit itself beareth witness with our spirit, that we are the children of God: And if children, then heirs; heirs of God, and joint-heirs with Christ; if so be we suffer with him, that we may be also glorified together.*

Walking in the newness of life it is important we grow. A baby that doesn't grow likely won't live long. When we are born in Christ we are like babies. We must grow. A newborn baby can't eat what adults eat. They need milk. The newborn Christian wouldn't be expected to understand all the scriptures. It was the common people who heard Jesus gladly. Babies need exercise to grow. Babies in Christ need to exercise to grow. Read the Bible and meditate thereon. Sing the good songs of Zion. Attend church meetings. Stay away from evil places. Visit with those who walk with the Lord. Remember, it is 'Christ in you'. Don't give Satan one inch. To willfully sin is to count the blood of the covenant wherewith we are sanctified an unholy thing. It is a fearful thing to fall into the hands of the living God.

Keep on praising and thanking the Lord, trusting in His grace, and looking to Jesus who is in Heaven. Some sweet day we'll see Him coming again.

Sometimes we sing the song, '*Yet there is room. The feast is spread, for every hungry thirsty soul*'. Today we have seen the working of the Spirit. Yet there is room. Sometimes there are meetings when the doors must be closed because there is no more room. It's hard to imagine procrastinating until it is too late. People going to events of the world, if they know there is limited space will go early to be sure to get in. Those events are only temporal. There is plenty of room in heaven for all who truly want to enter.

God shut the door of the ark. Was it because the ark had no more room? No, it was because man had become so wicked that God knew no one else would have a desire to enter. Why was this? Didn't they want to be saved? Noah was a preacher of righteousness. He warned them. It was because they didn't believe the preaching of Noah. It had never rained. Why would it now?

When God shut the door the time of decision had passed. The opportunity was lost. Are you looking into the ark? Do you believe the Holy Word of God? Are you shunning the Spirit? Today is the day of grace. Tomorrow may be too late. If you hear His voice, harden not your heart. Yet there is room. The Spirit and the bride say come. Whosoever will, let him take of the water of life freely."

After the meeting, instead of leaving right away as they did for years, the five new converts stood around visiting with their old friends. They were amazed by the joy of fellowshipping with the members. They hardly wanted to leave.

A Little Adjusting
Chapter Twenty Three

Carl's understood Joseph's desire to spend some time with his father and mother. Trying to look back that many years was hard for Joseph. Joseph and Lovina accepted his parents' invitation to spend their last night in Iowa at his old home. It was a difficult night as all the memories came rushing back to him from his old bedroom. He vividly remembered crying in his mother's arms the day his parents left for Virginia.

Early in the morning, while the children were still asleep, Joseph, Lovina, and his folks sat around the table enjoying some early coffee.

Gail, looking across the table at Joseph, asked, "Son, would you mind telling us the story of your life since we left you to go to Virginia?"

Joseph, looking reluctant said, "I'll tell it this once, but I would not like to tell it often. I feel the Lord was with me. Mortal man is inclined to sin. When we confess our sins to God, he will forgive, if we forgive those who sin against us."

Jake nodded his agreement.

"I know that is true," Gail replied, "but sometimes it is hard to do."

"It surely is," Lovina spoke up, "but my husband is a pro at forgiving. You must have instilled that attribute in him the first seven years of his life."

Joseph smiled as he responded to his wife's encouragement. "To read the Bible to children at a young age is to sow the seed of God's love in them."

"I believe that to be true," Jake cut in, "but Lois and I read to your older brothers and we prayed together. What did we do wrong?"

Joseph smiled, "It became obvious over the last few days that the teaching you and Lois gave my older brothers is still deep within them. I remember Simon told me one day after mother and I were planting seeds in the garden, how his mother explained the germ in the seed. How it would sprout and grow. How it reproduces itself in abundance. He told me how they took extra produce to mother when Paul was sick and helped can several jars. He told me how exciting it was to see the shelves filling up, as he and Rudy would take the full jars to Paul's basement."

"I remember those times," Gail said. "They were so excited that they told their mother about it. They could hardly believe that all those jars of food came from the little seeds that they had planted. Those boys helped us so much while Paul was sick. To us, that was 'Love in action'. At that time, I knew the boys were being taught to know and love the Lord. After Paul died, your father, Lois and your brothers came often and were such a big help.

When I received the sad news about Lois, I thought of your brothers. They dearly loved their mother. I, along with many others, brought food to them. But we couldn't take the place of their mother. Having also gone through the sorrows of death myself, I wept for them.

A couple of years later, when Jake asked me if I would be a mother for their family, I felt there was not a nobler calling. I loved your brothers, and still do."

Gail broke down and sobbed.

Jake put his arm around his wife and gave her a hug. "That love goes both ways."

"I'm so happy to hear the love Mother feels for us all," Joseph said. "This love can continue if we are willing to lay down the bad things of the past. We are called to forgive and cultivate the love of God in our hearts, as the scriptures teach. Moving forward, not looking back. That said, let me tell you what has happened over the last twenty-some years."

Joseph shared the whole story of his life. From the time he had said goodbye to his mother until the present time. When he had finished he said, "Now, in our hearts, let bygone be bygone. Let us be one happy family." He quoted one of his favorite verses, "*All things work together for good to them that love God.*" He put his arm around Lovina and gave her a hug, "In my journey, the Lord led me to a wonderful wife and three wonderful children."

"And gave us some wonderful grandchildren," Gail added.

The stair door opened and out bounded the three children.

"Good morning," they all chattered.

"It is time for grandma to get breakfast for my hungry family," Gail said, giving them each a hug.

They enjoyed a hearty breakfast of sausage and pancakes. Afterward, they spent some time of devotion, as they read from the Bible.

Jake wanted to show the boys the cow stable where their dad used to milk. Their little sister voiced her desire to go with them. Gail saved the day when she told Shelly, "Grandma wants to show you the dollies."

Walking to the barn, Jake held a hand of each of the boys, as their father walked beside them. When they got to the barn, Chad and Thad were sitting on milk stools milking a couple of cows.

"This is where your dad milked cows when he was seven," Jake told his grandsons.

"You milked cows like this?" Daniel asked looking up at his dad. In California, the boys had only seen cows milked with a machine.

"I sure did," Joseph answered.

"Do you want to show them how you do it?" Thad asked.

"Sure, is my stool still here?"

They found it hanging on the wall. Wiping the dust off, Joseph took a bucket, sat by a cow and started milking. The boys were impressed with the sound of the milk splashing against the bucket.

"Did you really do that when you were Daniel's age?" Eddie asked.

"I did it while sitting on this same stool in this barn," Joseph answered without missing a beat.

"Was it this cow?"

Grandpa chuckled, "No, cows don't live to be old like people do. The cow your dad milked has been gone for several years."

"Can I milk?" Daniel asked.

Joseph moved him in next to the cow and showed how to milk. Eddie, not wanting to be left out, wanted his turn. Grandpa grabbed another bucket and showed his little grandson the art of hand milking a cow. It was special having grandpa teach him. Both boys thought it was fun milking a cow.

They spent the day walking around the farm, reminiscing. Joseph, leaning on the garden fence, remembered helping his mother planting vegetables here. He kept telling himself, "The memories are good, just don't wallow in sorrows of the past."

****

Gail had the whole family in for supper. The table had to be extended as three of them were married and had children. It was a time of reminiscing about happy occasions in the past. There was talk of God's plan for His people in the future. Jake told the story of how they had acquired the farm. He also told how Jason got his farm. As the evening wore on they started singing some of the good ol' songs of Zion. It was the emotional mending of a love-filled family.

The sound of Carl's car coming up the driveway brought reality to the end of a life-changing visit. Jake and Gail thanked Carl and Rachel for the love and care they gave to Joseph. "It really puts a warm spot in our hearts to find out that while we thought he was lost, he was being raised by the hands of a Godly family." After a loving goodbye, they pulled away from the Bowman farm, leaving behind a happy family.

Homeward Bound
Chapter Twenty Four

Leaving his folks behind was hard for Joseph, but Carl's were his parents too. There would be a lot of time to discuss what had transpired during their visit to the Midwest. Joseph looked forward to the counsel he would receive from his adopted father and mother. They drove along in silence reflecting on the situation they now found themselves in.

Carl was the first to speak, "Son, I know there is a lot on your mind. This unexpected revealing of your siblings and your birth parents must be a shock to you. You and I have spent a lot of time counseling folks who have experienced various stressful times in their lives. We know it is good when we open up to someone. This helps to overcome the sadness associated with those times. We have several miles to travel. As father and son, I would encourage you to open up and pour out your heart. I don't want to pressure you. From the day we took you into our home until you were married, you often confided in us when you had questions. Son, I want you to know you may still share with us what is bothering you."

Joseph found himself staring at the distant mountains. How strange and confusing his life had become. One thing he knew for certain, the God who had seen him through this far was still with him. Finally, he opened up his heart. "I likely will never forget the day my mother was about to board the train. As I was crying in her arms, the sadness in her eyes, melted my heart. Many times while I was with the gypsies, I longed to be back in my mother's arms. When I cried, they punished me. To keep from crying, I remembered Dad's instruction. 'Look to Jesus,' he would say. The gypsies were very bad people. They tried to get me to assimilate into their lifestyle. I longed for my dad to come and get me. When he didn't come, I had a tendency to become bitter. As bitterness would work its way into my thoughts I would remember more of Dad's instructions. 'Bitterness is a tool of Satan's,' he would say. There were times I would dream about angels. These dreams helped me through the depressive wrongful thinking."

Joseph stopped speaking and stared out the side window. Carl let him reflect for a few moments before speaking up. "It is obvious God was watching over you as your journey brought you to us. We knew you were special from the moment we met you. We just didn't know the underlying story. The moment you came to the realization that you were in the presence of your childhood, what were you thinking?"

Joseph shook his head briefly as if he had no desire to share these thoughts. Knowing he had no choice, he answered: "When Jason was telling about the five brothers and it dawned on me that they were my brothers, everything started spinning. Suddenly I felt as if it was happening to me again. I was visualizing the hatred I had seen in their eyes. My disbelief that they could be so cruel was tearing me apart. I again was seeing the smirk on their faces as I pleaded for them to protect me. Hearing about my assumed demise was more than my spirit could handle. Everything was swirling throughout my mind and a deep chill came over me. My consciousness began to fade. I just could not believe they made up such a story. As I fought violently against what I was hearing, I still did not want to share the truth."

Silence prevailed while the reality of the previous statement sunk in.

"What changed your mind?" Carl asked.

"As my consciousness started to return, everything that happened from that day until the present flashed before my eyes. Suddenly, I thought I saw an angel standing at the foot of the bed. The angel spoke saying, 'Joseph, the Lord needs you to work for Him. There are souls at stake. Tell your family all that has happened. Keep no secrets and don't be afraid. I will be with you."

"Was it hard to tell your story?" Carl asked, looking briefly at his son sitting there wringing his hands.

"It was. I had been trying to put the whole thing behind me and forget it. You and Mother have been so good to me. With the blessings of a wonderful wife and children, I felt the Lord had caused me to forget my father and mother. I thought I would never hear from them again. Now, so unexpectedly, this comes up. I felt that telling it could be like living it all over again."

"That in itself is a reason to tell your story with your loved ones. Sharing your struggles will help you put them behind you. Holding them inside is detrimental to you moving forward."

"Lovina and I share a lot of things together. As you know, married couples discuss things that they would never tell anyone else. She ended up being the first one I told. It really wasn't hard to tell her. The hard part was not knowing how my brothers would react when they found out I was their brother whom they sold."

"We need to stop for fuel," Carl interrupted. "It looks like it's about noon. We should take a break and get something to eat." That sounded good to the others in the car. Everyone was getting hungry, especially the children.

With the car full of gas they found a small park where they could enjoy the sandwiches Gail sent. After eating, the couples lay back on a blanket in the grass, while the children enjoyed the swings and slide. Back on the road, the children were soon asleep, having worn themselves out at the park.

No sooner than they were up to speed when Carl wanted to hear more. "I interrupted you when I saw the gas gauge getting low. Do you want to tell us more?"

Joseph's face showed signs of thought for a couple of miles. When he spoke it was soft and with resolve. "I am very impressed with how you were able to bring my brothers to make a full confession. It was as though there was a locked door with 'Full Confession' written above the jamb. You revealed the key and unlocked the deadbolt. Holding open the door with one hand you beckoned them in with the other. You welcomed them to go in. With tears falling to the floor, they walked in. The confessions they made melted my heart. Dad, you were surely filled with the spirit of our Lord as you kindly led them to repentance."

"It is the Lord's work," Carl responded.

"It surely is," Joseph replied. "I am so delighted with the power of the spirit of the Lord in His faithful followers. To see the happiness manifested in my brothers since their conversion is so heartwarming. I do have a concern for them. There is no doubt Satan will try to make them fall. He tries us all."

"Yes, he does. When we are truly committed to following the Lord, we'll read the Bible often, pray daily, sing praises, and attend church regularly. These things will strengthen the inner man."

"That is so true. There is no doubt they wanted out of that prison for a long time. They are so happy to be walking with the people of God."

"They do have a very Christ-loving church. I believe the dear members will put a hedge of love around them the devil will have trouble penetrating. God protected Job so that he didn't fall. There are so many things that can try us. When we are rooted and grounded in faith, whatever happens, God will help us."

They drove along in silence for a few miles. There was a nagging question that Carl just wanted to know. How could someone be treated like Joseph had and deep down not harbor any feelings of bitterness? Finally, he decided he would explore that subject.

"Son, you have been mistreated and have been through a lot. Do you feel any bitterness in your heart?"

Joseph sat there a little with his head down, "I believe that all things work together for good to them that love God, to them who are the called according to His purpose. Dad, I want our father and son relationship to continue. You and mother have meant so much to me, not only while I was growing up, but also in the ministry. Not only the advice you give but also the life you and Mother live. You manifest the Biblical teaching of the Lord. That is priceless. Had I grown up in the home I was born in, I think I would have received the same teaching. Lovina's parents also are a living example of following the Lord. I feel so blessed. The only time we should look back is to the cross of Christ. My desire is that we move forward, with our eyes heavenward, looking unto Jesus and watching for his return."

Carl slowed down for a construction site. Keeping his eyes on the road he asked, "By what you say, I take it there is no animosity in your heart. Is that correct?"

"That is true. When we truly forgive, we don't hold onto any evil thoughts. We fill our lives with the spirit of our Lord."

Eddie, having stirred from his nap, was listening in to the conversation. "Grandpa, what does Heaven look like?"

Carl hesitated a little before answering. "We can only imagine what it looks like Eddie. Man has not seen Heaven, so we only see it through an eye of faith. From what we read in the Bible we know it is very beautiful. It is the place we all should look forward to spending eternity."

It was early evening when they pulled into a small roadside cafe. It had been a long day and they were tired and hungry. The chunky potato soup was soothing and satisfying.

Walking out of the café they were treated to a beautiful western sunset.

"Is Heaven prettier than this?" Eddie asked.

"This surely does give us a glimpse of the beauty of Heaven," Carl answered his grandson. He continued by quoting a familiar Psalm. "The Heavens declare the glory of God."

Shortly thereafter as they arrived at their cabin and the sun was slipping below the horizon.

Two long days later they arrived at Carl's. They were tired when they pulled in the drive, but thankful for traveling mercies. They had enjoyed the trip. Being together with Carl's had been special. They had sung a lot as they traveled.

As they had their evening devotions together, it was an emotional time, knowing this trip was over. They acknowledged that they had enjoyed their time together.

Early the next morning Joseph loaded up his family and they headed home. Goodbyes are difficult.

****

Coming home again is always a happy occasion, but it would take a few days to get into the routine of things. Joseph was relieved to see Wilbur had everything under control. He had done a great job but was glad to see Joseph.

Eston and Lucinda were anxious to see them and had invited them to come for supper. Even though the family was tired from the trip, Lovina was thankful for the invite. They enjoyed a delicious home-cooked supper and shared highlights of their trip. Joseph found himself having trouble tracking the conversations and as soon as the dishes were cleaned up he stood up. "If you will excuse us we need to get a good night's sleep."

"We'll come tomorrow afternoon to hear of your trip," Eston told his sleepy grandchildren.

Their own bed felt so good. Waking up early the next morning, Joseph told Lovina, "I feel as if all this has only been a dream."

"Was it the trip or the discovery of your family?"

"It still would have been a good trip without the discovery. It turned out to be a life-changing time in our lives."

Eston's came in the afternoon. The well-rested children were all over them, bubbling over with things they wanted to tell their grandparents. Their mother tried to calm them down. J.B. could see grandpa and grandma wanted to hear all about his grandchildren's experiences. He whispered to Lovina to let them unload their pent-up excitement.

Once the children had exhausted their excitement they headed outside to play. With the room quieter Joseph shared a few things about the trip and the Love Feast.

It was Lovina that shared the news about discovering Joseph's family. Her parents were amazed at how it all came about.

"It has to be an act of God," Eston said. "You need to invite your family to visit California. It would be good to meet them," he told Joseph.

Going about his work, Joseph could not get it out of his mind the things which had transpired on their trip. He felt, without a doubt, the Lord was directing their steps. What would the future bring?

Forgetting the Things Behind
Chapter Twenty Five

Back in Iowa, Jake called the five brothers together. "Boys, it would be nice if we could turn time backward, but we can't. We have to go on from here. Confession, repentance, and forgiveness have taken place. The next thing you must overcome is to forgive yourself. Forgiving yourself will take a lot of faith. We read in the Bible about a sin David committed. It was a terrible sin. In those days, the punishment for committing that sin was death. The prophet Nathan told David, 'God has put away your sin. You shall not die'. God loved David but, because of this sin, he had to suffer a lot.

We are living in the day of grace. God's love was so great, and seeing the fallibility of man, He sent His only begotten Son into this world. Jesus not only came to teach us how to live, He also shed His precious blood, to redeem us from our sins. David said, 'My sin is ever before me'. The rest of his life he had war, was chased by his son who tried to take his kingdom from him. He had wives unfaithful to him. David wasn't allowed to build the temple because of the abundance of blood he shed.

Today by the confession, repentance, and baptism, the blood of Christ does not only put away our sins but forgives us. Today you have a clean sheet, not only among your family but also in Heaven. Satan will try to make you think you are still sinners. In this life, we sometimes falter, but remember the scripture, 'If we confess our sins, He is faithful and just to forgive us our sins, and cleanse us from all unrighteousness.' Read the Bible daily, think on holy things, pray daily. Walk closer with the Lord. He will increase your ability to stand when temptation comes.

Remember the seed your mother helped you put in the garden. It was so small, yet it produced much. Your mother put a seed in your heart that is still there. That seed needs warm soil, for it to grow. Your mother's last words to you were for you to be good boys. Now I'm asking you to be good Christians."

****

The five of them were standing at the fence looking into the garden.

"This is where mother taught us the love of God," Rudy said.

"Remember the seed we helped mother put in the soil?" Henry asked. "This same soil has produced food year after year. It must be tilled, the seed planted, and the weed removed for that to happen. Remember how mother used to say, 'It is easier to remove the weeds every day than to let them get big'? That is true in our spiritual lives too. If we strive to follow God's will, He will be there for us."

"Let's go into the garden, kneel down on the good earth and open our hearts to our God," Simon suggested.

Henry opened the gate and they all went into the garden. There they knelt on the same soil where their mother, years ago, taught them about the germ God put in each seed. One at a time, they opened their hearts to the Lord in thankfulness and praise. When the last one had finished, they joined hands and together they prayed the Lord's Prayer.

To them, it felt as if their mother was there with them. They talked about how their mother used to sing as she worked in the garden. One of them started singing.

Jake, coming out of the house heard singing coming from the garden. Walking closer he witnessed his five oldest sons, sitting in a circle on the ground singing with all their hearts.

"And he walks with me and he talks with me, and he tells me I am his own. And the joy we share, as we tarry there, no other, has ever known."

As he heard these words ringing out across the yard, tears were running down his cheeks. He retreated to the porch, thinking back when they all sat on the bedroom floor singing together. In his mind, he could hear Lois singing that song.

The five of them talked it over and decided they would go separate ways in their occupation. They felt it was time to move ahead with their life. They did agree that Ben or Aaron should have the farm. Over the next few months, Rudy bought a general store and Simon rented a farm on the thirds. A short time later Henry went into the carpentry business and the twins took over the sawmill.

Before the paperwork was finalized on his store purchase, Rudy took a trip to see extended family in Ohio. The opportunity to visit with his mother's siblings filled his heart. It wasn't just family that touched his heart in Ohio. He became acquainted with a young lady that was eight years his junior. Rudy and Mary agreed to write.

Rudy lived in an apartment above the store and soon became friends with many of his customers. The general store was a good place to learn about the people in the community. He was always busy. Although he closed at five, there was constantly someone needing something after hours they thought was urgent. Rudy never turned them away. Many evenings as he was writing to Mary, a knock on the door would interrupt his thoughts. They were not always customers. He had a lot of friends and they liked stopping by for moments of fellowship. Rudy enjoyed his work, although it was tiring. There were times his father came by to help. Those times were especially heartwarming. He enjoyed working with his dad. On the days the delivery truck came, Rudy worked late into the evening stocking the shelves.

In one of his letters to Mary, Rudy asked her to please come to Iowa for a visit. He really wanted her to see what it was like there. A couple of months later Mary and her parents did make the trip. They stayed at Jake's, but during the day Mary wanted to be at the store helping Rudy. Mary's parents were impressed with the friendliness of the people in the community. Having received her parents' blessings, Rudy proposed to Mary and the following spring they married. In time their first son, Weston Rudy was born.

Simon worked long hard days. He badly wanted to get ahead and buy this farm if it became available. If that wasn't to be, he would find a farm somewhere to purchase. He lived alone in the big farmhouse. He was so busy that the loneliness didn't bother him. He had a hog operation with thirty brood sows. By the time he took care of the crops and the hogs, there was not much time left to do other things. Although he tried to be done with chores and in the house by dark on Saturday, he was always tired. Too often he would find himself drifting off to sleep in church on Sunday morning.

Jake talked to Simon about his tendency to overwork himself. He had the mentality that once he saved enough to buy the farm, then he would like to find a wife and have a family. Jake explained to him it doesn't work that way.

"Live the life you want to live as you live. Your desire to have everything perfect before you start your family is robbing you of years of blessings."

Financially Simon was making progress. He tried to do as his father told him. He would almost always go to a workday when one of the brethren needed help. He always helped at church workdays, only to work later in the night when he came home. He kept telling himself, "I must slow down." He awoke one night with pain in his chest. That alarmed him, but he thought, "It is just indigestion."

Jake stopped by early one day as Simon was eating his breakfast. Jake could tell that he was in a hurry.

"What brings you out so early?" Simon asked.

Jake cleared his throat, looking at Simon he asked, "Are you in a hurry?"

"Well, yes, I guess I am. The fat hogs are about out of feed and I need to husk some corn for them."

"Did you ever think about letting them in the field so they can husk their own corn?

Simon frowned, "Some farmers do that, but their hogs take longer to fatten out."

"Well, I have other reasons I think you need to slow down." Jake cleared his throat again as he frowned. "Son, over in Illinois this morning, Silas Boon was hurrying to get his chores done so he could husk corn. All of a sudden he fell over dead with a heart attack. It's a very sad day for his wife and eight small children. Just like you, he was working hard to pay off his farm."

Thinking of the pain he had been experiencing in his chest, Simon spoke up. "He wasn't very old. I think he's a couple of years younger than I am."

"He was only thirty, so I doubt he was even close to paying off his farm."

Simon decided to take his father's advice and slow down. He started by getting a neighbor to feed the hogs for a couple of days. Taking the train he and his parents made the trip to Illinois to Silas Boone's funeral. The five-hour train ride gave the two men time to go over the day to day operations of farming and how Simon could streamline his daily chores.

Simon changed his focus. He could never stop thinking of the children that were now without their father. He started writing to Silas' widow, Nova and two years later they married. He happily became a father to her eight orphaned children. The farm became a family farm where they lived the life they wanted to live, as they lived.

Henry got a job on a carpenter crew. He lived with Rudy for awhile. He saved his money and bought a forty-acre wooded parcel of ground. There were no buildings on it and he needed a place to live. He spent his first year cutting timber which Thad and Chad sawed into lumber. With that, he built a barn. At one end of his new barn, he fixed up a couple of rooms that was his home until he got a house built.

Henry had a likable personality. He was spiritually minded, yet witty. If someone needed help, he was there. If someone was down in the dumps, Henry was the one who would put an arm around him and help him out of the depression. He had walked down that road enough to know what was needed. For a while, Tuesday evenings found him helping Rudy stock shelves.

With his likable personality, he soon found a lady that was interested in him. After he had his house built, he and Marie were married. They enjoyed being with other newly married couples. He would usually lead the conversation into blessings told in the Bible. When they went to visit older folks they were encouraged by the experiences learned there.

Their home was blessed with four boys and three girls. He soon owned his own carpentry business.

The sawmill was Thad's dream. As long as he was milling logs he was happy. He built a house in the woods. He married Jane, a girl from Virginia. They were blessed with seven sons. They had two sets of twins. They had a happy energetic home. Thad provided well for them. Jane was disappointed they had no girls, but the sons took turns helping their mother.

Chad also enjoyed the sawmill. He built a house in the woods just a stone's throw away from Thad's. He and Thad were not only twins, but they thought alike. This made their work go smoothly. Chad's wife, Edith also came from Virginia and was a first cousin to Jane. They didn't have any boys but were blessed with five girls. This was a disappointment to Chad, but he dearly loved each one of his daughters. It would melt his heart when his three-year-old would put her arms around him and give him a kiss. He never got tired of hearing them say, "I love you, daddy."

The twins kept their priorities right in line. They would periodically shut down the mill and take their wives home to Virginia. They found it a joy to travel together.

All the brothers became pillars in the church, where the members treated them with love. No one ever mentioned a thing about their former sins.

Better Thoughts
Chapter Twenty-Six

Time moves along. It had been over two years since they were in Iowa. There were a lot of letters going back and forth. All five of his older brothers were married. Rudy and Henry each had a newborn son. According to the letters they received from Jake, all five of his older brothers were growing in the faith and were very happy. Aaron had a fiancée and soon would be getting married.

The letter telling about Aaron and Sue's upcoming wedding came from Ben. "Their wedding will be in a month," he wrote. "Aaron is still living at home and would like to buy dad out. We have been living in the little house and helping farm the place. Dad still helps quite a bit but would like to retire and move into our home. We have been thinking we would like to try living out in California. Do you think we could find a place to live? Could I find work?"

Joseph took the letter to Lovina. "You need to read this," he told her with a smile.

Lovina read through the letter and her eyes lit up. "Do you think you can find a job for him?

"I sure can!"

"Do you think we can find a place for Ben and Esther to live?"

"I sure can. I could also find a place for Dad and Mom Bowman too if they would come."

The following week Joseph received a letter from Jake. Jake wanted the family to get together and discuss the changes to the farm. He asked if it would be possible for them to come for Aaron's wedding. If they wanted to come by train they would let them use a car to get around.

That evening after devotions, Joseph and Lovina discussed the possibility of a trip to Iowa and what needed to be done before they could go. The children were excited to think they might get to see Grandpa and Grandma Bowman.

The children were thrilled with the train ride. Joseph felt that since they were traveling with the children it would be best if they rented a sleeper. The added security of having their family all together at night was worth it.

They arrived in Iowa on Friday at four in the afternoon where Rudy was patiently waiting. They arrived at Jake's at five-thirty just as the men were finishing chores.

"Enjoy your evening," Rudy told them as he handed them the last of their luggage. "We'll see you tomorrow morning."

Gail and Lovina went in to finish making supper while Jake and Joseph sat on the porch swing enjoying the pleasant south breeze. The children wanted to run around a little. The boys went running to the barn hoping to see the cows. They were disappointed that the milking was already done.

The call came for supper. After prayer, they enjoyed a supper of roasting-ears and ham sandwiches. You could see the joy in Jake and Gail's faces as they were surrounded by their grandchildren.

Looking at Joseph, Jake said, "Ben tells us they would like to try it in California. What do you think?"Jake asked.

Daniel and Eddie together said, "We'd like that and we want you and grandma to come too."

That brought a smile on grandpa and grandma's face.

"There definitely is an opportunity for Ben's out there close to us." Seeing a little frown on his father's face he continued, "There is a nice house close to us for you and mother too!" He thought he saw a little sparkle in his dad's eyes. "If you want to retire, maybe you could live the winter months out there close to us and spend the summer days here in Iowa."

"We're pretty sure we still want to live on our own," Gail spoke up.

"How would it be if there was a nice house just five hundred feet from ours? We have a car you could use while you are there. That would let you go back and forth by train."

It was evident this information was pleasing to both Jake and Gail.

The next morning all the family came together. The ladies brought in a delicious meal. Joe and Cassie with their family came over from Illinois. The children wanted to hold their two little cousins. They thought they were so cute.

As they all gathered around in the kitchen, Jake tried to keep his composure. It was a happy time to have his family all together. "Thank you all for coming. We are here as one happy, well-blessed family. God's love has been so great to us. We want our love to be great to him and each other." He suggested they sing the Doxology.

The house rang as they all, including the children, opened their mouths and lifted their voices in praise to God. Singing with their whole hearts, the five oldest sons thought back to years ago. Back to the day they were sitting on the floor in the bedroom singing "*Jesus lover of our soul*" to encourage their dad after their mother died. That flashback was for only a moment as their minds returned to the present day and the joy they were having. When the music died away, Jake asked someone to lift their voice in thankfulness to our heavenly Father for this day and the food. The boys all looked at each other and nodded to their eldest brother.

Rudy spoke up, "Dad, we are so thankful we all can be here at home as one happy unbroken family. All of us would like for you to offer this prayer."

Jake's mind flashed back through the years. He thought of all the joys and sorrows, through the trials and temptations. Now, to hear his oldest son say, 'One happy unbroken family' he thought, "How can I pray?"It was as though an Angel put an arm around him and whispered in his ear, "Looking to Jesus." With heads down and eyes closed, and with tears running down Jake's cheeks, he opened his mouth and in a quivering voice, praise and thankfulness rolled out. When he finished and said "Amen," all the men echoed "Amen". Tears of joy were flowing as they felt close to each other and the Lord.

They all enjoyed dinner together. There was talk about their work and everyday events. There was also talk about when the Lord returns to take up his bride. "We are happy here as a family. Just think how happy we'll be there when the faithful of all ages will be gathered around the marriage supper of the Lamb. No more sorrow, suffering, temptations, sickness or death."

"A land where we will never grow old," Simon said. "We were looking forward to today. How much more are we looking forward to that day?"

After dinner was over and the kitchen clean, Jake gathered the men in the living room in a circle with the women behind them. He told them of their desire to retire. He shared with them the offer Joseph made them about coming to California for the winter or all year if they wanted to.

"You know your family back here wouldn't want you gone all the time," Aaron said.

"We're planning to move out there this fall," Ben stated and went on to explain the offer Joseph had given them.

Aaron explained how he and Sue would like to farm the home place.

After the boys discussed it a little, Rudy asked their dad if they wanted to sell the farm, or would they rent it? Jake did not want to sell it at this time.

The brothers suggested that they rent the farm to Aaron's with an opportunity to buy it at a later date. If he and Mother wanted to go to California part-time and be in Iowa part-time, they could keep the little house for their home while they were in Iowa.

"And remember you can spend some time in Illinois," Cassie added.

Jake asked each of his children if they were satisfied with that plan. The consensus was, "If it is what mother likes."

"I don't like changes, but that is life," Gail responded. "I am excited about spending our winters in California."

Jake thanked them and said, "Now let's sing for a while."

The Wedding
Chapter Twenty Seven

A large crowd filled the meeting house on Sunday morning. Not only were several coming to witness Aaron and Sue's wedding, but word got out Joseph Bauman was going to be there. Several from Illinois remembered him at their Love Feast a couple of years ago. They came hoping to hear him again.

The wedding would be right after the regular Sunday morning service. Jason was to perform the wedding. The church service began with John Yoder, a young minister from Illinois, opening the service with thoughts of 'Walking a new life'. Joseph had the deacons read the fourth chapter of James. He stood up and, looking down at his Bible, read a part of the fourteenth verse. "For what is your life? It is even a vapor, that appeareth for a little time, and then vanisheth away."

Looking out across the congregation he spoke, "Greetings in Jesus' name. We came from far and near to hear the word of God preached and to sing praises to our Lord. Not only that but today we expect to see a couple become one. As we think about the plan of God, it makes us marvel to see the working of His love. Our text verse starts out 'For what is your life'. Looking at this large congregation, I think of so many of us here, and we each have a life. What is life? We each have our various challenges. We each have our goals. We each have our disappointments. Sometimes when things go wrong we hear someone say, 'That is life'. What are they saying? They are saying, 'Things happen during our life we don't like, but we must deal with them'. We don't let them get us down. This morning I am thinking of five things: Life, vapor, time, appear and vanish.

As a child, our life is surrounded by our parents and siblings. We look ahead to being older and learning things. Goals arise in front of us. A baby learns to coo, to smile, to recognize his parents, to crawl, to walk, to talk, to feed themselves. On and on it goes. Think about it. From the time a baby is born until he becomes an adult, how many changes he has made. These changes come about a little at a time. These changes come with him not choosing them. As that child is in the changing stage of his life, it is the parent's responsibility to teach him the road to take. He doesn't get very old before he notices there are different choices people make. Parental training instilled deep in his heart helps him to choose the right road. Before long he gets to an age when he needs to make choices of his own. He may lay awake at night thinking about himself and wonder, 'What is my life?' He has come to the point of choosing his destiny. Satan will tell him, 'There are a lot of horizons ahead.' He will paint pictures of worldly pleasures. Old age and death are so far away, he may not think about it.

The praying, serious youth when thinking, "What is my life?" will think, 'Even a vapor'. We all know what vapor is. We have seen steam coming out of a teakettle. The vapor soon disappears. Is it done away with? No, it just changes state. Thinking about our life as a vapor, we know it won't last long in the state we are now in. Old age may seem like a long way away. Time does go fast. Our text says it appears for a little time. Should we live to be eighty years old, how long is that compared to eternity? Older people will tell you time goes fast. It doesn't take long to get to be three score and ten years old.

What are we going to do with the time we have? Our choices determine our walk through life. The wise choice is to accept the Lord in our youth and be baptized. Then we receive the gift of the Holy Spirit to help us in our godly walk. A vapor rises upward. To be grounded in the affairs of this world could make us rich in carnal belongings, but we may not have treasures in heaven. Our life as a Christian is constantly looking upward. As a vapor rises, so should our thoughts rise upward.

When young people choose a companion in marriage, we need to choose one who has also chosen to be a vapor pointing toward heaven. When God blesses them with children, they are working for the Lord in bringing them up in the nurture and admonition of the Lord. Our time in this world is our opportunity to radiate the Lord. Our life, even a vapor of the Holy Word, will affect those who see it. Be it only a short time or fourscore years it will soon vanish away. Not to be destroyed, but to enter the climes of immortal bliss. Consider your life and choose to be a vapor pointing upward. Humbly serving the Lord for what time we are here, that when we do vanish away, we will leave footsteps others will follow."

Jason closed the meeting with thoughts on being blessed to have seen the vapor that faithful followers of the Lord have left for us. "Now they have vanished from our sight, but we know through an eye of faith they are eternally blessed. Today we have older folks whose life is still a vapor we can see. While we have the opportunity, let us benefit from their counsel. They are pointing us to the good way which will last forever. Let us pray."

$$****$$

Jason announced there was a couple getting married today and all were invited to stay for this ceremony and the meal afterward in the park. Aaron and Sue came forward and Jason gave them many well-founded words of counsel. Then he performed the wedding ceremony.

It was a beautiful day for an outdoor meal. Although they had the building reserved in case of adverse weather, they set up tables outside. Aaron and Sue with their parents and siblings sat around a large table. A simple meal was served by the young people of their church.

As they were eating, Sue asked Aaron: "I know what a teakettle looks like when it steams. I also know that when the heat is turned off the vapor is soon gone. If we stop reading the Word of God, will our vapor for the Lord go away?"

"It likely will," Aaron answered.

"In that case, now that we are joined together as one, let us read and obey God's Word together. In doing so, will our vapor be greater?"

Hearing these words from his new bride caused his heart to rejoice. He put his arm around her and giving her a hug whispered, "Yes it will. In doing so, we will be starting our marriage off on the right foot."

After they were done eating they planned to sing for a half hour. While they were singing, Gail took one of the grandchildren to the restroom. Coming back she noticed several folks sitting on park benches listening to the singing. Some of them had tears in their eyes. One lady told Gail she remembered her mother singing that song when she was a little girl. Gail stood there a little while listening to the beautiful singing. She thought, "A little vapor from a lot of people makes a large vapor to the Lord." Many hearts can be touched by a song on the lips.

As Life Moves On
Chapter Twenty Eight

After the time of singing, folks lined up to wish Aaron and Sue their blessings before they left for their homes. Jake and Gail went home to an empty house with many thoughts on which to meditate. Another day, another chapter closed. Joseph and his family came to stay another night before leaving for home. Daniel saw Ben heading to the barn and asked his dad if he could go too.

Gail spoke up, "Be sure to change to your everyday clothes."

"Do you think you can help milk?" Joseph asked.

"I hope," was the reply.

Running to the barn with Eddie on his heels, Daniel was excited to think that just maybe Uncle Ben would let him milk. As they entered the barn Ben had just gotten the cows in the stable.

"Here are my helpers," he exclaimed as the boys came through the door. "Before we start milking we feed the cows some grain. Do you boys want to help me do that?"

"Sure," they exclaimed.

There was a feed cart on wheels they pushed down the feed way in front of the cows. Ben showed them how to put one scoop in the box in front of each cow. He had Daniel feed the next cow. Then Eddie fed the next one. Ben pushed the cart while the boys took turns feeding the cows.

When that was done Ben said, "Now boys, we will milk."

He got the stool Joseph had used and a milk bucket. "Daniel, come over here and I'll get you started milking."

Daniel was a little nervous as he sat down by the cow.

"Talk softly to her so she knows you are here," Ben said in a soft voice. "Her name is Sophia."

Daniel spoke softly to her calling her "nice Sophia." She was a very gentle cow. He remembered how his dad taught him to milk. He started a little slow, but soon the milk was splashing in the bucket.

Joseph was surprised when he walked in the stable to see his older son milking just as he had done in this same barn years ago. Not only that, but Ben was helping Eddie milk too. Eddie was a quick learner and soon he was milking by himself.

Ben said, "I could just as well get another bucket." "Might as well bring one for me," Joseph said.

The boys thought it was fun to milk. It made it more enjoyable to be doing it with Dad and Uncle Ben.

When Thad came to help chore he was surprised to see the milking about done.

"Looks like you have a crew this evening," he said. "Those boys would be handy to have every day."

"They are, I don't know what I would do without them," their father replied.

Jake got to the barn just in time to see his grandsons finishing milking their last cow.

"Like father, like son," he remarked with a smile on his face. That made the boys happy.

As they were on the way to the house, Chad came up the drive. "By the time you all get to the woods, the fire will be just about right."

Simon had started burning a big brush pile back at the corner of the woods the day before and the whole family was showing up for a wiener roast. As they gathered around the remains of the smoking fire they found a lot of red hot embers glowing amongst some burnt-out logs and old stumps. In a barrel, there were long sticks sharpened on one end. After the prayer, the big folks showed the children how to roast their hot dogs. It was exciting to eat the hot dog they helped roast. As a treat, someone had brought marshmallows. The little ones found it interesting to watch the sugary treat catch on fire.

It had been a big day for Jake and Gail. They said, "Good night, we'll see you in the morning," and headed to the house. The family sang a few songs after the folks retired. The last one was, 'When Shall We All Meet Again'.

Joseph and Lovina were leaving early the next morning so they bid them all goodbye. When they said goodbye to Ben's, they added, "We hope to see you in a few weeks."

"Lord willing," Ben responded with a smile.

Joseph had trouble getting to sleep. He kept thinking about the family being united in Christian love and knowing how Satan likely will tempt us in some sort of way. The idea of Ben's moving to California and his folks coming in the winter. It was a lot of change. Even though he was in charge of a large estate and dealt with changes all the time, he found these life changes troubling. His anxiety kept him from relaxing.

The alarm sounded too early. The children came running shouting, "It's time to go to the train." They were excited about the train ride home. The hour-long car ride to the train station gave Joseph a little more time with his parents. It definitely was a blessing getting to know them better. He wanted them closer.

Traveling home on the train was enjoyable and relaxing. There were plenty of things to talk about. The children could hardly get over talking about Grandpa Bowman's and Uncle Ben's coming to California.

****

As usual, their home was a welcome place. Joseph had plenty to do to catch up. When he had a chance he talked to Eston about his folks coming for the winter. Eston suggested he build a little cabin close to their place.

That evening after the devotions and the children were in bed, Joseph told Lovina what her dad suggested. She thought that was a good idea.

"Out in the old orchard where those old peach trees used to stand would make a nice place for your parents," she told him.

"Good idea," Joseph responded. "Why don't we sketch up a plan?"

The two of them spent a couple of hours working on the cabin plans. It was getting late when they felt they had something Jake and Gail would approve.

Lovina said, "Tomorrow I will draw it up to scale."

"Thank you," Joseph said with appreciation. "Once you have them finished I will take them to the contractor. It would be nice to get it in his schedule, as soon as possible. Look, it's eleven o'clock already. We'd better get to bed."

There was a lot of catching up to do around the house and Lovina was a hard worker. In between doing the washing and canning fruit, she found time to draw the plans to scale. One evening after supper and the dishes were done Lovina told Joseph, "I have something to go over with you."

"Some prints?" Joseph asked as he winked at her.

"What prints?" Daniel asked.

"What are prints?" Eddie questioned.

"Boys, just stay here at the table and we will show you," Joseph told them.

Lovina brought the roll of plans and unrolled them on the table. Joseph was amazed at the thoroughness of the plans.

When the children saw the renderings, Eddie asked, "Are we going to build a new house?"

Joseph was engrossed in studying the plans and didn't hear him.

Lovina told the children, "We may build this house for Grandpa and Grandma Bowman to live in when they are here during the winter."

The children were very excited and full of questions. "Where will we build it? When will we build it? Will grandpa come out and help?" Even little Shelly was excited. Lovina calmed them down.

She told them, "We don't know the answers to all of your questions yet. We are thinking we will build it in the old peach orchard."

The children were overjoyed and could not keep quiet. To have two sets of grandparents close by!

"Why don't we build two houses so we can have grandpa Bauman's close too?" Daniel suggested.

Joseph raised his eyes from the prints. "It looks like we have created some excitement. Children, we are still in the planning stage. Try not to get too excited."

The boys had trouble keeping their minds in the Scripture that evening during devotions. After they were in bed, their folks still heard them talking. They were making all kinds of plans as to what they would do with both their grandpas. Lovina had to tell them to quiet down and go to sleep.

The next day Joseph took the plans over to Harry Unger. Harry was one of the well-respected builders in the church. He said he was very busy but would get back with him in a few days with an estimate and a time frame.

The next evening after supper, Joseph asked, "Does anyone want to walk to the orchard and see where we will put grandpa's house?"

That stirred up more excitement. As they were walking to the empty lot a couple of hundred yards from their home Eddie asked, "Why do we call it an orchard? There are no trees."

"When I was a little girl, there were a lot of fruit trees here," Lovina answered her young son. "There were apple, pear, cherry, apricot, and peach. My grandpa planted them and we had a lot of good fruit off of those trees."

"What happened to them?" Daniel asked.

"The trees got old. One at a time they died and had to be taken out. The peach trees were hardier than the others. For a while, they were all that was left. That is how it became known as the peach orchard."

"What happened to the peach trees?" Eddie questioned.

"They too got old and died."

Holding onto Lovina's hand Joseph spoke up, "When mother and I were courting, we used to walk out here in the evening as the sun was lowering in the west. We would pick a ripened peach and taste the sweetness of the fresh fruit. We would stand under one of the peach trees and enjoy the pleasant evening breeze as we would share stories with each other."

"Will Grandpa's house take up all the space in the orchard?" was Eddie's next question.

"Not at all," Joseph said. "It will take only a small parcel of the orchard. I've been thinking we could plant new trees in the back part. Would you boys like to help?"

Over the next few weeks, it became apparent that God was working things out. Harry had one of his jobs postponed giving him time to fit the cabin into his schedule.

It was the second week of June when Harry came with his crew. Things began to happen fast as it became evident they were used to working together. They put in the batten boards and strung up the strings. Ten men with spades and shovels throwing dirt had the foundation finished in a week.

While this was taking place, Jake and Gail were on the train heading west. They hoped to see their house taking shape. Joseph picked them up at the Bakersfield's depot. On the way home, he told them, "We have a surprise for you, but it will have to wait until morning." It was late when they got home and the children were in bed. Early the next morning the children were up, anxious to see their grandparents.

Harry, knowing why they wanted the little house, sounded it around there would be a house raising on Thursday for Jake Bowman's from Iowa.

When Jake's woke up it was to hear the sound of hammering. When they came downstairs, they were met with three excited grandchildren. They all wanted to talk at once. Eddie took Jake's hand and said, "Come with me." Daniel led the way and Shelly walked with grandma as they made their way to the orchard. They were amazed to see so many men and boys working on their house.

Harry came to meet them with a smile on his face. Welcoming them he shook their hand. "Don't bring your things yet. We still need a little more time." With a grin on his face, he added, "Maybe tomorrow night will be alright."

Jake responded by saying, "With this crew, you may be ready before noontime today." That brought a chuckle from Harry. By the end of the day, the exterior was finished. In three weeks it was done and Jake's moved in.

The Unforeseen
Chapter Twenty Nine

Jake and Gail spent the rest of that summer and the winter in California. Gail very much liked their new home. It was small, but so was the one they had moved into in Iowa. Eston's had furniture they weren't using, so they let Jake's use it. The summer heat was something they would have to get used to, but it wasn't as humid as it was back home in Iowa.

They so much enjoyed the apricots, peaches, and grapes. One thing they noticed was that to grow anything in the summer it had to be watered. There weren't rains like they were used to in Iowa.

That summer was a special time getting more acquainted with their grandchildren. Gail felt it was like turning back time. She had such inner feelings when she looked at Daniel. Although he was now eight, he still looked so much like Joseph did when he was seven. She loved all three of them, but she had to remind herself that he was not Joseph. Sometimes her mind went back to those years when she thought Joseph was dead. Coming out of her reverie, she was so happy to see her son Joseph and his wonderful family. Although she had walked through much sorrow in her lifetime, she felt she couldn't thank the Lord enough for the blessed joy she now had.

Jake was able to help Joseph and the boys plant a new fruit grove out the back of their house. Working with his son and grandsons was so wonderful. Eston came and gave instructions on how to plant the trees. Jake learned to know him as they spent time together. They seemed to enjoy each other's company.

Ben and Esther lived in a home about a half-mile from Joseph's. Ben had taken over managing the cheese plant and had been instrumental in turning it into a dairy processing plant as well. Their plant had installed the equipment to pasteurize and bottle milk. It was a hard sell for Joseph but once the benefits of pasteurization were proven he knew they would be required to comply eventually.

Jake was amazed at the operations that were in Joseph's care. Lovina and Gail had the opportunity to get more acquainted. During their conversation, Gail asked Lovina about their courtship and marriage.

"I went to the Love Feast down south," Lovina told her. "On Sunday afternoon the young folks were having a dinner where a boy chooses a girl to eat with him. I didn't think anyone would ask me as I was not as slim as a lot of the girls. The fact is I was pudgy. I was standing off to one side, kind of bashful when this boy cautiously came to me. I could tell he was bashful too. I wondered if he would ever get up enough nerve to ask me.

With his head somewhat down, he quietly asked me if I would eat with him. My heart was beating so fast I had trouble answering him. I don't think I actually said anything, I only nodded. We got our food and sat across the table from each other, giving us the opportunity to visit across the table.

I tell you, my heart was beating so fast I could hardly eat! I noticed he didn't eat much either. It took a little time before we could start talking. Once the ice was broken we had a good visit. I found out he was a dairyman. Being that I grew up on a dairy farm, we had something in common to talk about.

He was so kind and polite. It was easy to see he was a sincere Christian. Before he excused himself to go do his milking he asked if we could write to each other. Mother, I was so…, so…, I don't know how to say it. I guess I was so happy. I really don't know the best way to express myself."

"I know what you're saying," Gail said. "There are times we are so overjoyed there seems to be no words to express it."

"I guess that was where I was," Lovina answered.

"Did you write to each other?" asked Gail.

"Yes, we did. We wrote for the next two years until we got married. About every six months, Carl and Rachel, his adoptive parents, came up to our church meeting. He came along every time except once when he was sick with the flu. I remember well the day I got a letter from him asking for my hand in wedlock.

That day was another special day in my life. I had Mother and Daddy to read his proposal. Daddy knew Carl and at some time he had talked to him about Joseph.

I can still see the smile on Daddy's face as he read the letter. As is his way, he said, 'Don't be too hasty in responding. Pray about it and give it at least three days. After that, talk to us before you reply.'

Mother, I was on cloud nine. I wondered who wouldn't want a boy like Joseph. I did pray and read the Bible every day. The fourth morning after I got his letter, I told the folks at the breakfast table what I felt led to do. They gave me their blessing.

Joseph and I have been married now for almost ten years. That has been ten wonderful years. Joseph has shown a lot of respect for my parents. He grew up in a godly home as I did. He has the same attitude concerning spiritual things as my daddy. They believe the earth is the Lord's and the fullness thereof. Mother and Daddy both dearly love him. I have no siblings, so he is dad's only son."

One morning Lovina took Gail to see the cheese processing plant where her son Ben was the manager. When they got there Gail noticed the sign above the door read, 'Eston Cheese and Milk'.

"Did Eston start this cheese plant?" Gail asked.

"No he didn't," Lovina replied. "The original owner was planning to sell it and it would be closed. Dad bought it just to keep it in operation. This is where we sold our milk. It used to be named Robertson Cheese until we started to bottle milk. At that time the original owner asked that we no longer use his name. We had to come up with a new name and your son Joseph came up with this idea with respect for Dad. Dad didn't like the idea but Joseph convinced him to agree to it. Dad feels all praise belongs to the Lord."

Lovina said she would wait in the office, while Ben took his mother on a tour of the plant. The whole process was very interesting to Gail. She asked Ben if this whole place belongs to Eston.

Ben stopped in his tracks and turned to his mother, "I think everything here actually belongs to Joseph and Lovina. She is the only child of Eston and Lucinda. I think Eston's signed it over to them."

"Joseph and Lovina nor her parents act as if they are wealthy," Gail commented.

"Joseph has told me his father-in-law firmly believes all we have belongs to the Lord. We are His servants."

"With that attitude, I suspect the Lord will continue to bless them," his mother replied.

"Did you enjoy the tour?" Lovina asked.

"Yes, I did. It sure is interesting. Not everyone knows how much work and expense there is in the milk and cheese they enjoy."

Jake and Gail were enjoying their stay in California. They would go to garage sales and get more things for their little home. Gail soon made it look real homey. The foggy December days weren't too pleasant, but on those days they sat by the woodstove.

One warm sunny day in January, Jake asked Gail if she was about ready to go back to Iowa. Some folks were planting an early garden there in California. Then a letter came from Henry telling them about the twenty below zero and the snowstorm. It was hard to believe there was so much difference in the weather between Iowa and California.

Joseph told them they should wait until February and see the almonds in bloom. Jake enjoyed walking over to Eston's. He would pull a grapefruit off the tree, peel it and sit down and visit with Eston as he sucked out the juice.

Eston, with a twinkle in his eye, would ask, "Could you do that in Iowa?"

The third week in April Jake and Gail boarded the train and headed for their Iowa home.

****

"It looks like your father was right," Joseph told his wife as Lovina entered the kitchen. "He warned me against investing in the stock market a few years ago. A lot of people lost everything yesterday."

The stock market crash was only the beginning of a financial crash across the country. Within a couple of years, people panicked and banks failed, closing their doors. Manufacturers shuttered factories and laid off their employees. Unemployment rose to thirty percent causing prices of everything to collapse. Farm payments couldn't be made causing banks to foreclose on the farms. Banks found themselves in possession of hundreds of farms with no buyers.

In Iowa, Rudy had been doing well with his store, but things were beginning to change. He could see the handwriting on the wall as the continuous deterioration of the economy was taking its toll. People needed to eat, but without any income, they were in trouble. They came to the store and would get food and would charge it. Rudy felt it was his Christian duty to do all he could to help his customers, but knew that expenses without income could not be sustainable.

With no work available and with children to feed, people got in a bind. Some brought whatever they had and bartered for what they needed. Eventually, Rudy got into a bind. People were not able to pay their bills and, without money coming in, he had to cancel all orders for more supplies. All too soon the shelves became bare.

On the family farm, Aaron was feeling the pinch as well. The milk company that had bought his milk became a victim of the depression. They filed bankruptcy and shut down operations. Aaron did not receive the last two milk checks. He was still milking cows every day. What was he to do with all the milk? Part of it they took to Rudy to give to the people in need. The surplus they fed to the hogs.

Carpentry work came to a halt as priorities turned to survival. With construction at a standstill, the sawmill shut down. Farmers and folks living in the rural areas were better off than those living in town. The depression had drawn families and neighbors together. They planted large gardens and shared with those in need.

Things turned worse when county treasurers sold off farms to collect unpaid taxes. The county government was not interested in bartering. Many tax sales went unsold due to a lack of buyers.

Jake was able to keep the taxes paid on the farm, but Aaron became very discouraged with not having any money. With a big garden, producing vegetables and livestock for butchering they had food to put on the table. Constantly someone came knocking on the door, destitute of something to eat. The strangers never went away empty-handed.

After a few months of these conditions with no signs of improvement, Jake called his sons together. "Conditions here seem to keep getting worse," he told them. "With the drought across this part of the country, we may no longer be able to keep going. There are jobs and food in California. Go out there and talk to Joseph. He will find work for you. You will be able to feed your children."

Jake's whole family including Joe and Cassie moved to California. The depression had affected California too, but not as bad as in the Midwest. Although some had lost money in the stocks they had owned and their investments went down, they were still able to hang on. The economy was moving at a slow pace, but money was still available. Wages had to be lowered, but all employees had plenty to eat and a place to live.

The time came when Joseph felt it was necessary to lower the wages of their employees in order to keep as many as possible working. Several of his employees from Mexico decided they wanted to return home. They had a longing for their family and with what little cash they had saved, they felt what they had would go farther down in Mexico.

With the recent vacancies, there were plenty of jobs and housing available for all of Jake's family.

****

One evening during supper, Joseph and his boys were discussing the day's events. It was the first day of the month and Joseph had Daniel deliver the paychecks to all the employees.

"Dad, you once told us about a dream you had when you were seven. You dreamed that your brothers were working for you and had to do what you told them. I thought about that today as I handed them their paychecks. Is this the fulfillment of the dream you had?"

Joseph sat back in his chair with a faraway look in his eyes. "This may be the day the Lord was preparing me for. I haven't thought about your uncles working here as fulfilling that dream. I feel we are blessed to have our family working together. Son, I forgave my brothers a long time ago. God does move in mysterious ways. The foreknowledge of God knew this depression was coming a long time ago. It humbles me to think that we are instruments in God's hand doing what He wants us to do."

"Does God make His servants suffer as you did?" Daniel asked.

"Son, we don't always know the plan of our God. Jesus suffered for our sins, the just for the unjust. The scriptures tell us, 'who for the joy that set before Him endured the cross, despising the shame, and is set down at the right hand of the throne of God.'

Many years ago when I experienced that dream, if I could see the trials before me, it would have been hard to endure. Looking at the present and days to come, I know it has all been worth the struggle. Not only have we been blessed, but our family has shared in these blessings. Grandpa Jake instructed me to always look to Jesus."

Daniel, still trying to grasp the relationship between his father and uncles asked, "Do you think your brothers resent you being over them?"

"Not at all," Joseph answered with confidence. "After they made confession and were forgiven, they became members in the church. They study the scriptures and believe the inerrant Word of God. We are all servants of our Father in Heaven. We each have our place to fill."

"If you had not forgiven them, what would things be like now?" Daniel asked.

"I don't know what they would be like, but I would be in a bad condition with my God. To withhold forgiveness is not an option with the people of God. God is Love. There is no hatred in love. We need to show that kind of love towards everyone, although at times it's hard to do."

****

The next day just as Shelly was setting the table for dinner, Carl's came up the drive. It didn't take long for her to slip on a couple more plates. "I just had a feeling you would be here by noon," she told her grandparents. "I threw an extra potato in the pot."

That brought a smile on Grandma's face. As always there was a lot of catching up to do.

"Are you staying for church on Sunday?" Eddie asked. The children loved to hear their grandpa preach. He used a lot of the old Bible stories in his sermons. That made it interesting to them. He was happy to hear they were staying for a couple of weeks.

Grandpa's Sermon
Chapter Thirty

The sun shone brightly as they drove to the meeting house. The pleasant temperatures would surely give way to a hot day. Shelly noticed that Grandpa was unusually quiet. "Is Grandpa not feeling well?" she asked her grandmother.

"He is thinking about what he is going to preach today. He is getting older and the load is a little harder."

"Grandpa, would you tell us the whole story of Joseph? I've heard parts of it, but not the whole story at one time."

Grandpa just sat there stroking his beard. After a while Eddie noticed he got a sparkle in his eyes and smiled. "The whole thing might be a long sermon. Hopefully you're not hungry."

The meeting was opened with singing '*Nearer My God to Thee*'. Thoughts were advanced on walking close to the Lord or walking in our own way, far from the Lord.

As Carl stood his hesitation was noticeable as he surveyed his audience. How many times over the years he had been in this position. Not one of his asking but one to which the Lord had called him. He never wanted fame, his only desire was that people would hear and understand the Word of God.

"The brother spoke about two opposing positions in our world," Carl's older, but still booming voice finally broke the silence. "He shared the story of the prodigal son who ran from the Lord. We see too often in our world today our youth turning away from walking with the Lord. They seem to be trying to see how far away from God they can run. This morning I would like to share with you a story from the first book in the Bible. I will be speaking to the young people today but the truth that is in this story is one that applies to each and every one of us in this meeting house. My prayer is that you will see the differences in the hearts of the individuals in the story we share."

Carl could see that he had everyone's attention in the church and he needed to get into sharing the ancient story from the Word of God. One that was very applicable to the present day.

"It was a very nice day. They were on their way home from a mission that they had not wanted to go on. Suddenly one of them said, 'Look, someone is coming fast'. A cloud of dust rose from behind the horses that were running as fast as they could. Fear gripped the ten brothers as they watched the approaching riders. What could be wrong?

Jacob never intended to have more than one wife. He had an agreement with the father of the one he wanted to be his wife. He was to work seven years for her hand in marriage. After the seven years, he was tricked into thinking he was getting Rachel and ended up with her older sister instead. It was all due to the customs in the country where they lived. Jacob ended up working seven more years for the one he really loved.

His first wife, Leah started having children but Rachel, the one he really loved, did not. Each of these wives had a handmaiden. Rachel told him to take her maid, marry her and have children by her. This he did. She had two sons. Leah, seeing this and not wanting to be outdone also told him to marry her handmaiden and have children. This he did. She had two sons. Leah had a total of six sons and one daughter.

Rachel was grieved that she could not have children. God looked on her affliction and opened her womb. She bore a son. They named him Joseph. Jacob dearly loved that boy. Later they had another son they named Benjamin. But it was a sad day as Rachel died as she was giving birth. Jacob had such a love for Rachel and to lose her was such a sorrow. As a result, he loved Joseph and Benjamin in a special way. He loved their brothers too but the sons of his wife he worked so long for, and then to lose her, caused his love for her sons to be very deep.

Jacob made a coat for Joseph with many colors. No doubt he was favored above the older ones. They were a little jealous of him. One day Joseph told them about a dream he had. 'We were binding sheaves and my sheaf stood upright and your sheaves did obedience to mine.' His brothers not only were jealous of him but now they hated him. Then he had another dream, the sun and the moon and the eleven stars did obedience to him. When he told his brothers this dream it caused them to hate him all the more. One day his brothers did something very bad and Joseph told their father. The hatred got worse.

The sheep needed pasture. The ten older sons took them to find pasture. They went to Shechem. After they were gone a while, Jacob asked Joseph to go check on his brothers to see if all was well. Joseph was seventeen when he went to check on his brothers. He had no fear of anything happening to him. When he got to Shechem, he could not find them. He was wandering around hunting them when he met a man who asked him, 'Who are you hunting?' When he told him, the man said, 'I heard them say they were going to Dothan.'

Joseph had to go farther than he planned, but on he went. When he finely got to where he saw them he was no doubt excited. He must have gone running, thinking they would be glad to see him and to get word from home. I feel it had been a good long time since they left home. Around the home, Joseph helped them tend the sheep. He probably missed them in spite of their hatred.

Hatred was so deep within them, they could only think evil toward him. One of them in a bitter tone said, 'Here comes that dreamer.' Another said, 'Let's kill him and see what comes of his dreams.'

As he approached expecting to be embraced, they grabbed him by his coat a couple on one side and two or three on the other jerking one way then another, pulling tearing it severely. One of them, softening a little said, 'Let's not kill him because he is our brother. Let's put him into that empty pit.' That is what they did. The pit was deep enough he couldn't get out by himself. Still not knowing what to do with him they sat down to eat their lunch.

While they were eating some merchantmen came by taking their wares down to Egypt. Someone suggested they sell him to the merchants. The merchants offered twenty pieces of silver for him. Joseph pleaded, 'Don't sell me, I'm your brother.' But they wouldn't listen. Hatred could be seen in their eyes. In my mind, I can see a very sad young man being led away from his family on his way to a foreign land. Likely tears were falling down his cheeks.

Reuben was not there when they sold Joseph. He thought when his brothers weren't around; he would get him out and send him home. When he came to the pit and it was empty he got upset. He asked the others about Joseph. The Bible doesn't say, but I suppose they told him what they had done. Now they had to figure a way to make their father think Joseph was dead. They knew their father well enough, that if they didn't, Jacob would go find him. They decided to kill a young goat and put its blood over the torn coat and take it to their father.

When they presented it to Jacob, they fabricated a lie. They said, 'This we found. Can you tell, if this is Joseph's coat?' Jacob knew immediately it was. That part of their plan worked. Jacob said, 'No doubt a wild beast hath devoured him. Joseph is torn to pieces.'

Jacob wept for many days and couldn't be comforted."

Carl took a sip of water from the metal cup and set it back on the table. Every eye was upon him as the congregation was taking in the old familiar story. His booming voice again echoed throughout the meeting house.

"Joseph was taken to Egypt where he was sold. Potiphar, captain of the king's guard, bought him. He was a slave in Potiphar's house for some time. We don't know how long he was there. The Lord was with Joseph and caused everything Potiphar had to prosper while he was there. Potiphar put him in charge of everything. He must have been there for a few years.

Things were working out as well as could be expected under the conditions until Potiphar's wife fell in love with Joseph. She tried to entice him. He told her, 'How can I do this great wickedness and sin against God?' Joseph was going about his duties when she tried hard to get him to be with her. She grabbed him by his coat. He shed it and got out of there. Doing that made her angry. She hollered for help. She told the men servants that Joseph tried to force her and when she cried out he left without his coat. That was the second time he lost his coat to wicked people. She put up the coat until her husband came and she told him the false story. Potiphar believed her. It made him angry and he put Joseph in the dungeon prison.

How would you feel if you had been treated like Joseph was? Sometimes when we feel we have been mistreated, we are inclined to become bitter. Would you have? I don't think Joseph even considered becoming bitter. There is no justifiable reason to become bitter. How long was he in that prison? We don't know, the Bible doesn't say. I think of a dungeon as a dimly lit, damp underground place. Possibly there were rats and spiders in the dungeon. Joseph was there long enough for the jailer to notice God was with him. He put the other prisoners under Joseph's care.

I suppose Joseph wondered why his father didn't come looking for him. He would have been unaware of the lies his brothers had told their father.

There came a day when the chief baker and the chief butler offended the king. He put them in the dungeon under Joseph's care. This wasn't just one week or so, it was for a long time, maybe two or three years or more. Would you have become bitter being in those conditions for that long? Joseph didn't.

One morning he noticed the butler and the baker were not acting normal. They were sad and acted like they had something that was troubling them.

Joseph asked, 'Why are you sad?' They told Joseph they had dreams that troubled them, that no one could interpret it. Joseph told them to tell him the dreams.

The butler said, 'There were three branches came upon a vine and grapes on the three branches. I had the king's cup in my hand and I pressed the grapes into the cup and gave it into Pharaoh's hand as I used to do.'

Joseph told the butler, 'The three branches are three days. In three days Pharaoh will bring you out of this place and restore your position. When you are restored speak to Pharaoh for me. I was stolen out of my country and sold. I have done nothing to be in this dungeon.'

When the baker heard the interpretation of the butler's dream, he also told Joseph his dream. He had three white baskets of baked goods on his head and the birds came and ate the baked goods out of the basket.

Joseph interpreted the dream. 'The three baskets are three days. In three days Pharaoh will take you out of prison and will hang you. The birds will eat your flesh.'

Three days later was Pharaoh's birthday. He took the butler and the baker out of the dungeon. He restored the chief butler to his position and hanged the baker as Joseph interpreted. But the butler forgot Joseph.

I imagine every day Joseph was hoping someone from the King's palace would come and get him. Two full years passed and still no word from the butler. Would you be bitter yet? Joseph wasn't.

Pharaoh had a dream that troubled him. He called the magicians, but they couldn't interpret it. It was then the chief butler remembered Joseph. He told Pharaoh about Joseph. Joseph was called out of the dungeon, cleaned up and stood before Pharaoh. The Bible tells us he was thirty years old when this happened. He was seventeen when his father had sent him to find his brothers. For thirteen years he was a slave, a servant in Potiphar's house and in the dungeon.

When Pharaoh asked him if he was able to interpret dreams, he said, 'It is not in me. God will give you an answer of peace. Tell me the dream.'

Pharaoh had seen in his dream seven fat cattle grazing in a meadow. There came up seven sickly looking cattle and ate up the well-fleshed cattle. Pharaoh explained that he had had another dream. There came up a stalk of corn that had seven good ears, well filled out and very good. There came up seven thin stalks blasted with the east wind. They consumed the seven good ears.

Joseph told Pharaoh it is all one dream. That what God was about to do was very severe, therefore he showed him the dream twice. He explained that there were going to be seven very good years and the land will produce an abundance of grain. After that, there were to be seven years when it would not rain. During that time the land would not produce anything. Joseph told Pharaoh that he should find a man to take charge of things in the seven good years. He should build storehouses to put one fifth in storage during the seven good years. In doing so they would have food to eat during the seven year drought.

Pharaoh was impressed with the wisdom Joseph displayed. He asked his servants, 'Can we find such a one as this, in whom the Spirit of God is?" Pharaoh then appointed Joseph to fill that position. He put his ring on Joseph's hand, a gold chain around his neck and clothed him in fine linen. He gave him the second chariot to ride in. All authority over Egypt was given to him. Can you imagine? Joseph went from being a prisoner in a dungeon to being next to the king in power. Pharaoh commanded when Joseph passed by the people were to bow.

Joseph went right to work. The land yielded by handfuls. He had storage buildings built in all the cities of Egypt. There was so much grain in storage he quit keeping tally of it. During these good years, the king gave Joseph the daughter of the priest to be his wife. There were two sons born to them. The first was Manasseh and the second was named Ephraim. Joseph no doubt loved his wife and sons. He said God had made him forget all his toil and his entire father's house. The years of plenty ended."

The deflection in Carl's voice indicated a change. He continued on with the story in a slower solemn tone. "The drought began. People went to the king to ask for food. He sent them to Joseph. The drought was through all the land. People came from far and near to buy corn. One day as he was looking out over the many people, who had come to buy grain, he noticed his ten brothers standing in the crowd. It had now been over twenty years since they had sold him into slavery. They didn't recognize him. After all the years amongst the Egyptians, he spoke their language fluently. When it was their turn they bowed before Joseph. This act of respect and humility shown by his brothers brought back the dream he had had as a boy. Joseph communicated to them through an interpreter accusing them of being spies. He asked about their father and if they had a younger brother. When he found out his father was still well and alive, he turned and went into his house and wept.

I don't believe it was in Joseph to be hard-hearted. He remembered the mean look in their eyes the day they sold him. He wanted to see if that hatred was still in them. Still accusing them of being spies, he had them put in prison. Maybe the same prison that was home for him for several years. He told them to send one of them home and bring their younger brother and the rest remain in prison. If they did, that would prove they weren't spies.

After three days he had them brought out. He told them, 'I feared God.' He still accused them of being spies. He was gruff to them. He accused them of coming to Egypt just to see how naked the land was from the drought. They insisted they were the sons of one man and they came only to buy grain. Joseph finally told them that he would keep one of them in prison until they returned with their younger brother. 'If you don't, you will not see my face.' He told them. I would gather that statement meant they would not get any more grain.

In front of his brothers, he took Simeon and bound him. Why did he choose Simeon? The Bible doesn't say. He was the next to the oldest. Reuben, the oldest, had wanted to deliver Joseph back to their father before he was sold. Possibly that is the reason Simeon was held instead of Reuben. The other nine were sold corn and sent home. Simeon likely was sent to the dungeon where Joseph had been held. I wonder if Simeon had to sleep on the same hard cold damp bed where Joseph slept for years. The Bible doesn't say.

When the brothers got home they told their father about the harsh governor of Egypt. How they were taken for spies and put in prison for three days. How Simeon was bound and had to stay in Egypt until they returned with Benjamin. This made Jacob very sorry. He said 'Joseph is not and Simeon is not. All this is against me.' When they opened up their sacks of grain and found all their money in the mouth of the sack, they were scared. They knew something was wrong and they would have to pay dearly for this happening.

The day came when they were running out of grain and it was time to return to Egypt. Can you imagine how hard it was, not only for Jacob but also for the wives and children of the brothers to see them leave? Simeon most likely had a wife and children. There probably were a lot of tears shed in his home when he didn't come home with the others. The Bible doesn't spell everything out, but we know how it may have been. As a father and grandfather, I can just picture Jacob watching them go. Standing there watching until they were out of sight.

Thinking he may never see them again, he likely broke down and wept.

Think about that journey. I can see a very somber group of men walking along, fearing what lay ahead. After walking several days, the storehouses of Egypt appeared on the horizon. They knew the harsh governor would be there. I don't know if they had to stand in line like they had the first time, but I tend to think that Joseph had his guards go get the brothers and take them to his house. Joseph brought out Simeon. He had the ruler of his house make dinner for them. When Joseph saw Benjamin he went into his chamber and wept. He washed his face and came out. He seated them according to age. That made them marvel. I don't suppose they enjoyed the meal very well. They talked among themselves questioning why they were taken unto the governor's house. 'God has found out about our sin. What we did to our brother. Now he is going to take us for bondmen and take our donkeys.' All this time they didn't know Joseph understood their language as he was still using an interpreter.

The meal went well and nothing drastic happened. They paid the steward for the corn, loaded their bags on the donkeys and they all headed for home. I would wonder if they were a little uncomfortable as they walked along. The governor had been kind to them as they ate in his home. They marveled at how it was even the governor himself who brought Simeon out to them. Now they had full bags and nothing was said about them being spies. They were all going home.

****

The brothers stopped and watched in fear as the riders came to a halt half surrounding the caravan. The one that dismounted they recognized as one of the governor's steward. The rest were all guards. 'You have stolen my masters silver cup,' the steward scowled. 'After all the good he did for you,

221

why would you steal his cup which he divines in? Whoever's sack the cup is in, he shall be a bondservant. The rest can go on home.'

I'm sure the brothers were looking at each other, questioning which one would have done such a thing.

The steward demanded they take down their sacks starting with the oldest. One by one, they went through the exercise until at last it was found in Benjamin's sack.

Can you just imagine the sorry group of men trudging back to the city? What were they thinking as they made that mile or two journey? They had to be thinking about the expected outcome of their situation. They had to be thinking about the future; one that carried with it a lot of sorrow. Fear gripped their hearts.

Walking down the dry dusty streets the sound of the donkey's hooves against the stones riveted in their head. It was time to face their judgment. Arriving at the storehouse they were taken to the governor's quarters. Joseph studied the fear in the faces of his brothers. Through his interpreter, he asked them, 'Don't you know I am a man that can divine? How is it you have stolen my silver cup? The man in whose sack the cup was in, he shall stay and be my servant. The rest of you go home.'

Judah meekly stepped forward, and with humility told the story of their father's wife that he loved and her son that was dead. He told what Benjamin meant to their father. He asked if he could take the place of his brother and become a servant.

When Joseph saw the repentant spirit of his brothers, he cried out for everyone except the brothers to leave. Hastily, Joseph's steward and guards made their way out of the room. Once they were alone, Joseph looked around the group of confused, scared men.

I can just picture the group gathered in that room. They all were facing the governor who had shown an exorbitant amount of authority. Yet here in this moment he showed unexpected compassion.

'I am Joseph!'

How do you suppose they felt when they heard these words in their native tongue, coming from a man who previously had only addressed them through an interpreter? I imagine they questioned if they heard correctly. It was an unexpected statement.

'I am Joseph! The one you sold into Egypt. Is my father still alive?'

He told them not to blame themselves. It was God that brought him here. He wept on Benjamin's neck. He kissed them all.

He told them about the drought and how it was going to last another five years. He asked them to go home and get their father, wives, and children. Bring them down here to Egypt.

When Pharaoh heard, he told Joseph to send wagons to help with the move. Joseph sent his brothers away telling them to tell their father everything he had told them. The last words Joseph told his brothers were, 'See that ye fall not out by the way.'

I can imagine there was the temptation of wanting to blame what they had done to Joseph onto one of the others. I don't think they did. They had lived in the prison of guilt for twenty-two years. They didn't know how to get out of it. Now was the time to confess everything.

It was hard for Jacob to believe Joseph was still alive. When he saw the wagons he believed. Unlike the last trip down to Egypt, this one was a happy one. The confession had taken place. They had been forgiven. Can you imagine the caravan singing as they went along? They were no longer living in a prison of sin.

Joseph met the caravan as they arrived in Egypt. Think of the emotional reunion between Joseph and his father. It had been twenty-two years since he had parted from his father to go check on his brothers. Jacob had expected him to return in just a few days.

Jacob had never expected to see Joseph again. Likely, Joseph had never expected to see his father again either. They fell on each other's neck and wept for a long time.

Joseph gave his family a place to dwell in the land of Goshen.

Joseph brought his two sons to meet their grandfather. Jacob said, "'I never thought I would see my son again and now I have seen his sons.' Jacob lived in Egypt for seventeen years before he died.

Before Jacob died he blessed both of Joseph's sons. He told Joseph he gave him one portion more than his brothers. After the death of their father, the ten brothers were afraid of Joseph. They told him, 'Our father said for you to forgive us.' They fell down before him. When Joseph saw how they acted, he wept.

He said, 'Fear not; for am I in the place of God? You thought evil against me; but God meant it for good, to bring to pass as it is this day, to save many. Therefore fear not. I will nourish you and your little ones.' He spoke kindly to them.

What would you have done if you had been treated like Joseph? Remember, back home as a teenager, his brothers wouldn't speak peaceably to him. Joseph always trusted God. He believed what Apostle Paul would later write in Romans that 'All things work together for the good to them that love God, to them who are the called according to His purpose.'

It has been said, 'Joseph was a type of Christ.' Having a forgiving heart is a way to peace. Joseph spent time in a literal prison. God was with him. His ten older brothers spent years in a prison of guilt far away from God. Do you want to be like Joseph?"

In the car on the way home from the meeting Eddie thanked his grandpa for telling one of his favorite stories. "Grandpa when you were preaching, I really felt sorry for Joseph."

"That story made me cry," Shelly added.

Three Grandparents
Chapter Thirty-one

The fog rolled in. One could hardly see the barn from the house. Carl's had planned to leave early for home but he was uncertain about traveling in such fog.

"Why don't you stay for another day?" Lovina said. "Maybe the fog will lift and then it will be better for you to travel."

When the children got up, they were happy to see their grandparents had not left.

After a breakfast of sausage gravy on toast with coffee, Carl read the second chapter of Exodus. He then talked about how Moses was a descendant of Jacob. They were in Egypt for three hundred and fifty years when the Pharaoh noticed how many there were of them. He didn't even remember anything about Joseph. He reasoned if there was to be a war, and they joined in with his enemy, they could overcome the Egyptians. He decided to have all baby boys killed. This was the law when Moses was born.

"Grandpa, wasn't Moses' mother afraid when she saw she had a boy baby?" Daniel asked.

"We would think she was, however in the eleventh chapter of Hebrews the twenty-third verse it says his parents were not afraid of the king's commandment." Carl continued, "A long time ago, God promised Abraham that his descendants would be blessed. They would be in a strange land for four hundred years. After that, he would take them to the land he promised. I think Moses' mother somehow knew this baby of hers was the one God would use to take Jacob's descendants to the Promised Land."

Eddie asked, "Grandpa, what makes you think she may have known he was the one to do that?"

Carl responded, "It is recorded in the New Testament in the seventh chapter of The Acts the twenty-fifth verse, 'He supposed his brethren would have understood how that God by his hand would deliver them'."

"Then according to those two New Testament scriptures, Moses' parents likely instructed him about the plan of God," Joseph interjected. "The verse you quoted from Hebrews starts out 'by faith'. For a mother to put her baby in the water in a little ark would take a lot of faith. God likely revealed His saving love to them somehow."

"I believe God did, but not all the details. God keeps His promises," Carl continued. "You know, we too are on our way to a promised land. We don't know the very details of our journey, but by faith, we travel on. Be sure to remember, God keeps His promises."

Eddie said, "Grandpa, I like the way you explain the things in the Bible. You make us feel close to God. I would like for you to come sometime and preach to us about how Moses took the people to the Promised Land."

"Maybe your dad will do that," Carl responded.

****

The fog lasted for a week. Carl got a little jittery to leave, but Rachel was reluctant to go on the road in such a fog. They agreed there was no urgent need to be home. Shelly enjoyed the added time she had with her grandmother. One day all three of her grandmas spent the afternoon with her. She loved to hear them tell of events that happened in their lives. They had so many interesting stories.

Daniel suggested the whole family come together to sing some evening. Joseph asked Lovina if she felt the grandparents would enjoy a wiener roast. They could spend the evening singing around the campfire.

"It would depend on how heavy the fog is," Lovina answered. "If it's not too damp and cold, I'm sure they would."

Joseph asked Chad if the guys could bring a load of Almond wood up to the barnyard. He felt it better to have the wiener roast close to the house to accommodate their elderly parents.

"We have a brush pile from some old trees taken out," Chad said. "We'll bring a load up this afternoon."

Friday morning the fog showed signs of lifting. The fire was lit and word went out for the family and employees to come and bring their hymn books.

The boys brought up a flatbed wagon on which to put the food. Shelly helped make potato salad and other things to go along with a wiener roast. They were excited to have all their cousins come for the occasion, besides having all three sets of grandparents there.

Shelly's wish that Uncle Juniors would be there was answered when they showed up with their whole family. They had concerns about his parents driving in the fog and had decided to drive up and help them make the trip home. It made everyone's day to see Uncle Junior and Aunt Carol and their children, Rosy, Lloyd and Laban come.

"Your timing is great," Eddie told them. "We are having a wiener roast and singing this evening. Shelly just mentioned her wish that you folks would show up. Now the whole family is here."

"God works in mysterious ways," Junior responded.

****

The afternoon sunshine drove out the cold dampness of the last few days. The evening's pleasant temperature added to the excitement of the gathering. After the hearty greetings, Joseph said, "Let's all stand and sing the doxology." After the last note faded away one of the grandpas offered a beautiful prayer, thanking the Lord for a family in which love abounded. A family that was mindful of where their blessing came from. He thanked the Lord for the food.

Daniel decided the boys should roast the wieners for the grandparents. When Daniel offered one to Eston, he declined.

"I'm sixty-eight years old and never been to a wiener roast," he told his grandson. "I'd like to roast my own."

Daniel helped his granddad to the fire and assisted in steadying the shaky stick as Eston roasted the hotdog. When it was roasted with the small darkened burnt spots blistering around the edges, Eston felt happy with his accomplishment. He told Daniel, "I want to give this one to Grandma. I want to say that I roasted a hotdog for my sweetheart." As he handed the wiener in the bun to Lucinda and she looked up into his eyes, Daniel saw the gleam of love sparkle.

"Gleam in their eyes after fifty years of married life," he thought. "After years of joys and sorrows, toils and pain, disappointments and dreams fulfilled. And still a sparkle in her eyes for the love of her life doing a simple thing as thinking of her as he's experiencing something new." That gleam spoke a lot of words. Daniel walked away with tears in his eyes.

After they finished eating the hymn books came out. Jake called out the number for 'Precious Memories'. The old familiar hymn rang out across the barnyard as the family all opened their mouths in praise. Several of the employees joined in. The older folks had to dry their eyes by the time the song was over.

Over the next couple of hours, they sang, "Nearer My God to Thee", "Rock of Ages", "There is a Happy Land", "Blessed Be the Tie That Bind", "How Great Thou Art" and many more.

It was getting late when Rudy suggested they sing "In the Garden." As the melody drifted across the night, Rudy struggled to sing along. His mind went back to years ago to a time when he was a small boy in the garden with his mother. As she worked she sang this song many times. *And he walks with me and he talks with me and he tells me I am his own. The joy we share, as we tarry there, None other has ever known.* As these words rang out in praise, Rudy's thoughts returned to the evening. He noticed Joseph singing with all his heart and across the dying embers sat Daniel, the spitting image of his dad, singing with all his heart.

"To think we sold Joseph with hate in our hearts," he thought. "He suffered much from what we did to him. Now here we are on his farm in California with all our families, sitting around these dying embers, singing praises to our God. There is no sign of hate, only the Love of God. Had Joseph not forgave we could not have an evening like this." He was jolted out of his reverie as he heard them singing, *Jesus thou art a sinner's friend.* He joined in, *"as such I look to thee, now in the bowels of thy love, dear lord remember me."*

****

There was only a faint glow where the fire had been a few hours earlier when Eston's decided to turn in. An hour earlier, Carl's and Jake's bade them good night.

"This is my first time to experience such a thing as we have tonight," Eston had told them. "I want to stay until the last ember is gone."

When Carl's and Jake's had been walking towards the house, they heard the deep voices of the boys singing, '*The Love of God*'. They stopped and turned around. They were just far enough away and being a clear calm night, the singing was just beautiful. Finishing that song, they started another.

Carl, looking at Jake, said, "Children are a heritage to the Lord."

"Amen," was Jake's reply as they continued on toward home.

Everyone had retired except Jake's five oldest sons. Sitting there in the midnight hour their thoughts were drawn heavenward. The air was clear and the stars were so bright. Looking up one of them stated, *"The Heavens declare the glory of God."*

They talked amongst themselves about the Love of God.

"His love is so great, He doesn't want anyone to perish," Henry said. "Wasn't Joseph's love really shown this evening? No sign of hate, just total forgiveness. That is what Jesus did for us when He died on the cross, paying for our sins."

Rudy's response showed how much they had grown spiritually, "Yes He did. On the condition, we confess our sins and repent. Not only did He pay for fallen man's sins, but He rose triumphant over death, hell and the grave. He is now at the right hand of the Father interceding for us."

The Heavenly Home
Chapter Thirty-Two

Breakfast was a little late. The events the evening before were the topic of discussion at the table. Carl said they sure were glad to be with them on that occasion. When Joseph handed Carl the Bible, he passed it on to Junior as he had read for the last several mornings. Junior chose the fourteenth chapter of Saint John. After he finished reading, he talked about our Father's home. "It is time for us to leave this place and go to our earthly home. We know what it's like there. What will it be like when we get to our heavenly home?"

"We can only imagine through an eye of faith," Carl answered. "Jesus told us, 'If you love me, keep my commandments.' Last night as you were singing with enthusiasm around the glowing embers, what and to whom were you singing?"

"We were singing praises to our God," Lloyd was the first to answer.

"Singing from our hearts," Eddie added.

"It was from a deep belief in our Father God," Daniel said.

"In the first verse, Jesus said, 'Let not your heart be troubled. Ye believe in God, believe also in me. In my Father's house are many mansions.' What do we think about when we think of a mansion? We most likely would be thinking about a very large beautiful building or a house with lots and lots of rooms. We may think of a king's palace. We likely wouldn't be thinking about our home here.

'Jesus went on to say, 'I go to prepare a place for you.' What kind of place will it be? As the Lord looks down into our homes today, what does He see? Are we content with what we live in here? Will He provide us with something similar? People who hardly have a roof over their heads may think we are living in a palace.

The account Jesus gave about the rich man and Lazarus. They both died, and Lazarus was carried by the angels into Abraham's bosom. Where was that? No doubt it was a good place to be. It was the place where the righteous went when they died.

There is another account of a dying man. When Jesus was hanging on the cross, one of the men who were also being crucified confessed before all the people watching that Jesus was Lord. He said, '*Lord remember me when thou comest into thy Kingdom.*' That day Jesus told the thief on the cross, '*Today thou shalt be with me in Paradise.*' Where is Paradise? Is there a difference between Abraham's bosom and Paradise?

As the repentant thief hung there in agony he heard his savior say, 'It is finished.' Jesus then bowed His head and gave up the ghost. When Jesus died the veil of the temple was torn into two pieces and the Holy place was opened to all who would accept Christ.

Jesus said, 'I go to prepare a place for you.' When Jesus died on the cross, the sin of Adam was paid in full. He came not to destroy the law, but to fulfill it.

Those who obey Jesus' commandments, fully trusting and believing in Him, will no doubt enter into the Paradise of God that Jesus prepared for His faithful."

They pondered over the short message that Carl had shared. Each one around the table nodding in agreement with the truth they had received.

"This has been enjoyable, but we must head for home," Carl said.

Shelly and Rosa started singing, 'How Beautiful Heaven Must Be', as the rest joined in. As they were walking out to the cars, the children sang, 'God be with you until we meet again'.

There were lumps in their throats as they watched them go, not knowing if they would see each other again this side of Heaven.

The Love Feast
Chapter Thirty-Three

The years rolled by and one morning after devotions, the twenty-year-old Daniel told his parents that he and Wanda Sims were planning on getting married. "I received her parents' permission and would like to have your blessing."

Joseph and Lovina knew this day was coming. They had spent a lot of time in prayer and they were ready. The Sims' were a very stable family in the church. Although early in her life, Wanda had gone through a difficult time, she had been young enough to come out of it. Wilbur and Joyce had done a wonderful job in their care of her and her siblings. All three of them were good members of the church. Many times they hosted the young folks, always to have a clean and respectful day.

Lovina's mind flashed back to the day Joseph came home and asked her if they could help with the dilemma the children were in. Wanda had grown up to become a good, godly woman, nothing at all like her birth mother. Her character was much more like her adoptive mother.

They told Daniel they were happy to have Wanda as their daughter-in-law.

"When are you thinking of having the wedding?" his mother asked.

"Wanda and I would like to have it on Sunday afternoon after our spring Love Feast. Her parents approve if it doesn't conflict with anything." Looking at Joseph, he continued, "We thought there could be friends and family come to the meeting and attend our wedding. Dad, do you think that will be alright?"

"I'll take it up with our officials, but I don't see any problem with those plans."

"Where would you like to have the wedding?" Lovina asked.

"We are thinking we would like to have it in the almond orchard. The almonds are in full bloom at that time."

That evening around the supper table he shared the news with his siblings. There was excitement among them at the upcoming life event. When they were discussing the location of the wedding Eddie said, "We might want to schedule it with Uncle Chad. Flooding the orchard the day before could make for a messy wedding." That brought on some smiles.

After supper, Daniel drove over to Grandpa Jake's to share the news, and then on to Grandpa Eston's. They were all happy to hear the news. That night he sat down and wrote a letter to his third set of grandparents. He asked Carl if he would perform the wedding.

The winter months rolled by and soon February was upon them.

"It looks like the almond blossoms will be in full bloom by our meeting," Joseph told Daniel one morning at breakfast.

Daniel smiled from ear to ear and just said, "Great!"

"Are you sure you two want blossoms floating down around you during the ceremony?" Shelly asked.

"We discussed it and think we will like that," Daniel answered.

"What about the uneven ground in the tree rows? Will that interfere with setting up chairs?" Eddie asked.

"The ushers will have chairs for the older folks, everyone else will stand. The two of us and the preacher will be standing.

"Who all are you going to invite?" Lovina asked.

"That was a question Wanda's parents wanted to know," Daniel answered his mother. "After we discussed it with them, we made a list of who we wanted to give special invitations, but we will have an open invitation for anyone who wants to come.

It was Wilber who wanted to know about the seating. Wanda and I felt that not knowing how many will show up, we couldn't assure a seat for everyone. The service likely will not be any longer than it is at the grave when someone passes on. Most folks stand there.”

“Are you saying your wedding is a funeral?” Eddie grinned, making Daniel roll his eyes.

“It looks like you have done a good job covering your plans,” Joseph said. “What about the reception?”

“We wanted to talk to you about that. Wilber’s think they should host it, but they don’t have the space. Wanda wondered if we could have it in our barnyard where we have the annual wiener roast and singing.”

“You are welcome to have it here if that is what you want,” Joseph told him.

February fifteenth was a beautiful sunshiny day with mild temperatures. There was a large turnout at the meeting. Junior Bauman’s came and not only brought Carl’s but talked Charles Young into coming with them. The elderly brother Charles had been caring for had passed away two weeks earlier and he needed to get away. To keep busy he had started helping Carl’s by doing handyman chores around their home.

It made Joseph happy to see his old friends, Kenneth, Daryl, and Lester come with their families. He was especially glad to see Lester, as he was now a minister in Carl’s district. John Yoder from Illinois was another minister they had expected to be there. Carl was happy to see a minister from out of state at the meeting.

The meeting was opened in the usual way. Carl opened the meeting, and although he was getting old, he still had heartwarming words to encourage all to look to the closeness of our relationship with Jesus. John Yoder lead out, giving everyone the feeling of the blessing of being born again and sitting around the table of the Lord.

Saturday evening the meeting house was full as they communed with each other and the Lord. Jake, although old and feeble was still able to stoop and wash another’s feet. Tears came to his eyes as he saw his son Joseph stoop and wash Henry and Simon's feet, and place a kiss on their lips. He thought, "Oh, the beauty of a forgiving spirit." He also witnessed Jesse Sims washing the feet of his birth father. Jake couldn't help but shed tears thinking how God had orchestrated this moment. It was not man who determined who washed whose feet. We believe the church washes our feet. Surely it is a cleansing in preparation of partaking of the holy things. The bread and the wine are emblems of His broken body and the shed blood of our loving Savior, Jesus Christ.

Later as the cup was going around, they sang,

> *Come all ye chosen saints of God,*
> *Who long to feel the cleansing Blood,*
> *In pensive pleasure join with me,*
> *To sing of sad Gethsemane.*

Jake again shed tears, as he thought of his family. This evening they were all sitting around the communion table feeling the love of God, as they solemnly sang praises to him.

Sunday morning Lester started out on the farewell address. His subject was "This same Jesus" taken from the first chapter of Acts verse eleven. "God made promises to His people. He always keeps His promises. Years ago He made a promise to Abraham. God was prepared to keep that promise. I believe He is still planning to keep it. He said He would give Abraham the land of Canaan, a land flowing with milk and honey. They would journey in a strange land for four hundred years.

We all like the story of Jacob's son, Joseph. God has a purpose in all that He does. Before Joseph died he gave a commandment about their upcoming journey to the Promised Land. He wanted them to take his bones with them when that journey happened.

That promise came to reality some four hundred and thirty years later. God fulfills His promises in His time. That generation could have had it wonderful if they had obeyed the Lord. They did for a while, but little by little they drifted into apostasy.

God sent prophets who wrote about the coming of a savior. They were inspired by the Spirit to write. They may not have always understood what they wrote. Our brother yesterday morning read the fifty-third chapter of Isaiah. "Who hath believed our report? And to whom is the arm of the Lord revealed?" What was Isaiah writing about? It was 'This same Jesus'. Years later, when Jesus was born, the Jews who should have known the promise, were blind to know Him. He came unto His own, and His own received Him not.

It was the common people who heard Him gladly. When He was born, the angels informed the shepherds, who were watching their sheep by night, about 'This same Jesus'."

John Yoder continued on with thoughts about 'This same Jesus'. He will go away and prepare a place for His people, then He, 'This same Jesus', will come again.

Carl closed the meeting, putting emphasis on being ready to meet 'This same Jesus'.

New Homes
Chapter Thirty-Four

The appointed time of three o'clock came, bringing with it a slight breeze, as they gathered in the almond orchard. The trees were in full bloom. The ushers had a few chairs set up for the older folks and several ready for others who needed them. The grandparents were in the front row. Next to them were the parents and the siblings. Joseph lifted his voice and announced, "Let us sing hymn five hundred four." *Walk in the light! So shalt thou know that fellowship of love, His spirit only can bestow, who reigns in light above.*

After singing the remainder of the song, Carl arose and asked Daniel and Wanda to rise. He gave them a few encouraging words concerning their responsibility to each other and the Lord. He asked them to join right hands.

"Do you, Daniel Bauman, take Wanda whose hand you now hold to be your lawful wedded wife? Do you promise to love, honor, and cherish her in joy or in sorrow, in health or in sickness, in prosperity or in adversity, and forsaking all others cleave only to her as long as you both shall live?"

With a smile on his face he looked into her eyes and answered, "I do." Just as he answered a couple of almond blossoms floated down and landed on them.

Carl asked Wanda the same questions and she also looking into his smiling face said, "I do."

Then Carl said, "According to the laws of California and the authority invested in me by the church I pronounce you husband and wife. What God has joined together, let not man put asunder." They kneeled in prayer as Carl prayed a very tender, loving prayer asking the Lord's blessing on this new family. Arising from prayer, as he was introducing them as Mr. and Mrs. Daniel Bauman, a small breeze showered several blossoms down on them. Just after he had introduced the newly married couple, Carl noticed Charles walking away with his head down.

"All are invited to stay and enjoy the first meal with this new family," Wilber announced. After congratulating them, they were directed by the ushers to the place where a dinner had been prepared.

****

With each newly married couple, in time, there usually is a new life. Joseph and Lovina felt blessed to have grandchildren. It had been nine years since Daniel and Wanda were married. During that time, they were blessed with two children, Jacob Leroy, and Lucinda Joy.

Two years after Daniel's were married, Eddie and Linda were married. In time they were blessed with two children as well, Minnie May and Paul. A year after Eddie's were married Shelly married Jesse Sims. Three years later they were blessed with twin boys, Roy and Ray.

The house was so empty with all their children married. Joseph told Lovina, "When we were first married, there were just two of us, and we were happy that way."

She responded, "We were young then and not even thinking about the road ahead. Remember how the folks came over often. We were learning about starting up a home."

"Yes!" Joseph answered. "We were learning how two people raised in two different homes can become one. Remember the joy we had when we first looked at that little bundle God blessed us with?"

"I sure do. We were blessed with two more of those little bundles. How did those precious children grow up so fast?"

"I feel we enjoyed all of them to the fullest," Joseph answered. "And think how much they like their grandparents. Now we are the grandparents."

"They certainly are special, all six of them," Lovina sighed. "And to think Jacob just turned seven."

Joseph got a faraway look in his eyes when she mentioned Jacob being seven. "Mother told me this morning, when I took their breakfast over to them, how much she thinks Jacob looks like I did when I was seven."

"I didn't know you when you were seven, but he does look like Daniel did at that age."

Joseph was happy his sons were relieving him of much of the responsibility of the farms. At times he took one of the grandchildren with him when he needed to go get things for one of the farms.

"You're not spoiling them are you?" Lovina prodded.

With a grin on his face, he said, "Maybe a little."

The church was growing. Their old elder no longer was able to exercise in the ministry. The church was voiced if they felt to strengthen the ministry. It was united to do so. After the voice was taken it fell to Jesse Sims.

Joseph's mind went back to the time he and Lovina temporarily took those three children into their home. How Wilber's had adopted them and gave them a Godly home.

When Wilber received his son into the office of the ministry he broke down weeping. Thinking of the days when he and Joyce wondered if they were doing the right thing in adopting the children.

Now years later, the church, guided by the Spirit had called Jesse to preach the gospel. God moves in mysterious ways his wonders to fulfill.

Jesse and Shelly came over one evening to talk. Jesse felt the load was too heavy. He needed the encouragement of his father-in-law.

Joseph told him, "Try to live a Godly life. Don't look to man, but look to the Lord for your strength. Except the Lord build the house, they labor in vain that build it."

The Accident
Chapter Thirty-Five

It was a nice summer day. Two years passed since Jesse was called to the ministry. Joseph had been a good mentor to him. Jesse was doing well but, being humble, didn't think so.

Jesse and his father were in the hayfield. As Jesse pitched a fork of hay up to his father on the wagon he asked, "How do we know if we are doing the will of the Lord?"

"Read the Bible regularly," Wilber answered as he placed the hay around on the wagon. "And pray the Holy Spirit will guide you in the way of understanding. Always look to Jesus. Have faith in the Lord. Preaching is the Lord's work. If you obey the Holy Word, He will be with you. Give Him the glory. When troubles come, look up from whence our blessings come."

The wagon was loaded and just as they were going through the gate, the doubletree snapped into two pieces. Wilber holding onto the reins toppled off the loaded wagon onto the ground head first. Jesse was walking beside the wagon when it happened. He saw his dad was alive and tried to help him up. He soon realized his father was not able to move. He ran to the house as fast as he could to get help. Joyce called the emergency. Shelly called her mother and told her to send Dad quick.

Wilbur was taken to the hospital. They found he had a broken neck. He could look around but couldn't move. The Doctors said there was not anything they could do for him.

Jesse was able to keep his composure even though inside he was torn apart. He asked his father to blink his eyes if he wanted to be anointed. The rapid blinking was an obvious answer. Joseph came and Jesse told him what he did.

Joseph said, "Blink your eyes to answer yes."

He asked him the questions for the anointing and each time Wilber blinked. Joseph and Jesse anointed him and prayed over him. Wilber got a smile on his face, his eyes brightened up and he was gone.

Joyce, Wanda, Jesse and Ella, all broke down weeping. In Jesse's mind were the last words his father had told him, "When troubles come, look up from whence our blessings come."

It was a very sad funeral. Joseph called Lester to see if he could come to help. They came and brought Carl's. Carl and Rachel were hardly able to travel anymore.

Carl did have the opening. He didn't have many words, but they were words of deep meaning. Lester gave an encouraging sermon on 'Looking to Him from whence our strength comes'. Joseph closed and spoke a few words at the grave, talking about when the graves will be opened and the saints will come forth.

Carl's spent the night with Joseph's. He and Joseph had a very nice visit. They did a little reminiscing. Rachel didn't talk much anymore. She was so forgetful. Carl's mind was as good as always, but his strength was about gone.

Joseph asked Carl about Charles.

"He has been doing well. I consider him a pillar in our church down home. He always comes to meeting, since brother Sol passed away. Sol never had anything but good to say about him. Charles was just what Sol needed those twelve remaining years of his life. As long as he was able, Charles brought him to meeting. When Sol got to where he couldn't get out anymore, Charles had folks come in from time to time to sing. Sol was a people person and enjoyed having company. When his wife was still living and was able, they had company for Sunday dinner often. Charles would tell Sol on a Sunday morning, 'You invite whom you will and I'll fix dinner.'"

Joseph said, "That was a big undertaking wasn't it?"

"Yes, but they both thoroughly enjoyed it. Sol's last year he suffered considerably. His mind was clear, so when brethren came to visit, they went away getting more than they brought. After Lester was called to the ministry, he often visited Sol."

"Did he like families with children to come?"

"He dearly loved them but, suffering much, his nerves couldn't handle their childish ways."

"Was there any conflict between Charles and Sol all the years they lived together?"

"Not really," answered Carl. "The only time of trial was when Charles got word that his former wife had overdosed and died. He sobbed for a long while when he got the word."

"How did he find out about her passing?"

"Her siblings kept in contact with him. One of them called and told him. Although he knew he could never have her again for his wife, down deep he loved her. Not only that, but he dearly loves and misses his children."

"Did he go to her funeral?"

"No, he didn't. Lester's offered to take him, but Sol wasn't doing too well at the time. Charles felt devoted to taking care of him."

"Do Wilber's children know that Charles is their birth father?"

"I don't think so," responded Carl. "He told me he promised Wilber and Joyce he would never tell them. He told them if they ever wanted to tell, they could, but he wouldn't do it. He has kept an eye on them from a distance all the years they were growing up.

One of the hardest times for him was when he came up to your Love Feast. It turned out that Jesse washed his feet. Charles told me, 'When that young brother finished washing my feet I could just feel the love in his heart. Then he placed a kiss on my lips, I wanted to give him a hug.'"

"I believe I would have cried," Joseph said.

"Some of the brethren sitting close, who knew the situation, did shed some tears. Charles was at Daniel and

Wanda's wedding standing in the back of everyone else. Soon after I introduced them as husband and wife, he walked away. His head was down. I feel he was shedding tears."

"Since Sol passed away what does he do?" Joseph asked.

"The family rents the house to him. He does odd jobs for folks. I hire him a lot to do things I can't do anymore. He is very dependable and kind. He is liked by everyone in our church. He is very appreciative of the forgiveness of his former sins."

Generations Passing
Chapter Thirty-Six

Lovina thought she was ready to give up her mother. Seeing the tiredness in her eyes and knowing she hurt so much made her think she wanted her to go to her reward. It had been a year since Joseph had lost his mother Rachel. Just six weeks ago Carl passed. It had been hard for Joseph to lose the parents who raised him, even though they knew this time would come.

For years, Joseph would call Carl to help him through the stressful times. Many times Carl and Rachel would come and help. While Jake and Gail still lived close by and were helpful in their counsel, they were getting feeble.

For Lovina, being an only child, it was especially hard now to lose her mother. She had always lived close by and they were with each other regularly. Joseph was a comfort to her, and she was thankful to have her children close.

Joseph and Lovina's children and their grandchildren were all there. Joseph picked up the Bible and turned to the ninetieth Psalm. He asked Jesse to read it. Then Joseph called Lester and asked if he could come and help with the funeral.

They came and brought Daryl's along. Daryl had been installed into the ministry three years ago. The two of them had the services. Thoughts were advanced about the brevity of this life. Now is the day of salvation. To see a loved one who has lived a life, working in the Lord's vineyard, pass on in peace gives us comfort.

Charles came to the funeral. Eston asked if he would consider moving in with him. He wanted to stay at home but knew it couldn't be if he didn't have someone to help.

Charles talked it over with Joseph and Lovina. Lovina was thinking she would take care of her father in their home.

Eston made it plain he wanted to stay at his home as long as possible.

The week after the funeral, Eston came over and wanted to talk to them. It was early in the morning and Joseph and Lovina were enjoying their early coffee. Joseph pulled a chair for him while Lovina poured him a cup of coffee.

Eston got right to the point. He wanted them to know he and Lucinda had signed everything they owned over to them a few years ago. He and Lucinda had told them that when they did it, but he forgot.

Later Lovina told Joseph, "I don't know if he forgot, or he just wanted to come and visit over a cup of coffee."

Joseph and Lovina both told him, "We enjoy seeing your smiling face. You come anytime."

He took them at their word. He and Charles started coming early for coffee at least twice a week. One time Lovina asked Joseph if they could go to her father's house and surprise him for early coffee.

"We might catch them in their nightclothes," Joseph said.

Lovina laughed, "We'd have to be awful early if we did."

It had been three years since they laid Lovina's mother away. Eston and Charles were doing fine. Eston would tell him the same thing over and over again, but Charles was kind and just acted as if he hadn't heard it before.

Once in awhile, Eston had Charles take him around to the different farms to look things over. The farms were all he had ever known. He would say, "The Lord made the earth to bring forth food for His people. To see men happy in their labor, tells me they are abundantly provided for. To put our money in the bank doesn't feed anyone. In my ninety years, I've never seen those laboring in the soil go without food. Only God could make the same soil produce a crop year after year." As they passed a worker, Eston would wave and they would wave back.

One time on their driving around, they happened to pass Wilber Sims' place. Joyce was working in the garden. They waved and she waved back. Eston remarked, "It is such a feeling of sorrow about that family. He was taken so suddenly. The children are so good to her, but she has some long lonely hours."

As they came around a curve, a wagon load of hay had just pulled out onto the road.

"That was what took Wilber," Eston said. "The doubletree snapped and the reins pulled him over the standards. He went down head first and broke his neck."

When they passed, they noticed it was Jesse on the hay. He wasn't standing up, but sitting down.

"If Wilber had been sitting down, he likely wouldn't have fallen," Charles remarked. "I wonder why farmers stand on top of the loaded wagon while driving the horse."

"They stand on the empty wagon, and I suppose that is just what they do. In our area, ever since Wilber's accident, they don't stand on a loaded wagon."

As they got back home Eston said, "Well, if Mom were still here she likely would have supper about ready."

"It won't take long," Charles told him.

While they were eating their supper, Eston remarked again about Joyce. "I have someone to eat and converse with but Joyce doesn't. I'm so thankful to have you to help me. At my age, it won't be long until you will be here alone. Then what will you do?"

"The Lord will supply something," Charles replied.

Eston with a twinkle in his eye said, "Maybe you could help Joyce?"

****

"How will I handle this?" Was a question in Joyce's' mind as she reread the letter she had received in the mail.

Two weeks ago was Eston Spitler's funeral. Charles took it so hard. For three years, he had been taking care of him. Eston was a grandfather of her daughter-in-law and also her son-in-law. Daniel and Wanda spoke often of how happy grandpa was having Charles to help him. Jesse and Shelly likewise spoke well of him.

Now here came this letter from Charles asking her to be his wife. "You know about my former life," the letter said. "I am very ashamed of my past. You and Wilber made much better parents for my children than I could have under the condition. I was so happy when they came into the church. When two of them married Joseph's children I rejoiced. It was Joseph who kindly directed me into the Lord's vineyard. It was he who taught me the value of a forgiving spirit. It was Joseph I would go to when I was feeling low, and I'd always go away feeling built up. He and his adoptive father got me to know Brother Sol. I learned compassion and forbearance while I was there those years. After he passed I worked for Carl until he passed away.

It has been about three years now that I've been helping Eston. All three of these brethren I worked for taught me lessons of love and peace. They all had a forgiving spirit. Before Eston passed away he suggested I should consider getting to know you.

I have never told your children I am their biological father. I did not want to disrupt their happiness as your children. If we were to marry I feel I would have to tell them everything about my life and ask them to forgive me. Also, I ask you if you can forgive me. May the Lord direct us in His way?" It was signed, 'Charles Young.'

Joyce read this letter a couple of times. Her mind rolled back to the day Joseph asked them to come and get the children. How Joseph prayed with them. How he had Lovina's dad to get a hired girl to help. Then she thought how hard it was for Charles to come to church and try not to notice his children. How he moved away so she and Wilber could fully adopt them and they could become their children. She remembered Wanda's fourth birthday how they felt the love the children were to them. She decided to go get Joseph and Lovina's council. Likely Charles had already done that.

Bitter Sweet
Chapter Thirty-Seven

After her meeting with Joseph and Lovina, the decision was made. She invited her children over for supper one evening. After the last of the chicken was wiped from greasy lips, the children were playing and the babies were sleeping, Joyce told them she had something to tell them.

She began by reminding them about their being adopted. They had revealed that to the children years ago when they had reached an age to understand. Even though the children were inquisitive, they were never told the identity of their birth parents. The children all felt so loved that they never pressured their parents for more information.

Joyce shared with her children about the many lonely hours she was experiencing now that their father was gone. "I do appreciate how often you children stop by, but there are many hours I'm alone and lonely. I called you here tonight to tell you I plan to get married."

Wanda's face blushed as she asked, "To whom?"

"Are you going to make us call someone Dad who is not our dad?" Ella asked quietly.

"I assume it is someone sound in the faith?" Jesse questioned.

"One question at a time," Joyce knew her children well enough to know what to expect. "It will be your decision as to if and when you call him Dad. He has proven to be strong in the faith. He will be here in a few minutes and Wanda your question will be answered. I told him to be here at eight to discuss our decision with you children. I just wanted to tell you before he came."

A number of other questions were answered before a knock on the back door interrupted the interrogation. "I'll be right back," Joyce told them as she got up to go answer the door. The three siblings were apprehensive as they waited, not knowing what to expect. It wasn't long until in walked their mother accompanied by Charles Young.

They all were perplexed as they took in the idea that their mother was marrying Charles. They had known Charles for as long as they could remember. They knew he was single, but never asked why. Jesse remembered washing Charles feet at a love feast just a few years back. It was Jesse's first time to commune after he became a member of the church. What made that experience so vivid in his mind, he being so young, felt unworthy to be washing an older brother's feet. When he gave him a kiss, the tears were running down that brother's cheeks.

Joyce let her children work through the revelation as to who she was marrying before hitting them with additional life-changing information.

"Not only is Charles the man I plan to marry, but he is also your biological father."

They were stunned. Slowly questions appeared on their faces. It would not take long before those looks turned verbal.

Charles looked with compassion into the eyes of his children, "I know you need time to absorb this news. When you were all small children, I was a wayward lost soul. Satan had us in his grips. We were living an ungodly lifestyle when your birth mother left. I tried to take care of you the best I could, but I lowered myself to stealing just trying to care for you. I was working for Eston at that time. Joseph had recently taken over running the farms. One day things got so bad I went to him and confessed everything. I admitted I was not able, nor worthy, to be a godly father to you three.

Joseph was a great counselor and instructed me on how to amend my ways. He sent me to the deacons of the church. They were firm but kind. One of them went with me to make amends.

It was Joseph I had wronged the most. He taught me the spirit of forgiveness.

It was through much counsel it became evident to me that you children deserved a good, godly home. That was something I was unable to provide. Joseph and Lovina kindly took you in for a while until your parents adopted you. Joseph has helped me over the hard places in my life. He helped me to become a new child of God."

"You were gone for a long time," Jesse asked. "Where did you go?"

"After I came to know the Lord, I attended your church. Seeing my little children every Sunday was more than I could handle. Joseph and his adoptive father set me up to go south and move in with an old widowed brother. He was lonely and I helped take care of him until he passed on. It was there that I learned true godly love. After that I was depressed and lonely myself, so Carl hired me to help them around their house.

It was during that time that I came up here with them to the Love Feast. Jesse, I couldn't believe it was just a coincidence that it fell your place to wash my feet. I felt so unworthy. When we saluted, I couldn't help but shed tears. I just wanted to hug you."

"I remember that," Jesse said. "I was wondering why you were so emotional."

"Over the years I've been so thankful that Wilber and Joyce became your parents. No doubt there has been love in this home as you were growing up.

I felt very sad when your father had an accident. I wondered 'Why did it have to happen to such a loving father and a good Christian?'

After Carl's were gone, I came to help Eston. One day while we were out for a drive we came down this road and there was Jesse with a loaded hay wagon pulling out onto the road."

"Was I standing?" Jesse asked.

"No, you were sitting. Eston commented about how farmers started sitting down after your father's accident.

Soon before he passed away, Eston saw he was getting weaker and asked me what I would do after he was gone. He told me that I spent many years helping make lonely widowers happy. With a twinkle in his eye, he told me that maybe it was time I made a lonely widow happy."

"What about our birth mother?" Wanda asked. "I'm to assume you would not remarry with her still living."

"That is correct," Charles answered. "She lived an extremely difficult and bad life. Sadly she passed away many years ago. While I always had compassionate feelings for her, those feelings were not reciprocated. I will not dwell on or share negative attributes of your birth mother as that is not a Christian thing to do. You have been blessed being raised here in this godly home, for which we all should be thankful.

"I have shared with you about my past while keeping nothing from you. Your mother and I have, through much prayer, decided to get married. I can understand if you have mixed feelings and possibly don't even want me around. Now, I'll bid you goodnight and give you time to discuss our future with each other. May the Lord keep and guide us as we journey towards the Promised Land. Good night."

****

"Supper's ready," Lovina called from the porch and the children came running. It was always happy children to eat at grandma's table. Besides Joseph's family, all of Joyce Sims' family, Jake and Gail came along with Charles. The table was stretched out almost to its limits.

After they sang a verse, Jake in his quivering voice, thanked the Lord for their blessings and asked Him to bless their food and bless each one there.

256

The roast beef was very tender and, to put gravy on it, made it almost melt in your mouth. Everyone and especially the grandchildren loved Lovina's mashed potatoes and noodles.

After they were all finished eating, the ladies quickly cleared the table, moving the food to the kitchen.

"There is pie and homemade ice-cream yet to come," Joseph announced, "but first we have other business to take care of. We are together this evening to witness the joining together of two lonely people into one. This is not only a marriage, but it will also reunite a family."

Joseph asked Joyce and Charles to come to the head of the table. He stood to one side and asked them to stand at an angle so all at the table could see their faces. Joseph opened his Bible and read some familiar scriptures concerning the marriage.

He asked them to join right hands and then performed the marriage vows. Standing to one side he introduced them as Mr. and Mrs. Charles Young. Looking at Jake, Joseph motioned for them to come. Jake and Gail gave them words of encouragement. Both had lost their first companion and although it had been a long time ago, they still knew the sting of death. They could understand the need for a helpmate. Next, he nodded to Daniel and Wanda.

Daniel pulled the chair back as his wife stood. He put his arm around her as they walked to the end of the table. Wanda threw her arms around her mother and sobbed. Turning to Charles, she looked into his eyes, said, "Daddy, I do forgive you. Even though I've only known you as my father for a short time, I love you." In an embrace, they wept for a long while.

Next Jesse and Shelly came forward. Taking his hand he kissed him with the salutation as brethren do. Then he gave him a hug and said, "Welcome back dad. I forgive you for any wrong you did. Thank you for putting us in a home where we were taught to love the Lord and to have a forgiving spirit. From this day forward you are my earthly father."

Turning to his mother, he gave her a hug. Tears were flowing as his mind flashed back over his early years. The love they experienced in their family. The sorrow they had gone through when they tragically lost his father. "God does all things well," he whispered into her ear. "I'll support you in this marriage. May the Lord bless you two."

Fred and Ella were next. Ella took Charles' hand and placed a kiss on his cheek. "Thank you for placing us in such a God-loving home when you knew you couldn't care for us. I forgive you for all the past wrongs in your life. Whom mom loves, I love. It may take a while to call you Daddy."

Turning to her mother she kissed her and wept on her. "Sorry I didn't come more often. Now you have someone to be with in the evenings while we are enjoying our families. We'll still try to do better spending time with you two." Fred also congratulated them and gave them his blessings.

The grandchildren followed shaking hands and hugging their grandparents.

Room was made at the end of the table for Charles and Joyce to sit. Lovina and Shelly started dishing up homemade ice-cream as Eddie served it to the table. Just as they started, Jesse started singing *God moves in a mysterious way, His wonders to perform. He plants his footsteps on the sea and rides on the storm.* All the others joined in.

Cherry, apricot, apple and pecan pies were passed around to compliment the ice cream. The rest of the evening was a time of rejoicing. By all appearances, the family was willing to consider it God's leading. After the wedding party and the guest left, Jesse and Shelly stayed to help clean up and put things back in order. As they finished up, Jesse gave Joseph a big hug and said, "Thank you for all you have done for us."

Jakes Blessing
Chapter Thirty-Eight

It had been years since the beginning of the depression and things had picked up. Jake received a letter from Jason, asking him if they would consider moving back to Iowa. "Bring your sons and come. You belong here." Jake's had been in California for several years and it had become home. They did miss the friendliness of the neighbors in Iowa. Even though the brethren were friendly on the west coast, many of the worldly folks had the mentality of every man for himself.

Joe and Cassie moved back to Illinois two years earlier when his father had a heart attack and badly needed his son to run the farm. Now Gail dearly missed her daughter. When she read the letter from Jason, it sounded good to her to move home.

They talked it over with the family. Benjamin and Aaron felt they wanted to stay where they were. Joseph had given them an opportunity, and they were satisfied to stick with it. The five older sons wanted to think it over and pray about such a decision.

Before Jake could make a decision his health started failing. He called his sons to come. He told them he felt the time was upon him to die. He shared at length about the joys and sorrows he had throughout his life.

He talked about the blessings the Lord gives to those who obey him. He talked about Jesus coming into this world to save sinners. He talked about the blessing His people have when they have a heart to forgive anyone who wrongs them.

He told them about the attitude of a man named Joseph in the Bible. "He was a type of Christ. He manifested a forgiving spirit. It is important that we forgive and teach our children the importance of forgiving.

In the biblical account of Joseph, they were in a strange land. They were in that land for four hundred and thirty years. God told them that the day would come when He would take them to a land that flowed with milk and honey. Before Jacob died he blessed his sons. He told them he wanted to be buried in his home country.

Boys, when I am gone, I don't want to be buried here. Take me back to Iowa and bury me beside my first wife, Lois. The account of Joseph in the Bible gave them hope of the land of freedom. It would be a land where everyone would eat under his own vine and fig tree. Before Jesus left He said He was going away to prepare a place for His people.

Someday He is coming again to take us with him to the marriage supper. The Church, that is, the people of God, will go to a land where we'll never grow old. We don't know if it will flow with milk and honey but we do know that it is a land of love and peace. It will be a place where we will praise God forever.

Boys, in the Old Testament God blessed His people when they obeyed Him. Several didn't get to go into the Promised Land because of their disobedience. Jesus came and opened up a more perfect way. The Bible tells us all have sinned and come short of the Glory of God. In the first chapter of First John, it says, 'If we confess our sins, He is faithful and just to forgive us of our sins, and cleanse us from all unrighteousness.' We are living in such a blessed time. When you fail, confess your sin and repent. We know that it's through the precious blood of Christ that we are forgiven. In thinking of this, surely we will want to have a forgiving spirit.

When Jesus comes, it won't matter where we live on this earth. The Holy Word says, 'Every eye shall see Him.' How we live is what matters. Wherever you choose to dwell, be a light to Jesus. Your life may be the only Bible some folks will read.

In the Bible, Jacob wanted to be buried in the land God promised to Abraham. While it doesn't matter where our bodies are buried, I want to be buried by my first wife. When the trump of God sounds, the dead in Christ will come forth and we shall meet Him in the air. So shall we ever be with Him. I am not Jacob, but I will endeavor to bless you before I die."

Jake sat on the edge of his bed and asked Rudy to come to him. Rudy knelt in front of his father and Jake laid his hands on his son's head and prayed that the Holy Spirit would guide him through his life. That Rudy would be a shining light amongst the people. Jake repeated this prayer with each of his sons.

As Joseph was before his father, Jake broke down for a short moment. In his prayer, he made mention about his son being taken away for a season in his life. How he had not expected to see him again this side of Heaven. He thanked the Lord for His marvelous work in taking care of Joseph through all the absent years. He praised the Lord for bringing them together again, not only to see his son but also to get to know his grandchildren.

After Jake finished praying a blessing on each of his sons, he said, "Now I want you all to stand in a circle and hold hands. Joseph, I would like you to stand between Rudy and Simon. Benjamin, please stand between Simon and Henry. Aaron, you go between Henry and Thad. As they all found their places according to their father's desire, Rudy took hold of Jake's right hand and Chad took his left. Jake, in his feeble voice, asked that they pray the Lord's Prayer together. When they said "Amen", Jake started singing and the rest joined in.

> *Oh when shall I see Jesus,*
> *And dwell with him above!*
> *To drink the flowing fountains,*
> *Of everlasting love?*
> *When shall I be deliver'd*
> *From this vain world of sin,*
> *And with my blessed Jesus,*
> *Drink endless pleasures in?*

But now I am a soldier,
  My captain's gone before,
He's given me my orders,
  And tells me not to fear;
And if I hold out faithful,
  A crown of life he'll give,
And all his valiant soldiers
  Eternal life shall have.

As they started this last verse, Jake indicated he wanted to lie down. Rudy and Chad helped him into bed and heard him trying to continue singing. They motioned for Gail to come to Jake's side. She could see he was slipping away as she went up to his bed, she leaned over him and their eyes met for an instant, telling each other words that couldn't be uttered. She felt the love which she had seen many times in their married life. She put a kiss on his cheek and sat back down and sobbed.

Through grace I am determin'd
  To conquer though I die,
And then away to Jesus,
  On wings of love I'll fly;

There was a sense of peace as they felt the presence of the angels while Jake took his last breath. Tears began to flow as they finished the last verse.

Farewell to sin and sorrow,
  I bid it all adieu;
And you my friends be faithful,
  And on your way pursue.

After a memorial service at their church in California, Jake's body was taken to Iowa for his final resting place. There in the church where he had spent a majority of his years worshiping his Lord, a crowd gathered. Every seat was taken and a number of people stood just to be part of Jake's life. Although Jason was now old and feeble he stood and preached the funeral. His mind was still keen and with clarity, he delivered the message, "I have fought the good fight, and have kept the faith."

At the grave, Gail grieved quietly. After the service was over, she walked over to Paul's grave and stood there reflecting back over her life. She felt love and support as Cassie and Ben stood beside her.

It had been arranged for the families to all come to the home place. Few people knew that Joseph had bought the farm from his father a number of years earlier. The church sisters provided a meal for the family and others that joined them there. Early in the afternoon, Gail walked over to the little house where she and Jake lived after their children were gone from home. As she walked in the door, she was not prepared for the onslaught of emotions. She stood there looking at the little table where they ate their meals and conversed. She broke down and sobbed.

Amongst the rest of the family, there was a lot of reminiscing. With all the grandchildren and now great-grandchildren the house was full and loud. Joseph needed to find some solitude, so he slipped out to the barn. The barn had been vacant of livestock for a number of years. Opening the door to the old cow stable, he saw his old milk stool hanging on the wall, covered with spider webs and dust. He pulled it off the wall and dusted off years of neglect. As he sat on this antiquated stool he leaned up against the wall and let his mind whirl back through the years of his life. He heard footsteps approaching and the creaking of the old hinges revealed his five older brothers. Anxiety momentarily struck him as he flashed back to the day they sold him for ten dollars. He jumped to his feet as reality replaced fear.

The six of them stood there talking about the years gone by. Joseph sensed his brothers had something else on their minds that they were uneasy about. "I know you are grieving the loss of our father like I am. What else is bothering you?"

Henry cleared his throat and sort of stuttered, "Before Dad passed away, he told us he asked you to forgive us for what we have done to you."

It brought sadness to Joseph when he saw the fear in the eyes of these now elderly men. "Even after all these years, do you still not understand? I forgave you a long time ago. It is true that while I remember what you did, I no longer hold it against you. It is God who forgives sins. Remember it is Christ in you the hope of glory. When you made confession before the church and were baptized you were forgiven.

Do not fear me. I will take care of you and your children. If you get in a bind, if I can, I will help. We are brethren, not only in the flesh but in Christ. Eston taught me that anything we have came from God. We are responsible for how we use it. Let us pray that it is for the glory of the Lord."

After Joseph embraced each of his brothers he asked that they join hands and he prayed for all of them that they would have a full understanding of forgiveness. After he finished he told them, "Let us all press on, not looking back to our shortcomings, but looking up from where our blessings come."

Walking back to the house, the five of them stopped by the garden. There they discussed what their mother had taught them about the germ in the little seed. How it reproduces its kind.

"I feel like I am still a little seed needing the warm soil and someone to get the weeds out of my life," Rudy said.

"Don't we all," Chad responded.

"Our children may follow our example. We must show them the fruit we are from," Henry added.

Later that evening Gail shared with the family that she planned on going home with Cassie. She would likely make that her home the remainder of her years.

The five older brothers revealed their plans to move their families back to Iowa.

"Remember what Dad said," Joseph told them. "It doesn't matter where we live, it is how we live. Any of you that would like to continue to live in California will be welcomed to do so."

Ben and Aaron said that they were planning on staying out west.

Joseph told the rest of them, "We are all one family. Lovina and I would like to help get you established. If you find a place you like and need help getting it, let us know."

"Chad and I walked back to the old sawmill," Thad said. "Weeds have grown up around the mill and everything is rusted beyond use."

"If milling lumber is your desire, we'll help you get an updated sawmill," Joseph told them.

Rudy wanted to look into reopening his store. Simon wanted to farm and Henry was certain that he wanted to get back into carpentry work.

The next evening they sat around a campfire. After roasting wieners and enjoying a lot of food they started singing. The good old songs were named one after another. The stars were bright. The cool evening air brought their chairs closer to the fire. Joseph let a tear slip down his cheek as he thought about the changes that were taking place. No more would they be together as they were tonight. He remembered what Carl told him, "Unless we have a forgiving spirit, there will never be true Godly love and union." That night they were there with love in their hearts. They all had that love that Jesus taught. *He loves us and we love him and therefore we love each other.*

The crisp quiet night air was interrupted as someone started singing, *I'm pressing on the upward way, new heights I'm gaining every day.*

The end